Sing Me To Sleep

A Ghost Story

CHRIS SIMMS

Other novels by Chris Simms:

Psychological thrillers
Outside the White Lines
Pecking Order

DI Spicer series
Killing the Beasts
Shifting Skin
Savage Moon
Hell's Fire
The Edge
Cut Adrift
Sleeping Dogs

DC Iona Khan series
Scratch Deeper
A Price To Pay

6/16

PROLOGUE

The men stared at the hole in grim silence.

She turned away from the hushed group to gaze across the dull field at a finger of bright snow. It clung stubbornly to life in the shadow of a dry-stone wall. She realised, wrapping her shawl more tightly about herself, it was the last visible evidence of the brutal storm from a fortnight before.

From below their feet a disembodied voice called out. 'OK, carry on!'

The firefighter holding the winch started turning it once more, winding in a length of rope that dropped like a plumb-line into the dark cleft.

The heads of his colleagues stayed bowed, as did those of three policemen, a man in an overcoat and a vicar. A funeral, she thought. It looks just like a funeral. But no body was being buried. The reverse, in fact.

A yellowish glow broke the blackness at their feet. She looked on impassively as the dirt-smeared head and shoulders of a man rose slowly out of the ground. In the harsh light of day, the lamp on his miner's helmet was suddenly useless. His arms came into view. They were cradling something loosely wrapped in blue plastic sheeting.

She knew exactly what it was.

The man had now been winched high enough to get a knee on the brick-lined rim. He held the bundle out.

1

Reluctantly, a policeman took it. Without looking at it properly, he laid it on the wiry turf and backed away.

All eyes went to the man in the overcoat. After sending an uncomfortable glance in the lone woman's direction, he crouched down and tentatively lifted the corner. A collective jolt passed through the group and the vicar's legs suddenly folded. He sat down in the long, cold grass and started to claw at his dog collar, only stopping when his shirt was torn open. Moaning weakly, he turned in the woman's direction.

But she was already striding away, shawl now pulled over her head. A veil.

CHAPTER 1

The doctor crossed his legs and the folds in his corduroys reminded her of the undulating land surrounding her new home. 'So, tell me about this...dream of yours.'

She hesitated before replying. Was it his tone? He just didn't feel very doctorly. From somewhere outside his surgery came the shrill sound of a startled bird. She glanced nervously at the frosted glass before looking back at the doctor. Bushy brows formed an unbroken crest above his narrowed eyes. She felt pinned by his unblinking stare.

The window behind him glowed with late autumnal sunlight. It caught on the thick hairs protruding from his ears. Like antennae, hanging there in space. Antennae not very well attuned to more delicate thoughts and feelings, she suspected.

Her right hand lifted and fingers moved slightly as she began to speak. 'It feels so similar to the one I used to have.'

He reached for her medical notes, causing her words to falter and stop. She thought: he surely read the top sheet before I opened his door. Any good doctor did that. So he knew the basics. The surface detail. Laura Wilkinson, thirty-nine years old, five feet eight, excellent physical health, no allergies, blood type O, a shade over nine stone.

As she'd first stepped inside, he'd half-risen from his chair, directing her to the empty seat beside his desk with a flash of palm. His eyes touched her face in a cursory sort of way. Then they'd returned for another look.

She'd often been told she was attractive – though why people said that she never could fathom. She liked her hair. Long and pale and windblown when she let it hang loose. Combing it and arranging it had always given her so much pleasure – always, ever since she was very young. But she was convinced there was too much of a gap between her eyes and she found the bones of her face harsh. When she closed her lips, she could see the swell of her teeth behind them.

Her husband, Owen, had assured her many times that her bone structure was beautiful. Sometimes, she just sensed her skull when she looked in the mirror. Lurking there. Waiting, one day, to show itself.

'Carry on, I'm listening,' he prompted, leafing back through the pages. There were lots. 'Your dream...'

'It feels so similar,' she tentatively repeated. But eye contact had gone, and with it the feeling he was taking her words in. She persevered. 'A tunnel. Narrow, dark, cold. Horribly cold. The same sense of abandonment, of needing warmth and comfort – but being so alone. This time though, the child – it's too indistinct to tell if it's male or female – isn't lying at the end of the tunnel. And it's not curled in a foetal position, either. It's nearer –'

'This previous dream. The one from six years ago?'

'Yes.' His head was still down as he studied the pages. She could see her previous doctor's handwritten additions. The elegant, neat letters somehow conveyed how kind she was. Dr Ford added something in a harsh scrawl.

'The time when you and Owen were trying to start a family?'

'Yes.'

'And you began to feel anxious and unhappy when that proved unproductive?'

There it was again. Unproductive. How tactless of him, she thought, considering whether to lean forward and yank one of the monstrous hairs from his ears. She wondered if he'd yelp. 'That was all prior to the series of fertility tests I underwent.'

He looked up with a questioning expression.

'There was nothing wrong with me, you see. That wasn't the problem. Which means – you know – that the reason I couldn't conceive...that was down to Owen. His sperm count.' Introducing Owen into the equation seemed to unsettle the doctor slightly, judging from the way he shifted in his seat. He looked down at her notes once more.

Twenty-three years, she thought. The age difference between Owen and me. It had seemed so utterly irrelevant when they'd first met. Back then, the attention of an older man – and one widely tipped for greatness – had, if anything, been a thrill. Her mother had her reservations. Gentle hints about the long term which Laura – made giddy with love – had blithely swept aside

Her eyes drifted to the bright pictures on the wall above the examination couch. Images from fairytales, placed there to make younger patients feel more comfortable. Her favourite was right in the middle. Snow White. Rabbits gambolled at her feet and birds fluttered about her head. Before the witch appeared and ruined everything.

'And when you made the decision not to have children, the dream faded away of its own accord?' Doctor Ford asked.

Faded? Of its own accord? It was obliterated, she wanted to yell. By the drugs they pumped into me. And we didn't make the decision not to have children. Owen decided for both of us when he refused to undergo any tests. 'I went to see a dream therapist. My previous doctor – Helen Evans – she put me in touch with him.'

He sat back. 'A dream therapist?'

'Yes.' She wondered if it was his accent that made him seem so...unfeeling. The northern gruffness.

'Down in London, was this?'

She nodded. 'He said the image of the curled-up child – its position in a cold, dark passage – that was my mind trying to represent not being able to get pregnant. The passage was my womb, the lack of warmth my perceived infertility –'

'Well, I'd prefer not to conjecture on the symbolism of dreams. If you feel that you need to be referred for some counselling, I'm sure –'

'No.' The word came out with too much force. 'Sorry. No. I feel fine. Happy. The whole thing about having babies doesn't bother me any more. I mean, I'm thirty-nine. It would be silly.'

'But this dream bothers you?'

Her fingers started to flutter once more. She saw his eyes intently tracking their movement. The psychiatrists used to do that, too. She placed her hand back in her lap. 'Yes. It's similar, not the same. The figure – I'll call it a him because I sense its male – is much nearer to...to what I can tell is the opening. The way out into the world. But his position is all awkward; the knees are apart, an elbow is jutting out. One hand is bent back behind the head. Like he's jammed. He can't move. It's a horrible image.'

She heard the thin whistle of air passing up his nostrils. It must, she thought, be hairy up there, too. 'Have you discussed this with your husband?'

She shook her head. 'No – the dream has only started recently. The last month. Since we moved into Lantern Cottage. I'm not sure if it isn't related to the funny noise that I've been –' His eyebrows twitched and, for the briefest instant, she spotted something in his eyes.

'What noise?'

'It's like a bird singing. It comes and goes. Owen hasn't heard it yet. But I have. It's not unpleasant – it's too beautiful for that. But it's started to frustrate me.' She paused. 'No, the fact I can't figure out where it's coming from has started to frustrate me. It seems to float.' His eyes were moving about and she realised they were following her fingers. She thought: I'm motioning again. Reaching for thistledown, as Owen calls it. 'It's always too indistinct to pinpoint. I can't tell if it's in the house or not.' She glanced at his computer terminal. 'I had a look on the internet.' She laughed nervously. 'You don't think it could be tinnitus, do you?' The thought of developing the affliction filled her with dread. 'Sufferers usually hear whistling, hissing or buzzing. But apparently people hear other types of noise, too.'

He picked up a pen and tapped it quickly against his notepad. She guessed it must be so frustrating to be a GP. Everyone coming to their appointment as an armchair expert.

'You've just moved to rural surroundings. From the edge of London. I think you'll find the sheer range of sounds up here overwhelming at times.' He smiled. Patronising. 'During the summer, the dawn chorus can get to be quite a nuisance.'

She contemplated telling him that Richmond Park also had a healthy bird population. Including wild – and very raucous – flocks of parakeets. 'At night?'

'Sorry?'

'This birdsong often happens when I'm lying in bed trying to get to sleep. It's not a nightingale, charming as it is. Not in November.'

He was silent. From the waiting area beyond his door came a cough. It seemed to rouse him and he glanced at his watch. 'I'm very sorry, we've run over. You need another appointment if you want to discuss a second issue. Just book in again at the reception; when you come back I can examine your inner ear, check for infection or a build-up of wax. In the meantime, try a hot milky drink directly before bed. Perhaps a bath, too.'

She tried to hide her sense of disappointment. She hadn't the chance to broach the other issue that was bothering her. She hadn't had her period. It had been due within days of moving into the cottage. And her cycle had run like clockwork all her adult life. The word she dreaded nudged its way to the forefront of her mind. No, she thought, forcing it back. Not that. Too soon for that.

He gave her a reassuring smile. 'Laura, you're in totally new surroundings. There is bound to be a degree of feeling unsettled. Owen – he's back on familiar ground. Maybe that's why he can't hear anything. How are his rehearsals going, by the way?'

'Fine.'

'It must be very exciting for him, to be conducting the Hallé. And in the Bridgewater Hall.'

She reflected on the reasons behind their move. With Owen's appointment as Senior Fellow of Composition at the Royal Northern College of Music was a commissioned piece. Its performance was to form the highlight of a concert in just six days' time. 'He's certainly looking forward to it,' she replied, reaching for her shawl; the part of the appointment concerning her was clearly over.

'Do tell him my tickets are booked. I can't wait.'

'I will.' Her smile felt tight as she stood.

'And for you? Give it a few days and see how things are. If sleeping really is a problem I could...' He gestured at his prescription pad.

'No,' she said, waving a hand, astounded he was even offering her pills. It was all the proof she needed. He hadn't read her notes properly. He hadn't a clue what she went through six years ago.

On the way out, she paused at the rack in reception and removed a leaflet entitled *The menopause*.

CHAPTER 2

The road rose steadily, taking her away from the river the little village sat beside. She glimpsed the Cheshire Plain below her. In its middle, the massed buildings that were Manchester. It was a still afternoon and a hazy brown band wreathed the city. She wondered if its residents were aware of what they were breathing in.

Disquiet flared. Owen's forthcoming concert meant he had become a virtual commuter since their move. His chest could get bad enough in winter without the aggravating effect of air pollution.

A terrace of cottages now obscured her view. Squat things with poky windows. Half-way along was a little row of shops, including a butcher's run by two brothers. She pulled over and reached for the cotton shopping bag on the passenger seat. The leaflet on the menopause was next to it. She shoved it into the glove compartment, telling herself she'd read it later.

'Afternoon, Mrs Wilkinson, enjoy this nice weather while it lasts.'

'I am, don't you worry,' she smiled back, surveying the trays of meat beneath the counter.

'What can I get you?'

She couldn't decide. The chicken looked pale and insipid. Perhaps it wouldn't on a warm summer's evening, but it did now. From the rear of the shop came a heavy thud. David, she thought. The younger, more flirtatious brother. Dismembering something substantial, by the sound of it. 'Not sure, Matthew. Maybe something dark?'

He gestured to a couple of skinny corpses hanging from the hooks behind him. 'Some nice wild rabbit there.'

'Oh no.' She could feel the grimace on her face. 'I couldn't. Poor little things.'

He held his hands to his chest and bunched the fingers in. 'That's not what Mr McGregor said when he saw the state of his vegetable patch.' His nose twitched up and down.

The reference to Beatrix Potter suddenly clicked and before she could stop it, a deep belly laugh burst out. She clapped a hand over her mouth.

David poked his head through the doorway of the backroom, a mixture of surprise and amusement on his face. 'Was that you?'

She gave a demure nod.

He grinned. 'I bet that gets you into trouble.'

'What do you mean?' she replied, knowing full well the effect her laugh could have on men.

Also smiling, Matthew looked down at the counter display. 'How about a nice bit of venison? It's local – from Lyme Park. Mushrooms, red wine, some roast potatoes on the side...'

She thought of the spinach Owen had recently put in. They were all big plants, several with leaves ready for harvest. 'That sounds lovely.'

'A pair of medallions?'

'Please.' He had her routine already. A month of living here, she thought, and he knows my name, where I live, and how much I'll order. Such a far cry from London. As he wrapped her order, she noticed the collection box on the counter. On it was the face of a lovely little girl, marred by a tube coming from one nostril. Help Molly Get Her Operation, said the red lettering.

'Who's Molly?' she asked, retrieving her purse.

'Molly? Lovely little lass. Never sad, always full of

sparkle. She lives not far from here. The doctors said she should be dead by now.' He half-turned and tapped a thick knuckle against his sternum. 'Rare kind of lung condition. Such a little fighter. But the only treatment is in America and – of course – it isn't cheap.'

She gazed at Molly's smiling face, amazed at how fierce the seed of life was, once it took hold. She felt her thoughts slowing, deepening. Could I still deliver a baby into the world? It wouldn't matter how it turned out, my love for it would be...

'Anything else?'

She turned to him. 'Anything else? No. Thank you.' She extracted a ten-pound note for him and a twenty for the collection box.

Matthew sucked air in through his lips. 'That's very kind, Mrs Wilkinson. Her dad will really appreciate it.'

'It's nothing,' she said, taking her change and heading for the door. 'See you soon!'

Driving up the steep and narrow lane to Lantern Cottage, she regarded the hawthorn hedge close on both sides. So thick, she thought, it trapped the lane in perpetual shadow. Its dark depths made her think of the barrier of thorns surrounding Sleeping Beauty's castle.

Then she was out, into the rolling farmland surrounding her home. The views across the Cheshire Plain were now unbroken. Like termite mounds on the savannah, a cluster of tall pale buildings marked the centre of Manchester. Lights were starting to speckle the darkening landscape and, on the horizon's far edge, the sun was sinking behind the purpled hills of Wales.

A few of the closest lights were by the church on top of a nearby hill. They're still there, she thought, working away on all fours in the grass by the graveyard. Some kind of excavation was taking place and, once again, she told herself she really must pay a visit to see what was going on.

Owen's shock of white hair stood out in the fading light as he appeared round the corner of the cottage. A mallet was swinging from one thin arm and he was not looking happy. She turned the engine off and climbed out.

'Bloody badgers,' he announced in her direction. 'They've got in at the far corner. Menaces. The vegetable patch has been completely stripped.'

'No,' she replied. 'Everything? Including the spinach?'

'Spinach, curly kale, winter cabbage, the lot. If I had my way, we'd be allowed to bloody shoot them.'

Crestfallen, she looked down at the shopping bag containing the venison. She had the feeling there were some broad beans in the freezer.

'They even tried to topple your bird table. Must be able to smell the seeds on it. I've banged it back in lower, but the base is all splintered from their dirty great claws.'

'Well, I suppose they were living here first...'

'No wonder the last lot didn't do anything with the garden,' he grunted, before disappearing into the large shed that jutted out from the side of the house.

Her eyes lingered on its arched double doors. Like so much of Lantern Cottage, the shed was slightly odd. Picturesque, but still slightly odd. The side facing the road had a hatch built into it, the windowsill consisting of a large slab of stone that extended out a good half-foot. Above the shuttered opening, an ornate wrought-iron hook had been bolted into the brickwork. This, the estate agent had told them, used to hold the lantern which gave the cottage its name. Steep eaves jutted out. Clinging beneath them, a row of swallows' nests awaited their owners. Already she longed for spring and the birds' return.

Her eyes travelled over the rest of the building. Extra bits had been tacked on over the years: a small conservatory at the back of the kitchen, a little extension consisting of a snug sitting room and box room above it at the cottage's far end. There were swallows' nests beneath the extension's eaves, too. Or at least the beginnings of them. But, for some reason, the birds had abandoned their work. The shallow crescents resembled sad smiles, she thought, now shrouded in cobwebs. What was it that had put the birds off from nesting there?

When they'd found the property back in the summer it was empty. They put an offer in considerably below the asking price and, to their delight, it was accepted. That gave them a five-month period before they moved in to have various renovations done. It was Laura's idea to have the ageing conservatory knocked down and replaced with a larger orangery which looked out over the rear garden.

It was there they'd sit with a glass of wine, music playing in the background, contentedly listening to the sheep bleating in the steep, tussocky fields that sloped down to a thickly-wooded valley. It still seemed scarcely possible such an idyllic property cost less than half of what they'd got for their town house back in Richmond.

Raising the latch on the outer porch, she let herself in, removed her shoes, unlocked the inner door and paused. Despite telling herself not to, she couldn't help doing it. Listening for the mysterious trickle of birdsong.

In the first few days after moving in, she'd assumed it was Owen playing a recording in his study; some sort of last-minute adjustments to the piece he'd spent so long on. When she questioned him and realised it wasn't, she'd become convinced it was the ring-tone of a mobile phone, accidentally left by one of the recently-departed builders. She could picture the device, fallen beneath a floorboard or inadvertently sealed behind a freshly-plastered wall. After all, the batteries of modern phones could last for ages, couldn't they? But enough time had passed for her to be certain it was no phone. Yet still...on the occasions when she heard the noise, it seemed to be emanating from so deep within the house, she found it hard to conclude anything else.

Savouring the absence of sound, she padded across brand-new carpet to the kitchen. Above her stretched the old timber beams which finally swayed her in favour of the place.

A step led down into the flagstone-floored kitchen where a battered pair of sheepskin slippers awaited. She slipped them on and placed the shopping bag on the side. Broad beans; she was certain there was a bag in the freezer.

The door in the far corner opened and Owen stepped in from the garden.

'Darling, I'm sorry, I've got badgers on my brain. How was it at the doctor's?'

She see-sawed a hand. 'A bit of a mix-up, to be honest.'

'Oh?'

Bending before the freezer, she examined the frosty shelves. At the back, was her bottle of *Grey Goose* vodka. She kept it there for special occasions: like moving into a new house. Fat chance of that, she thought. Not with Owen's concert so close. 'I wasted too much time going on about my rubbish sleeping. By the time I got to the noise, my slot was up.' She glanced back to see his attention had wandered to the shopping bag.

'Slot was up?'

She stood, the bag of frozen broad beans in her hand. 'Afraid so. I've got another appointment booked for next Tuesday. We'll see if there's any change before then.'

'Right,' he said vaguely, lifting the folds of the shopping bag. 'What's for supper?'

She didn't know if it was his stooped posture or the tiny creak that ran through his final word, but a profound sense of sadness suddenly engulfed me. Not sadness: something stronger than that. Despair. A shrewish voice in her head rang out. Your mother was right, he's old, he's old and he'll die leaving you without a child and you'll be alone, alone in the world, too old to marry again, too old for a family with anyone else, no one will want you, you should never have married someone so much older –

'Darling?'

She blinked to see him looking at her with a kindly smile. 'Is it beef?'

'Venison,' she replied, crossing quickly to the huge porcelain sink. 'From a local place.'

'Lyme Park?'

'That was it. Lyme Park.' She turned the tap on, needing to have her back to him, just until the horrible urge to weep had passed. 'Isn't that butcher's good?'

'Crofthouse? It's been in the family for generations, that place.'

She heard the chink of a bottle and knew he was contemplating a red for their meal.

'I'm wondering whether to open a Côtes du Rhône. Plenty of punch to stand up to the venison.'

She continued rinsing the beans under the tap, even though there was no need. Just until my hands stop trembling, she thought. Just until this ugly surge of emotion subsides. 'Maybe a Barolo? I'm grilling them.'

'A Barolo it is, then.'

'Lovely.'

A rattling noise from the drawer, the squeak of a cork and a hollow pop. 'I'll leave that to breathe.'

She felt sufficiently in control to glance over her shoulder. 'Oh, Dr Ford wanted me to tell you his tickets are booked. He can't wait.'

The mention of the forthcoming concert caused a troubled look to pass across his face. She knew he was agonising over the finishing touches, as he always did. She turned back to the sink. 'Does it seem strange to be registered again at the surgery you went to as a child?'

He didn't reply and she knew his mind was elsewhere. Pre-performance nerves. There was once a time, she reflected with a pang of regret, when I was familiar with them, too. 'And to be under a doctor who was a couple of years above you at school.'

He eventually responded. 'That doesn't bother me. We always got on. Darling, do I have time to do a little more work? I'm having some problems with the dynamics at the end of the second movement. I'm beginning to wonder if

13

it's my notations.'

'What problems?'

'Oh, it's the blasted sopranos. I want them to come in *pianissimo possibile* after the crescendo. They just don't seem capable of getting it right.'

The tensions of working with a new orchestra, she thought. A process he seemed to always forget about. 'Of course. This will be at least three-quarters of an hour.'

'Good.'

She listened to his footsteps recede down the corridor then looked round the room. Where on earth did that ugly voice in my head come from? The lilies she'd recently bought were beginning to flower: shiny green casings being split by the waxy white petals within. Weird how the ones she'd placed on the windowsill up in her studio hadn't done a thing.

CHAPTER 3

Birds chattered and squabbled outside the kitchen window. She watched them flit to the bird table where they rapidly pecked at the seed-covered platform before returning to less exposed perches.

Is there, she wondered, an order to their visits? The blue tits, robins and chaffinches all seemed to get along well. The nuthatch or tree-creeper — she was not sure which — was shy, timing its visits to when no others were feeding. The starlings were like hyenas, swooping in as a noisy group, plundering all they could. Steaming, she thought. That's what they called it in London: when gangs of youths went mugging en masse.

She'd woken in the night. Not from a dream. She wasn't sure, at first, why. Owen was sound asleep, his gentle rasp too light to have bothered her. Then she spotted the glow at the edges of the curtains. The security light overlooking the back garden had clicked on. Something outside made a scraping noise. Plastic clattered on stone. Quick footsteps and a huff of breath. Heart beating slightly faster, she climbed out of bed and lifted the corner of the curtain just as the floodlight went out. But in that brief instant before the darkness surged back, she'd spotted movement. Something dark and bulky lumbering across the lawn.

'How big do badgers get?' she asked Owen over

breakfast.

He looked at her for a moment, the muscles in his jaw flexing as he slowly chewed. 'Big enough. They used to put dogs against them. Still do in some parts, I imagine.'

'So they can be the size of a dog?'

'I've seen old brocks – the males – not far off the size of a sheep. Why?'

'The bin-lids were knocked off in the night. I heard one of them go and looked out the window. Something was making for the shadows just as the security light went out.'

'Badger,' he nodded. 'We'll have to put up a special fence if we want to grow anything in the summer. It's a big job, too.'

She gave him a questioning look while reaching for the cafetière.

'The fence has to go about three feet under the ground then out at ninety degrees for another couple of feet. Stops them digging under. I think they've got this place marked as a meal stop on their nightly rounds.' Stiffly, he climbed down off the stool and brushed at the corners of his mouth as if smoothing an invisible moustache. 'Right, I'd better be off. Don't load the bird table with too much food; that only encourages the bloody things to sniff about.'

'OK. What time will you be home?'

He lifted his leather satchel from the side, checking the brass buckles were secure. 'Seven, eight? I'll call you after lunch; I'll have a better idea by then. What will you do today?'

'Not sure. Poke around on the internet for a bit. See what else I can find on tinnitus.'

He frowned slightly. 'Have you been hearing it again?'

'Only once or twice,' she lied.

'OK.' He bent forward to kiss her. 'Try not to dwell on it – I'm sure it will only make it worse. Speak to you later.'

She sighed with exasperation. There was just too much

information on the internet. It was now after ten and she was still sitting at the breakfast bar, flicking through screens.

Increasingly, she liked the forums best. Something about the actual experiences of others. The official stuff was fine: she now knew that tinnitus was a very common condition – one that affected about a tenth of all adults in the UK. Its onset could be linked to a stressful event – like moving house. It often occurred in later life. Some sufferers resorted to wearing a WNG – or white noise generator – to mask the sound. Please, she thought, don't let it come to that.

But for her, it was real people talking about what it meant for them that resonated most.

The DJ who woke one morning after a festival to the sound of Morse code beeping in both ears.

The travelling salesman who had given his collection of noises different names: the Seven Dwarves for the chorus of whistles, the Flock of Pigeons for the barrage of fluttering, the Motel TV for the barely audible drone.

The pensioner who slept next to her aquarium to find solace in the gentle fizz of bursting bubbles.

Outside the window, the birds scattered and the garden was suddenly quiet. Strange, she thought, craning her neck to try and see what might have scared them off.

And that's when the singing started. It was so insubstantial as to be almost the hint of a sound. An echo that hadn't quite died. She fixed her stare on a distant plane creeping stealthily across the grey sky. Was the sound carrying from somewhere far away? Or was it in her head? She inserted the tip of a forefinger in her ear, wiggled it and listened again. The cascade of notes continued. She raised her hand and gently banged the heel of it against her temple, then did the same to the other side. It failed to dislodge the noise.

The mere act of getting off the stool – the whisper of her silk dressing gown – was enough to drown it out. She opened the window and remained motionless, listening for it again.

Now, she thought, I've let the sounds of the outside world in. An engine revving from down in the valley behind the house. A metallic clanking sound. A sheep bleating plaintively and, as if in response, a crow's mocking caw. None of them loud, but enough to make pinpointing the trickle of notes impossible. Which meant it was coming from inside the house, surely?

She closed the window and then her eyes. Behind the faint whirr of her laptop she heard a snatch of it again. She looked down. It was coming from below her feet. The cellar! It was down in the cellar. But even as she started towards the narrow door in the far corner, her certainty lost strength. Now it seemed to be coming from behind the wall to her right. On the other side of that was the shed with the arched doors. Was it able to move, this bloody sound?

'First things first,' she muttered, turning back to the cellar door. The light switch was to the side. She turned it on before pushing the door open. The steep flight of stone steps led down to another flagged floor. She pulled her gown tighter and, as she took the first step, kept a handful of material clutched at her throat.

She remembered the first time they looked around the cottage. She'd recoiled at the cellar's cold and clammy atmosphere. Owen had said that, if it was to be ever free of damp, they'd have to have it properly tanked. She'd had no idea what that meant.

The yellowish paint on the walls was peeling away, like the skin on a sunburnt back. The slabs making up the floor were covered in a moist sheen. On the bottom step, she looked uneasily about. At face level to her immediate right was the fuse box. The rows of switches were all down. Little labels below them read: cooker, smoke alarm, lights first floor, lights ground floor, lights basement, security alarm. At the end of the row was a large red one labelled

Main Switch. A mass of grey wires sprouted from the top and ran up the wall before disappearing through the ceiling.

At the top of the wall on the far side was a small window that, according to the estate agent, swung inward on the hinges along its upper edge. The panes of glass were thick like the bottom of jam jars. Mildew or lichen had stained them a faint green. A low wall of misshapen bricks closed off a narrow rectangle of floor immediately below it. For coal, the estate agent had explained. In times gone by, the window – which was just below ground level outside – would be opened, allowing the delivery to be poured straight through.

Now the only thing in the bricked-off area was a layer of dead leaves that had fallen through the gap at the base of the window above. As she stepped off the bottom step, the leaves rustled and shifted. A shudder gripped her. Toads. Living among the decay. She found the animals repugnant. Owen said he'd removed them, but they must have got back in. Surviving on...it was too disgusting to even contemplate.

Elbows tight at her sides, hand still clutched at her throat, she stood perfectly still and listened. Shelves lined one wall and on them they'd piled various things. Crates of spare plates and crockery. A toolbox. Salad bowls, walking boots and tennis rackets. Tins of paints the decorators didn't use up. Books on gardening. Paint rollers in their trays. A box containing spare batteries, light bulbs and Owen's old mobile phone, before he was persuaded to upgrade to something with a touch screen.

A fragment of birdsong wafted across her ears and she looked up at the underside of the kitchen floor. Web-shrouded wires and pipes were tacked to the criss-crossing beams. Did it come from above? She thought it did. Quickly, she climbed back up the stairs, relieved to be out of the dank pit. Standing in the kitchen, she readied herself to listen once more. But she knew – and she had no idea how – that it was gone. For now.

She realised the birds had also begun returning to the garden and she moved to the side of the room with the views over Manchester. Small splodges of colour were in the field beside the nearby church. The people, continuing with whatever they were doing. Time, she decided, to discover what they were up to. Maybe see if the vicar was there, too. Moving to a place like this, it seemed the right thing to do – even though she only ever went to church at Christmas.

CHAPTER 4

Her car plunged into the shadows of the lane and when she eventually reached the main road, she turned back towards the village. After crossing the river, the road rose sharply, taking her past a canal that led, in a series of locks, up to an ugly-looking cliff face of bricks. At its base was a row of three arches.

It was, she remembered Owen saying, and old battery of kilns for burning lime. Canal boats once transported the stuff from quarries in the nearby Peak District. It was fed into the top of the kiln and the temperatures inside reduced it to something powdery that farmers spread on their fields or builders used in cement. Now the canal lay still and brown, the kiln's arches long since sealed up with grey blocks.

A small sign directed her to Oldknow church and, turning off the road, she found herself on a narrow lane bordered on both sides by head-high dry-stone walls. The road continued to climb before twisting round to reveal the church itself. Stone, darkened by passing years, made up its sombre walls – but warm light was shining out from the half-open front doors.

She parked alongside the cluster of vehicles in the small car park and made her way across the graveyard. She wasn't sure whether to poke her head into the church or continue straight round to the field on the far side. A voice speaking from inside the porch caused her to pause on the path.

'Hello?' she tentatively called.

A youngish man – early thirties perhaps – with a head of thick brown hair stepped out. He was wearing a fitted jacket, jeans and brown leather shoes. As he looked at her with inquisitive eyes, he pointed to the mobile phone held to his ear. 'That sounds splendid, Marjorie. Lovely. Yes. Absolutely. No, no – I think you're right. Yes. OK, I really must – yes? No I agree. Marjorie? I –' He rolled his eyes at her.

She tried to suppress a smile: it was just like when her mum used to ring at an awkward time. No amount of polite hints could get her off the phone, either.

'Splendid. That's wonderful. See you then, Marjorie. OK. Thanks. Bye, then. Goodbye.' The hand holding the phone to his face lowered and she spotted his dog collar.

'Sorry about that; one of my older parishioners. She does like a chat.'

She couldn't think what to say: there were a whole load of reasons why she didn't think he was the vicar. Age, good looks and nice dress sense, for a start.

'Martin Flowers.' He was holding out his hand and smiling. Nice teeth, too.

'Sorry.' She lifted her own hand and felt it grasped briefly. A firm grip, warm, smooth skin against hers. 'Laura Wilkinson.'

He glanced to the side. 'Are you helping with the dig?'

'The dig? No...is that what's going on?' She pointed a finger behind her. 'I can see them in the field from my kitchen. We've just moved in…'

He looked over her shoulder. 'To Lantern Cottage? So you're the new owners.'

'Yes.' She turned round and there, clearly visible on the hillside across the valley, was her new home. The sun was shining through scudding cloud; large blotches flowing soundlessly across the landscape. As one swept the cottage, the smile fell from her lips.

She could see a dark figure up on the roof. He stood, stiff and sentinel-like, staring in her direction. Staring, she felt certain, at her. She turned to the vicar, confused and alarmed.

He caught her eye. 'Is something…?'

She pointed her finger and looked back to the cottage. The cloud shadow had moved on and now the solitary building was bathed in bright sunlight. The figure had been replaced by the chimney. She frowned. 'How odd.'

'Sorry?'

'The chimney – it looked just like a man up there on our roof. I thought we were being burgled.'

He laughed gently. 'Trick of the light, as they say. Such a pretty little place.'

She checked the chimney again. The slightly flared upper part and rounded pot on the top had formed – for a second – the head and shoulders of a person. *Funny*, she mused, *how I was so sure it was a man.* 'Yes it is,' she murmured.

From this distance, she was able to see the farmland rising up behind the cottage. She realised she didn't even know who owned it. After a few hundred metres the carpet of rough fields stopped. As if an ancient farmer, confronted by the increasingly steep slopes, had swung his plough round and thought: enough. Any further is futile.

The moor beyond was raw and untamed. Its surface had been divided up, true. But the dry-stone walls seemed little more than a network of thin lines scarring it. Interconnecting welts. Beneath them, the land's solid bulk continued to dip and swell, buckling in places to rocky ridges. Above these high points, a few dark birds floated. They gazed silently down on the brooding terrain.

'I'd been planning on dropping by and introducing myself,' Martin said.

She looked back at him. 'Oh – that's very kind. It seems a lovely area. I feel very lucky.'

'Isn't it? I only took over here a couple of months ago,

but I've been made to feel incredibly welcome. Where have you moved from?'

'Richmond – we lived in a place on the edge of the park.'

There was a knowing smile on his face as he started slowly along the path round the church. 'I grew up near Dulwich.'

'Really?' she asked, falling in beside him. She found his relaxed manner calming; a welcome contrast to her husband's current tense state. 'So what brought you to this part of the world?'

'I was a student in Manchester. Here is just great.' He nodded at the city's massed buildings on the flat land laid out before them. 'Manchester twenty minutes in that direction, the heart of the Peak District twenty minutes in the other. Perfect.'

She found herself nodding. 'It is nice, though the weather is a bit different from down south.'

He laughed. 'You mean wetter? Well, that's true. So, the Archaeological Society has caught your interest?'

They rounded the corner of the church. Visible in the field beyond the graveyard wall was a line of poles linked by fluttering white tape. Inside the perimeter, the grass had been mown short. Sections of the turf had been peeled back. Revealed beneath were swathes of rich soil. This, in turn, had been dug away in places. About a dozen people were gathered in one shallow trench, some kneeling, others lying on their sides.

She just stopped herself from saying that things seemed all quiet on the Western front. 'What are they doing?'

'It's an iron age hill fort. Aerial photographs revealed its presence in the summer: apparently rays of the setting sun caught on what was left of the foundations.'

'That's fascinating. What have they found so far?'

He spoke out of the corner of his mouth. 'Not much actually. Much to their annoyance. A few fragments of pots. One bit of metal which might be the tip of an arrowhead. I think they were hoping for something more dramatic. You know, King Offa's last stand against the Romans or similar.'

She giggled. 'King Offa? You're about a millennium out.'

He clicked a finger in mock frustration. 'Bloody hell, you had to be a historian.'

Laughter was rising up and she tried to keep it down. What emerged was a throaty chuckle. She stole a glance in his direction. He wasn't like any vicar she'd ever met.

Suddenly, his hand went up. 'Adrian? You have a visitor.'

She looked back at the field. A stocky man in combat trousers and an orange cagoule was making his way over.

'This is Adrian Moore – head honcho on the project. Adrian – Laura Wilkinson. She's just moved into Lantern Cottage.'

His eyes shifted momentarily to the side, but he avoided looking fully in the direction of her home. Then he leaned his forearms on the top of the graveyard wall and interlinked his fingers. 'Lantern Cottage? We've seen the builders coming and going these past few weeks.'

'Yes.' The breeze had grown stronger and she smoothed a stray strand of hair, suddenly conscious that looking across the valley was a two way thing. We'd been a source of interest, she realised, before even moving in. 'There were a fair amount of things that needed to be fixed.'

'Well, it had been empty for some time.'

She thought of the previous occupants; from what the estate agent had said, they were an older couple who had moved out when the cottage's remote location had become a problem. 'I'm just glad we found it before anyone else snapped it up. It's so cosy and quiet.'

He breathed in deeply through his nose. 'Rain's on the way.' He turned his back on us and lifted his chin. 'Thought so. Coming in off the Irish Sea.'

Had he, she thought, smelled it on the wind? She looked across the Cheshire Plain: he was right. Moving inland from the west was an ominous band of grey cloud. Veil-like ribbons hung motionless below it.

'Better get packing up.' He ambled away, leaving her feeling like she had somehow offended him.

'Man of few words,' Martin quietly said. 'A lot of the older men around here are. We could pop into the church hall.'

'Thanks,' she replied, watching Adrian's retreating form. Was that really the reason he had suddenly walked away? 'Are you sure you're not too busy ...'

'Only putting the kettle on for that lot,' Martin replied. 'Come on – you can even see that prize arrowhead.'

There was a hint of sarcasm in his voice and she couldn't help smiling. 'Well, now you've mentioned that, how could I refuse?'

CHAPTER 5

'Your husband is, I gather, very respected in the world of classical music.'

She stopped blowing into her mug of tea and looked up. 'He is.'

'A few older members of my congregation – they remember him being the church organist here,' he explained. 'One or two even remember him as a choirboy.'

'I'm still getting used to the change from living in London. It's so much more anonymous down there.'

'True. But also rather lonely, don't you think?'

She met his eyes, wondering if it was a subtle reference to her past. She hoped the time when she'd become ill wasn't common knowledge, too.

'Big cities,' he added breezily. 'The sense of community can struggle to survive.'

It was the first time he'd actually sounded like a vicar. 'Yes,' she responded, deciding his earlier comment had been an innocent one. 'I couldn't have named anyone on our street in Richmond other than our immediate neighbours.'

On the wall in front of her was a row of three noticeboards, each one covered by photographs of the excavation. Pins in the pictures had been connected by lines of coloured thread to little squares of paper. Inner Rampart. External ditch. Six post holes. Raised platform. Area of vitrified stones.

In a small glass cabinet, the various finds had been lined up. Martin was correct; not much to show so far. The rather hopeful question mark added to the label reading 'fragment of arrowhead' made the meagre display seem even sadder.

'So, everyone knows all about Owen Wilkinson,' Martin said, now perched on the edge of a table. 'But what about you?'

'Me? Oh, I don't know…' She hated talking about herself.

'How did you two meet?'

'He was conducting the orchestra. Hair flying all over the place, arms furiously waving around.' She smiled. 'He was a bit younger then.'

So you're a musician? Let me guess – flute or violin? No, I know: harp.'

She realised her hand had been drifting about in the air. 'Neither – I was a ballet dancer. It was a performance of Swan Lake. But no one can be a dancer for ever. It takes a terrible toll.'

He nodded. 'Don't they say dancers die twice? The first time being when they have to give up their profession.'

Every time she heard that comment it made her feel miserable. As if she were a cat, halfway through her allotted lives. She turned back to the display cabinet. That was miserable, too. 'I was ready. Mid-twenties. It was time. There were so many other things I wanted to do.'

'And what were those?'

She kept her face averted. Start a family, she wanted to say. Become a mother, watch my children grow up. Not be…not be a spare part. A childless appendage to a successful man's career. 'Just live a normal life, I suppose. Stroll on beaches. Lounge in bed. Eat ice cream.'

'Escape the regime of being a dancer, then. I take it you were pretty good?'

She spotted a collection box on the windowsill. That little girl again. To avoid answering him, she walked over, lifted it up and read the sticker. 'Help Molly get her operation.'

The vicar sighed. 'We're getting there … slowly.'

The collection box, she noticed, was almost empty. 'Who is she?'

'Molly Maystock? She lives back towards the village. Her dad is a firefighter – he enters every running race going to raise funds for her.'

Laura recalled that the butcher hadn't mentioned a mother either. 'Is he a single dad?'

Martin nodded. 'The mum walked out when Molly was still tiny; before the diagnosis. New husband now, apparently. Lives near Edinburgh.'

Laura shook her head. How heartless. To abandon your baby like that, how could she? She stared into the little girl's eyes. And someone so angelic, so beautiful. Whoever the mother was, she didn't deserve to be called that. A mother should never, ever –

'It wasn't easy for her,' Adrian added. 'It was before my time, but I gather she had issues about the fact she had even got pregnant in the first place.'

Replacing the collection box, Laura looked at Martin. 'That's no excuse.'

He opened his mouth then closed it. Laura realised how much venom had been in her voice. The silence began to stretch and she suddenly knew he was aware that she didn't have children. She could see the knowledge in his eyes. He took a sip of his drink and she did the same.

'So, do you continue with any ballet? You look very…' A hand was held in her direction. He struggled to find the appropriate word.

'Thank you. I do yoga and Pilates – but just at home. Before moving up here, I taught part-time at a little prep school in Richmond. That certainly kept me on my toes.'

He leaned forward. 'Ballet classes?'

'Dance in general – simple stretches, posture-related exercises. Music and Movement, I called it.' She could tell he was thinking about something.

'There's a respite centre near here. In a big old farm out near Rowarth. It's all been converted and modernised. There are even a few residential units. It's for kids with disabilities – some quite severe. Molly?' He gestured at the collection box by her elbow. 'She goes there some afternoons. I know they're always looking for volunteers – especially people who can offer forms of therapy.'

Laura looked down at her drink. The children she'd taught had all been perfect little things. Princesses-in-training; that's how she referred to them with Owen. All of them had wealthy parents, nannies – some even chauffeurs. 'What sort of disabilities?' she asked uneasily. 'I don't have experience of…'

'Oh, trained medical staff are always on hand. That wouldn't be a worry. Some are autistic, others have medical conditions. Quite a few are in wheelchairs. One or two need walking frames. The place survives on a shoestring budget.'

A thought jumped into her head. 'Why don't I talk to Owen about a fundraising event? He could come here and do an organ recital – all proceeds to the…what's the centre called?

Martin's eyes were almost popping out. 'The Skylark Trust. Would he consider doing that?'

'Why not? As you said, he was the organist here once, wasn't he? The prodigal son returns.'

He placed his cup of tea down and raised both hands. 'Laura – they'd be queuing out the doors for that. Really – it could raise a huge amount of money. You really think he'd consider it? It's the sort of thing the local papers would love. Even the nationals, probably!'

'Why don't I ask him? Leave it with me,' she said flippantly, finishing off her drink.

'This is…' He fumbled excitedly in his jacket pocket. 'Here, take my card. It's got my mobile and landline.'

A silhouette of the church and, in white lettering,

Martin's details. The church even had a website address and a Facebook page.

Through the window she could see members of the Archaeological Society climbing through a narrow gap in the graveyard wall. With their different coloured fleeces and assortment of hats, they looked like a group of retired ramblers. 'Thanks for the tea. I'll make a break for it before that rain blows in.'

'I'll walk you round.'

'No need,' she replied quickly. 'Besides – that lot will be wanting their tea.' She pointed out the window.

Adrian Moore was out there, standing next to a furred tombstone. He was staring at her through the window with an intense look.

CHRIS SIMMS

CHAPTER 6

Laura let the music filling her car wash over her. Hey la, day la, my boyfriend's back. She loved these girl groups from 50s and 60s America. The Chiffons. The Shirelles. The Ronettes. Joyful lyrics she sang along to if Owen wasn't in the car. He said the music was naive and silly; she found its innocence a delight.

He couldn't understand why she never listened to the music she once performed to. The thought of Tchaikovsky made her shudder. She'd heard it was often the same with professional sportspeople when they retired: tennis players who never lifted a racket again, swimmers who forever avoided the pool.

Hidden inside a CD case for Diana Ross and The Supremes was *Never Mind the Bollocks* by the Sex Pistols. She loved that music because it simply didn't give a shit. She smiled: if Owen knew about that, he would have been absolutely horrified.

She let the song finish then turned the engine off. The dispiriting sound of rain on the car roof replaced it. She looked at the dark windows of Lantern Cottage and wished she had left a light on inside; it was so horrid coming home to a cold, empty house.

Once in the kitchen, she turned the central heating on then made her way round the ground floor, flicking on lamps. In the living room she looked at the protruding bricks of the hearth and thought of the chimney jutting out of the roof above. Had it been deliberately designed to look like a figure? It had certainly fooled her earlier on.

She peered through the little window set deep in the thick wall. Strange spiders, with bodies like grains of rice and impossibly long legs, had spun their webs in the corners of the window frame. However much she vacuumed them away, others soon appeared. The field by the church was empty and she pictured them all in the little hall. A few could be looking across right now, watching the cottage lights going on.

Back in the kitchen she realised the phone was blinking. A message from the doctor's surgery – an appointment had become free the very next day. The joys of a rural GP practice! How long, she wondered, would I have waited back in Richmond? She called back to confirm, then looked at the clock. 12.20. Just time for some exercise before lunch.

The fact her first-floor studio was at the back of the cottage filled her with relief; all the window faced was empty farmland. No church, house or anything else overlooking it. Her privacy was complete.

After changing into shorts and a baggy top and tying back her hair, she selected Taffetas on the i-Pod. As the pleasant guitar melodies began, she checked the lilies on the windowsill. Spots of black had started to break out at the bases of the large green flower buds. The flesh of the stalks also seemed to be losing their firmness. Perhaps they'd been infected with an airborne fungus, she thought, wondering if the flowers inside were still alive.

She went into a series of light stretches before the floor-to-ceiling mirrors. She'd had them mounted on the wall that separated the studio from their bedroom next door. Like the rest of the cottage, the wall was of a solid construction; she'd exercised in here during the evening while Owen was reading in bed and he hadn't heard a thing.

Once warmed up, she stood in the neutral position and

gauged if any part of her felt like it needed any more loosening. Her neck and shoulders. She spread her exercise mat across the floorboards and decided on a few yoga poses: svanasana, gomukhasana and the namaste.

As she worked, her mind wandered to the conversation with Martin Flowers. He seemed nice; young, positive, perhaps too eager to come across as unconstrained by traditional expectations of what a vicar should be. Joking about in his own graveyard certainly didn't feel right.

His comment about the Skylark Trust came back. Taking a class for severely disabled kids.

She got to her feet, lifted one knee to hip level, then raised the big toe of the foot still on the floor. She lowered it slowly back down and lifted the toes next to it, keeping her big toe flat. The skin of her lower shin flexed out as the tendons and muscles beneath contracted. The novelty of exercising in bare feet still hadn't completely worn off – so many years wearing ballet shoes. She sighed. It was no use pretending otherwise; the only reason she'd suggested Owen's fundraising event was to deflect the vicar's attention from herself. Severely disabled kids. What did that mean? He'd mentioned wheelchairs and walking frames. She pictured twisted spines and wasted legs. Heads that lolled, wrists curling in on themselves. Drool.

She admitted it: she didn't think she'd be able to do it. It felt awful. If the kids' problems were less extreme, then maybe. Like that little Molly: her disease was hidden away inside. She looked...she looked...well, normal.

She swapped legs and as she started working her other toes, looked guiltily at her reflection. It wasn't as if she didn't have the time to take a class. But you needed training, surely, to deal with people who were so disabled? Especially children. Or am I, she wondered, just being selfish? Not much better than Molly Maystock's mum.

By the time the album approached its finish she'd worked her way through another dozen poses. She was breathing lightly. The endorphins released by the exercise were coursing through her, creating a sense of energy and wellbeing – along with a strong urge to eat.

After crossing over to the docking station she cut the music. But silence didn't return. The singing was there. She stared over at the mirrors. Her reflection stared back with a frown. The singing had returned. How long had it been masked by the music? Carefully, she let the breath seep silently from her mouth. The notes were faster, more insistent. They'd never felt this clear before. Where the hell were they coming from?

On tiptoes, she moved towards the window, closed her eyes and leaned her forehead against the glass. No, it was not coming from outside. She felt sure of that. She looked at herself again. Is it in my skull? She lifted her chin and gargled air at the ceiling. She shook her head, causing her ponytail to swing about. The sounds continued to hover at the far limit of her hearing. Was it coming from their bedroom?

She stepped quietly into it and looked around. Her eyes travelled along the timber beam spanning the ceiling. But now it seemed to be in the bathroom. She turned round and crossed the corridor. The tiles felt cold beneath her bare feet. Air in the pipes, maybe? She turned both sink taps on full, shut them off and listened again. Water slid down the plug hole with a slight choking sound. Silence. It had gone.

As she breathed out with relief it started again. Scratching at her scalp with both hands, she looked about. 'Ssshhhhh! Be quiet!'

It continued for a few seconds more, slowed and stopped. But she knew it wasn't because of anything she'd said. This is ridiculous, she thought, trotting down the stairs and opening her laptop.

Once the website for the Tinnitus Sufferers' Association had loaded, she clicked on the tab marked Forum. 32,781 members. Over 600 people currently online. 143 of them unregistered – including herself. She looked at the discussion topics.

Advice for tinnitus newbies.

Tinnitus…a way forward.

Tinnitus in one ear.

Tinnitus and TV.

Tinnitus or not?

Corticoid injections.

Success with grommets.

She picked at her lower lip. Should I join? Should I share my experiences? She snapped the laptop shut. The noise I've been hearing isn't coming from in my head. I don't want it to be in my head. It is real. I want it to be real.

CHAPTER 7

The noises came back in the night; scratching sounds, the scrape of a patio pot being moved. She was awake anyway, lying on her back with one hand cupping her lower stomach. She was awake because the dream had forced her from the depths of sleep.

It had been about the curled figure once again. The knees splaying outward, one arm twisted back behind the head. She lay in bed puzzling over the image. Her viewpoint in the dream was odd. The figure seemed suspended in space, allowing her to circle about it at will, observing it from below, above, side on, in front. She couldn't work out how gravity was affecting the figure. Was it lying on its back, with its knees raised up? Or was it on its front with the arm bent behind the head – almost like in a yoga pose?

In her other dream – the one from when she became ill – she knew that figure was lying on its side in the foetal position. And she knew it was at the end of a long tunnel. But this, newer, dream? It felt the same: cold and dark. But there was something different about the tunnel itself. It made her feel disoriented and unbalanced and, because of that, unsettled. Frightened, even.

'I heard movement again last night. Outside.'

'Mmm?' Owen looked up from his breakfast. 'Movement?'

'Like the other night. Something poking around in the garden.'

He dipped the tip of a teaspoon into the sugar bowl and stirred a minute quantity into his coffee. 'Did you cut back on the amount of bird feed you're putting out?'

'I don't think the noises are out on the grass. It's from nearer the house. The back patio.'

'But badgers do that – they forage about. The bird feed could be what's luring them in.'

She thought about this. Owen was probably right. 'How did things go yesterday? You seemed exhausted when you got in.'

His eyebrows lowered. 'I'm going to have to start banging heads together soon. The same issue keeps coming back.'

'Dynamics at the end of the second movement?'

'Dynamics at the end of the second movement,' he raised both hands, eyes fixed on the far wall. 'We build to the crescendo; I've brought everything in: all the strings, the entire brass section,' he gestured to his right, 'tuba, French horn, trumpet.' He lowered his voice. 'The bass drum is thundering. Boom da da boom da da boom! Then the cymbals, then the timpani and then,' he pinched the air, 'silence. Silence for an instant before I want the sopranos to come in.' He began a high-pitched whisper. 'So far, so far, so far to the sea.' Dropping his hands he looked at her angrily. 'They won't do as I say: and now I can see them – the bloody prima donnas – looking to the blasted first violin and not me. I can see the glances going between them. Well, if he wants a battle, too, he can have one. The end of rehearsal yesterday? He put his violin away and walked out. Not a bloody word said in my direction.' His jaw was tight as he reached for his drink.

This isn't good, she thought. Owen needed the first violin on his side. As leader of the orchestra, the first violin's body language alone could influence everyone else's mood. Nothing needed to be said; just the way he lifted his bow decided how all of them performed. 'Can't you have a quiet word with him? Get him to explain to the sopranos exactly what you're looking for at that point?'

'Not if he marches out the moment rehearsals finish,' Owen retorted, lifting his cup with a sulky look.

Neither said anything for a moment.

'I drove across to Oldknow church yesterday,' she announced. 'To see what's going on in the field next to it.'

'The church? I see.' He glanced at his watch.

'Those people we've noticed are archaeologists – amateur ones. It's an Iron Age hill fort, the site they're excavating.'

He looked at her and blinked. 'A hill fort?'

'Yes, next to Oldknow church. Makes sense really, given its elevated position.'

His eyes turned to the window. 'I haven't been back to the church in – I don't know how many years. I bet it hasn't changed.'

'Some of the congregation remember you as a choirboy, apparently.'

He raised an eyebrow. 'They do? How do you know that?'

'I was chatting to the vicar. Youngish man called Martin Flowers. He took over the church not long ago.'

'It's got a lovely organ, you know. I pretty much learned to play on that organ. Before winning my place at the RNCM.'

'I know.'

He smiled a nostalgic smile. 'We should go up there some time.'

She brushed at an ear, deciding now would be a good time to mention it. 'They are trying to raise money for a little girl who lives locally. She needs a particular treatment that's only available in America.'

'Reginald Burridge. That was the name of the vicar when I was organist. Succeeded by a fellow called Dobby. Now that is going back a bit.'

'This little girl they're raising money for. Molly Maystock, she's called. The vicar and I discussed the possibility of you doing some kind of fundraising event.'

His smile vanished. 'He what?'

'An organ recital possibly? They could charge for tickets, all proceeds to the little girl's medical fund.'

'Who the bloody hell does he think he is approaching you directly like that?'

'I suggested it, as a matter of fact.'

'You did? Jesus Christ, Laura. You said I'd do an organ recital?' The thread veins across his cheekbones are showing, he's gone so pale.

'No, I said it was possible you might consider it.'

'I've got a bloody performance this Sunday evening and you're committing me to other events?'

'Owen, calm down. No details were discussed; it was mentioned in passing. That was all.'

He marched across to his leather satchel, muttering to himself.

As he gathered up his things she looked at the back of his neck. There was a latticework of wrinkles showing in the red skin. 'What time do you expect to be home?'

'What time?' He flashed an angry glance at the church. 'God knows. Depends on whether the sopranos decide they would actually like to follow my instructions.'

The satchel was under one arm and he kicked off his slippers. 'Owen – the organ recital was just a suggestion for the future. That was all.'

'Well, isn't that a relief?' he said sarcastically, picking up his jacket by the collar and jiggling it up and down. His keys chinked. 'Where are my bloody keys?'

'In your jacket – I heard them.'

He patted a pocket. 'So they are. I need to go.'

'OK. Good luck today. I'll see you later.'

He paused in the doorway and drew in a deep breath. 'I didn't mean to snap at you. Let's discuss it when I get back.'

That's fine.' She took the bowls and plates over to the sink.

'I'm sorry.'

'I said it's fine.' She felt silly now; a schoolgirl who'd taken offence at being scolded. His footsteps came across the room. A hand slid up her neck to the side of her face and he pressed his lips against her ear. His softly murmured words were huge, more vibration than sound. 'I'm sorry, my love.'

She cupped a hand over his, turning her head so their temples touched. 'Owen, it's your gift. And I love you for it.'

He sighed, wreathing her lips in warm air. She could taste his muesli in her mouth. 'It's such a bloody rigmarole.'

'It is now,' she whispered back. 'But when it's over, the clouds part. They always do.'

His chin lifted and he perched a tiny kiss on the tip of her nose. 'I couldn't do it without you. Really.'

'Go on, you'll be late.'

His fingers squeezed her arm then he set off once more. She stayed where she was, watching him hurry from the front porch. He's forgotten to comb his hair as usual, she thought. Strands were standing out at the sides. As he took the steep step up to the gravelly road, he avoided putting too much weight on his weaker right knee.

Look at him, the cruel voice suddenly said. Look at the pathetic failure of a man. Look at him hobbling up those steps. His thin legs are hardly strong enough to carry him. He's old and feeble and he'll die soon, he will, he'll die soon and you'll be all alone, all alone. Your life will be sad and empty –

She clattered the spoons into the sink, purposefully trying to drown out the ugly torrent of thoughts. She thought: it's like they're being streamed into my brain through an invisible earpiece. Owen had left half a piece of toast and she walked over to the kitchen door, opened it and stepped outside. Thank God, the words had stopped. She couldn't believe she could think such bitter, resentful things. Why would I look at my husband – a kind, thoughtful, reserved man of incredible talent – with such…she didn't even want to admit to the emotion: but it was there. Loathing. Pure loathing.

Owen's car grew quieter as it trundled off down the lane. The bird table was in front of her but something at the edge of the patio caused her to pause. As she suspected, the ceramic pots used for growing herbs had been disturbed. A trickle of soil had spilled from one and another was standing slightly away from the others. Next to it was a crumpled red object. She bent down for a closer look: a little box. The words on it said, *Sun Valley Raisins. 100% natural. 15g.* Snack-sized, like for a child's packed lunch. Owen didn't eat raisins and neither did she.

Her eyes swept the rest of the garden and then the fields beyond. No one was out there, watching. After putting the bit of toast on the bird table, she turned round and glanced up. Her heart lurched. A figure was looking down at her. The bloody chimney, she realised. It loomed there, silent as a sentinel.

She stepped back into the kitchen with a sense of unease. Standing there with an ear cocked, she half expected the birdsong to start up. Don't be silly, she told herself, with a quick look at the clock.

The appointment with Dr Ford wasn't for another forty minutes. Her eyes moved to her laptop at the end of the breakfast bar. Go on then, she thought. You may as well.

The sign-in screen for the Tinnitus Sufferers' Association asked her for a username and password. Seconds later, she was in. The discussion topic, 'Tinnitus or not?', had been initiated by someone experiencing a series of crackles, whistles and pops accompanied by intermittent feelings of nausea. Ear infection, the consensus seemed to be.

Laura opened up a new message box and got ready to type. Her fingers hovered. What do I say? That I'm hearing a sound – faint to the point of inaudible – that seems to come and go at will? A noise that, if I'm honest, seems to emanate from the very bricks and mortar of my home? She pinched at her lower lip, eyes on the blinking cursor. Then with a little nod, she began her message.

Does anyone hear birds singing? Hi there, ever since moving into my new home, I've been hearing little bursts of what I am certain is birdsong. I know tinnitus often sounds like buzzing, hissing or humming – but does anyone else ever hear a bird singing? It's really starting to get to me!!!

She pressed enter and immediately logged off. Why, she thought, do I feel this sense of trepidation? I've opened something, she realised. Not just a line of communication on my computer. By sharing my experience, I've opened something in my mind. And I have no idea what might now come in.

CHRIS SIMMS

CHAPTER 8

Dr Ford peered at her from beneath his bushy brows. 'Come and take a seat,' he said without getting up. She saw her medical notes were spread out before him.

She sat down and tried to give him a pleasant smile. His brusque manner had already set her on edge.

'Right, how have you been sleeping?'

'Not so well.'

His eyes were on whatever he'd written down after her previous appointment. 'Because of the dream?'

'Partly. I also think we may have badgers in the garden. Noisy things.'

He smiled. 'Welcome to the rural life. Did you try a hot drink before bed? Ovaltine always does the trick for me.'

'No. I'll get some after this.' She wanted to move things on: it was the damned noise that concerned her most. That and her lack of a period. But she didn't feel comfortable enough to mention that.

'Has the dream come back?'

'Last night it did.'

'The figure trapped in some kind of tunnel?'

'Yes.'

'Something's obviously making you feel anxious.'

'Funnily enough, it didn't seem to leave me feeling so unsettled,' she lied. 'Perhaps it's losing its power.'

'Through repetition, you mean?'

'Maybe.'

'What are your thoughts about counselling? Sure it couldn't help? I was looking back through your notes; to the time you became unwell a few years ago. Your sessions with a psychiatrist appeared to help you then.'

She pushed the memories away, fogged as they were from the volume of drugs they forced down her. 'Let's leave it for the time being. See if it doesn't fade of its own accord.'

'OK,' he breathed in through his nose, filling the room with a thin whistle. He could definitely do, she thought, with some nasal hair trimmers. 'You also touched on a problem with your ears, did you not?' He leaned back and crossed his legs.

I can hear birdsong inside my house, she wanted to say. I think it might be following me around. 'That's right.'

'Have you any pain in either ear?'

'No.'

'Feelings of nausea or dizziness?'

'No.'

'You don't seem to have a blocked nose or the beginnings of flu?'

'No.'

'Have you noticed moisture or any kind of discharge coming from the inner ear?'

'None at all.'

He leaned to the side, opened a drawer and removed a small black case. Inside was a piece of apparatus that looked to her like it belonged in a TV show. Dr Who's sonic screwdriver.

'This is an otoscope. It allows me to see into your ear.' He got up and moved behind her. He clicked his fingers next to her left ear. 'Did that sound clear to you?'

She nodded.

He clicked at her right ear. 'And that?'

'Fine.'

Good, I'll take a look inside now. It's not painful.'

She felt the nozzle of the thing pressing down on the

lower part of her ear. Part of her wanted to jerk her head clear: the fear of one's outer body being breached.

'Nothing amiss there.' He did the same on the other side. 'Fine there as well.' He came back into her field of vision and retook his seat. Removing a wipe from a pack on his desk, he began to clean the end of the otoscope. 'Your inner ear is absolutely fine. There is a healthy shine to the tympanic membrane –'

'Tympanic?'

He glanced at her. 'The eardrum.'

'Of course. Sorry – Owen was describing a crescendo earlier on. He mentioned the tympani; those tuned drums.'

'Latin,' Dr Ford smiled. 'Gets everywhere, doesn't it? All going fine with his preparations?'

'The usual last-minute niggles. He's such a perfectionist.' She left her answer at that.

Dr Ford nodded respectfully. 'Well, I'm glad to say your eardrums are perfectly fine. My guess is you have a mild viral infection. They normally settle down of their own accord after a week or so.'

'A virus? So this noise is just a symptom of a virus?' She felt giddy with relief. Just a virus.

He broke eye contact to carefully replace the otoscope. 'That would make sense. You've heard the noise again?'

'Yes. It was actually becoming quite annoying. Annoying and…actually, a little bit distressing.' She smiled, but his head was still bowed as he fiddled with the catch on the case. 'I was so afraid I'd developed tinnitus. Some people hear music or birdsong, apparently. I couldn't imagine anything more tormenting.'

He looked up at last. 'I don't think you need worry about tinnitus. Anything else you'd like to raise?'

She tried to summon the will to tell him about her disrupted menstruation cycle. The first thing he'd ask was when she'd last had sex. But it wouldn't be that: she and Owen rarely bothered any more. Certainly, not when he was preparing for a concert.

'Laura?'

She shook her head. 'No, that was all.'

'OK. Let me know if the Ovaltine helps with your sleeping and let's see you again in a fortnight.' He nodded at the door. 'You can book another appointment with the receptionist on your way out.'

'OK, thanks,' she got to her feet.

'And Laura?'

She looked back. He was already at the keyboard, getting ready to type up the details of her appointment.

'Let me know if you experience any changes.' He glanced at her for the briefest instant. 'To the noise.'

There was something furtive about his manner. 'Changes?'

'If it increases in frequency or volume...that sort of thing.' He was now focusing on his monitor.

'Right,' she replied, feeling a little mystified. 'Of course.'

She closed the door behind her and looked at the next person waiting. A young mum cradling a pale-looking baby. The little thing's limbs were so limp, it could have been dead. Then she heard a rattling wheeze in its chest. She hesitated, wanting to run her hand over the soft hair on the infant's head. The mother looked exhausted.

'Sorry if I kept you waiting,' Laura said, eyes drawn to the little thing once again. 'Your baby's beautiful.'

Thanks.' The mum's smile was forced. 'She kept me up all bloody night.'

Her answer irritated Laura. The woman didn't know how lucky she was. A thought flickered in Laura's mind. I could offer to care for the baby. While the mum goes back to bed and sleeps. I could cradle the little thing in my arms, sing her songs, stroke her face. Smell her.

Dr Ford's door creaked. 'Bernadette Morrison?'

CHAPTER 9

Across the valley, she could see them in the field, brushing at the earth. Sifting for secrets in the soil. Before driving home, she'd popped into the convenience store just along from the doctor's and bought some Ovaltine.

The small glass jar seemed from another age: rationing in the lean years after the war. She wasn't sure if she'd actually bother drinking the stuff, but after the relief of Dr Ford's diagnosis of a viral infection, she'd felt happy to follow his advice.

Coming out of the shop, she'd paused at the noticeboard in the post office next door. A photo of six little kittens arranged on a blanket jumped out at her. So sweet! They seemed to be nudging blindly about and she could almost hear their mewls. The message beneath the image said they were free to good homes, ready for collection mid-November. Just over a week ago. Wandering toward her car, she guessed they'd probably all been snapped up. Such a shame Owen couldn't stand cats.

Jar in one hand, she unlocked the porch door to a mass of letters on the floor. Once in the kitchen, she put her slippers on and started to flick through them. She realised she was humming a song to herself. Her shoulders weren't slightly raised and she didn't have one ear turned, anxiously listening for the sound. It was all being generated by a virus, that was all. Thank God.

Among the junk mail was a stout A4-sized envelope

addressed to Owen. It had been franked by a machine that identified it as having come from the Bridgewater Hall. Publicity, no doubt, about the forthcoming concert.

Below it was another letter, also franked. She frowned – this one had come from the High Peak Primary Care Trust. The letter inside wasn't aligned correctly and she couldn't quite see the name above the top line of their address. Was it to her or Owen? Putting it to the side, she turned on the kettle and removed her coat.

She really didn't like coming home to an empty cottage so often. In Richmond it was never as quiet as this. Down there was a constant flow of traffic, the occasional siren in the distance, the bustle of a nearby city. Here it was all solitude and silence. Too much of it.

There seemed to be a bit of a commotion going on by the church. Two figures were hurrying across to a group of three others. Arms were even waving. My, my, she said to herself, perhaps they've found the rest of that arrowhead.

She opened the laptop and, out of habit, immediately checked her emails. Top one was a message with an unusual subject line. Hi there Laura, please don't worry. She was about to consign it to the junk folder when she realised it had come via the Tinnitus Sufferers' Association forum.

Of course, she thought. The message I sent in. Someone has already replied. She perched on the bar stool and clicked the envelope.

Welcome to the forum, Laura! My name's Tamsin Harper and I'm one of the moderators. I live in San Francisco.

Laura paused. San Francisco. I went there once, on tour with The Royal Ballet back in the mid-nineties. *The Sleeping Beauty. Romeo and Juliet.* I had just made first soloist and my sights were already on principal. She carried on reading.

We're eight hours behind you in England, so what am I doing sending messages at 2 o'clock in the morning? Well, my T has gone acute, in fact it's been driving me nuts all night. Currently I have my maskers in to help, but the noise is still like a hurricane blowing through a keyhole!!!

So, you're hearing birdsong? Want to swap with me?! Seriously, I've traded messages with a few fellow sufferers who hear birds singing or music playing. Even specific songs sometimes. Over here, when it's not standard whistling, buzzing, or hissing – but tunes or song instead – we refer to them as musical hallucinations.

Laura stopped reading. That single word was enough to make the stool feel like it was toppling over. She gripped the edge of the breakfast bar tight. Hallucinations. Hospital memories surged back. Some for the first time. The smell of baby lotion on the hospital sheets. Water that tasted of formula milk. Sometimes it even appeared white. She didn't want to read the rest of Tamsin's message. Placing the cursor in the reply field, she began to type.

Thank you so much for your kind message. I've just returned from seeing my doctor and he told me I have a viral infection that should clear up on its own very soon. Sorry to have bothered you, but it looks like I'll be OK. Good luck with your own problem, kind regards, Laura.

She pressed send and then closed the laptop and pushed it away. I knew, she said to herself, that joining the forum was a bad idea. Why did I do it?

Over by the church, all of them were now gathered round one spot. Huddled in close. Something had caught their attention. She contemplated driving over to see what it was. They'll have enrolled me next, she smiled.

The letter from the High Peak Primary Care Trust stared up at the ceiling. She tried to push back the upper edge of the cellophane window. It was too well attached to let her see anything. She cocked her head: why would Owen have been sent anything from them? He certainly hadn't had any medical appointment since we moved up here. It must be for me.

Feeling slightly guilty, she extracted the smallest knife from the drawer and sliced the top of the envelope open.

It wasn't to either of them. It was to the parent or guardian of William Hall. She recalled that the old couple who lived in Lantern Cottage before them were called the Halls. She knew she should return it to the envelope for resealing. She knew she shouldn't read it. But now she was intrigued. She wanted to know more.

RE: William Hall, DOB 17.5.1996. Lantern Cottage, Coal Lane, Mill Brow, Oldknow, Derbyshire.

Assisted travel entitlement.

Dear Parent/Guardian,

Our records indicate that the assisted travel entitlement for William is due for review at the end of this year. It will help us to determine whether William should still qualify for assisted travel if you can confirm the following –

Does William still have a statement of Special Educational Needs?

Does he still attend the Skylark Centre in Rowarth three afternoons a week?

Do you still receive disability living allowance for William's continued care?

She scanned down to the letter's base. It had come from the Special Educational Needs Transport Team. She went back to the top. The date of birth given there put William in his late teens. What, she wondered, was wrong with him? Something profound, judging by this.

She wasn't sure what to do; obviously the Travel Team needed to update their records. Just scrawling 'return to sender' on the envelope and putting it in the post didn't seem enough. I should call them direct, she decided, explain I opened the letter in error and let them know William was no longer at this address. William Hall. She tried to remember the name of the parents. Edith and Roger? Yes that was it. Edith and Roger Hall – that's what the estate agent said. Odd he'd mentioned nothing about a son.

CHAPTER 10

The wind was tugging at the last few leaves clinging to the trees which lined the graveyard's lower edge. A couple finally lost the battle. They were whisked over the wall and banished to the wild grass beyond. Soon all the branches would be bare.

The church doors were shut so she continued on to the end of the graveyard. There were eight of them from the Archaeological Society and they were still congregated at one spot. An elderly lady saw her and several heads turned in Laura's direction. They conferred quietly before Adrian Moore broke off from the group and made his way over.

'Hi there,' she smiled, pushing some hair from her face. The wind was being a nuisance. 'Have you found something interesting? Only, I noticed the commotion from my kitchen window.'

He shot a glance in the direction of Lantern Cottage. 'Ah – yes.' His face turned back to her and she could tell he was weighing up what to say. The rest were watching and she got the feeling her presence there wasn't particularly welcome.

She stepped back. 'I didn't mean to pry. Sorry.'

He looked at Lantern Cottage again. 'No – you needn't apologise. We're in view from your window, simple as that. We have found something, yes.'

She wondered if it was an item of jewellery; something they'd like to keep quiet while they catalogued its position or whatever archaeologists did. 'If you're worried I'll say anything, you needn't be. I won't say a word.'

He studied her again. 'Well…'

'Go on Adrian, for goodness sake, spit it out! We're not a secret society!'

The comment came from an elderly lady in a red anorak. Adrian looked over his shoulder and she made a shooing motion at him with one hand. 'Go on!'

He turned back. 'It looks like it could be human remains. A skull.'

Oh, thought Laura. That isn't what I expected. 'A skull?' All of a sudden the site didn't seem quite so innocent. In fact, the shallow trenches now had a touch of something sinister.

He registered her troubled look. 'It's probably a peacetime burial. Wartime ones were normally dug outside the ramparts. It's simply a grave – like the ones behind you.'

She looked briefly at the ranked tombstones.

'It could be the offspring of a chieftain or other important person.'

'The offspring? It's not… not an adult skull, then?'

'Doesn't seem to be. Now, Mrs Wilkinson, I'm sure you appreciate there are people with less honourable motives than ours or yours. So I'll have to ask that you treat this in the strictest confidence.'

'Absolutely. What will you do – try and move it somewhere safe?'

'Once we've ascertained what else is in the vicinity, yes.' He moved away. 'And we're fast running out of light.'

She crossed her arms, unsettled by their revelation. 'Can… can I bring you over some tea? Biscuits?'

'Martin's on the case now. But I imagine he could do with a hand.'

'Hello!' she called out, nearing the doorway of the church hall's narrow kitchen.

'Hi!' He smiled, arranging cups on a tray. 'I didn't hear you come in.'

He'd got the same jacket on, but was now wearing brown corduroy trousers. They went well together.

'Isn't it exciting?' she announced.

'They told you? Adrian is treating it like they've unearthed the Holy Grail.'

'He had to – once he realised I had seen across from my kitchen.'

Martin laughed. 'Sworn to secrecy, though?'

She pressed a finger to her lips.

Grinning, he placed a few teaspoons on the tray.

'Can I help?'

'Would you? There are biscuits in that cupboard.'

'OK.' She squeezed past him. He was wearing aftershave: something woody. 'Shall I just bring out the whole box?'

'Good idea, we needn't bother with plates.' The two kettles clicked off and he started pouring water into each mug. 'Who'd have thought they'd unearth something this interesting?'

'I know. It's all very dramatic.'

He continued pouring water. 'Did you mention anything to your husband?'

She felt herself blush and was glad he was occupied with filling the cups. 'I did – but he's very focused on the coming performance. It's a big thing for him: conducting his own piece.'

'Specially commissioned by the Royal Northern College of Music, too. It's a sell-out, isn't it?'

'Apparently. And he's only got three more days to get things perfect. Best we wait until it's out of the way.' She smiled conspiratorially. 'I'll start working on him then.'

Martin looked awkward. 'Please don't feel in any way obliged. He must be incredibly busy.'

'He is. But he also has a soft spot for your church.' She reached for the fridge door. 'Milk?'

'Yes the whole carton, I suppose. How about the dance class? Did you have any more thoughts on that?'

She took her time locating the plastic container. 'I've been so busy getting things sorted at Lantern Cottage. I need to dig out my folder from when I took the classes at that prep school – see if anything could be appropriate.' She knew she was stalling, avoiding the question. It was pathetic. But she couldn't admit that the thought of a group of kids with severe disabilities terrified her.

'OK, it was just a thought.'

She could tell from his voice her dissembling hadn't gone unnoticed. She straightened up, milk carton in hand.

'I haven't mentioned anything to the people at the Skylark Trust,' he added. 'It's not like there's any hurry.'

Skylark Trust. She'd seen that name mentioned somewhere else. Where William Hall was going for his therapy. 'By the way, did you ever meet the last people who lived in Lantern Cottage?'

'No. Why?'

She waved a hand. 'Just curious. The estate agent mentioned that they were an elderly couple. I think they moved because of the location. The narrow lane up and awkward steps inside. At least that's what he said.' She kept looking at his profile. His head was bowed as he fished teabags from the cups.

'They moved out before my appointment. The cottage was empty – until you moved in.'

He glanced at her and she didn't see anything on his face to suggest he was concealing information.

'I could ask my congregation after the service this Sunday. Lord knows plenty of them like a chinwag, bless them.'

She picked up the biscuits. 'Would you mind?'

CHAPTER 11

Dusk had fallen by the time she pulled up outside the cottage. All its windows were dark and the chimney loomed up against the sullen sky.

She finished reading the leaflet and looked sadly across the valley. A cluster of spots glowed in the field. One or two shifted, winking out then reappearing as the lantern-carrier moved about. The scene should have had an enchanting quality, she thought. But it failed to stir her. She felt flat. Despondent. They'd cleared more mud from around the skull, and as she left, were preparing to cover the spot with a tarpaulin. Adrian Moore was even talking about pitching a tent and sleeping there to guard his find.

She'd peeped into the shallow pit, glimpsed the curve of bone showing in the earth and felt a worming sensation in her spine. It had risen rapidly up and caused her shoulders to hunch. But she'd also felt intrigued: who was the child? How old had it been? Why did it die? Grubbing around in a cold, muddy field suddenly made sense. To discover the answers to these questions must be fascinating.

With a sigh, she looked at the leaflet again. *The menopause.* It didn't make sense. She reread the opening lines. Fifty-one was the average age for when a woman's ovaries stopped producing. She closed her eyes. I'm thirty-nine. Menstruation could sometimes stop suddenly. She lowered the leaflet and became aware of her hands pressing against her lower abdomen. Was this it, then? Is my time over? She imagined her insides, empty of eggs. It made her feel like something within her had died.

It wasn't fair! I'm too young, I'm not ready. She turned a hand over and felt with her fingertips. I don't feel empty. She went through the list of symptoms again. Hot flushes, mood swings, palpitations. She had none of those. No night sweats or urinary infections. Everything felt normal. Some problems sleeping, yes. But that's to do with this place, she thought with a glance at the dark cottage. Not me.

She angled the rear-view mirror to examine her face. I don't feel old, or exhausted or...less of a woman. Oh God. Will Owen still find me attractive? Will anyone? She remembered the visit to the butchers'. How the brothers had reacted when she'd laughed. And the vicar; she'd spotted a few sparks in his eyes, too.

For some reason, her mind switched to the part-built swallows' nests at the chimney end of the cottage. Crumbling little mud ruins. Like the nesting birds had suddenly decided it was all futile. She shoved the leaflet back into the glove compartment.

Once in the cottage, she switched on the lights in the entrance hall then turned left to do the same in the lounge. It was only when she reached the far side of the room that she sensed something wasn't right.

That plant pot in the opposite corner was lying on its side. Small lumps of soil were spread across the carpet. She knew that particular palm had grown top-heavy, but it had never toppled over in their place down in Richmond. Her hands were frozen on the curtains, ready to draw them across the main window. She looked down. There were dark droplets on the windowsill. Blood. It was still wet. She felt the skin of her scalp tighten and everything suddenly sprang into sharp focus.

Heart hammering, she turned round. The magazines on the coffee table were all askew. Someone had been in the –

she swallowed back a wave of sickness. Someone could still be in the house.

Standing perfectly still, her mind shot into reverse. The porch had been locked. So had the front door. She thought of all the other ways of getting in: the kitchen door, the patio doors, the orangery doors. Ground-floor windows. Oh Jesus, she thought, why didn't I bother with the burglar alarm? Oh Jesus.

She hoped the person was upstairs, going through her jewellery. Please God, let him be upstairs. What was the quickest way out? The door into the snug was on her left, just the other side of the fireplace. There were speckles of soot scattered all over the hearth. What were they doing there? The door to the snug was ajar. The patio doors into the garden were just through it. But she didn't want to go into a dark room. No way was she going into a dark room. She decided to tiptoe back the way she'd come and slip out the front door. That way, she knew for certain no one was hiding between her and the way out. It meant getting across the length of the lounge then the hallway and into the porch. Twenty steps or so. That was all.

Her eyes crept to the right and she hardly dared breathe as she slowly lifted a foot. She stopped.

A tapping sound came from beyond the doorway into the snug. A fingernail making contact with glass? Tap. Tap. Tap. Something rustled. It sounded like the hem of the curtain dragging over the carpet. The noise came again. Was someone coming out from behind the curtain in there?

She leaped over the coffee table and started sprinting across the room. An image of a man – a dark silhouette – was in her mind's eye. He was coming out of the snug and pursuing her. Closing the distance. She got to the lounge door. There was no noise of movement behind her, no heavy breathing, no hand grabbing her hair. She didn't dare look back as she careered out into the hallway, slamming the door shut behind her. The rug shifted and she fall to one knee, a hand connecting with the oak floor. He would be just behind her now, about to crash through the door and dive on her back. It took all her balance not to go over completely. She regained her feet, tugged the porch door open and then the front door. Cold air. Out! Out and running away from the cottage. The lane stretched away before her. Too far back down to the junction. The hedge reared up on each side and she knew she'd be trapped there. Hemmed in. She swerved to the side, vaulted a waist-high wooden fence and ran out into the field. After a few seconds, she looked back.

No one was there. The front door was wide open. No one was there. She slowed to a stop, breath rasping in her throat. There was no one there, but there was no one to help, either. I have no neighbours, she thought. I'm alone up here. My phone. Thank God I have my mobile phone.

Not taking her eyes off the house, she eased it out of her jeans pocket and lifted it up.

Who the hell to call? Owen was in Manchester, miles away. The police? She could dial 999, but how long would it take for them to arrive? Who else, she thought, do I know nearby? The brothers who ran the butchers, but she had no idea of their number. Then she remembered Martin Flowers handing her his card. Her fingertips slipped into her back pocket and she felt it there. Oh, thank God. Keeping one eye on the cottage, she keyed his number in.

CHAPTER 12

'This is really embarrassing,' she murmured, sending another mortified glance at the police car and fire engine parked on the track before the cottage. 'There's no one in there.'

'We don't know that for sure,' Martin said. 'Are you warm enough?'

'Yes, thank you.' She had his ski jacket on, hands tucked into its pockets.

He'd taken less than five minutes to arrive, roaring up the narrow lane in a red sports car. At first, she thought he was going to rush straight into the house: her phone call had been jumbled at best. So she shouted across, one hand waving above her head.

He'd looked shocked to see her standing in the field, shivering in just a linen shirt. Removing the ski jacket from the back seat of his car, he'd set off towards her, speaking into his phone as he did so. The patrol car took less than quarter of an hour to arrive, shortly followed by a fire engine.

Watching the cottage windows, Laura could see people moving about in the house. Most seemed to be in the lounge. Then they began to make their way across the room, towards the hall. Seconds later, figures started pouring from the porch.

One of the police officers smirked. 'It's OK, madam. We've found the culprit.'

'Is it safe?' Martin asked. They were both the other side of the fence, long grass up to their ankles. Laura's feet were cold and wet.

'Safe?' The officer said, looking back at the cottage. 'What do you reckon, lads? Is it safe?'

The firefighters were laughing among themselves as they started climbing back into their vehicle.

'Yes, it's safe.' He addressed her directly. 'Your house is secure; no doors or windows have been forced.'

She knew there was a joke in there somewhere, but couldn't work it out. He said they had found the culprit. Another firefighter stepped out of the porch. He approached, holding something in his hands.

'Mrs Wilkinson? I think you need a cowl over that big chimney.'

He was holding a bird. A live bird. Light from the kitchen window glinted in the dark sphere of its eye.

'What is it?' Martin asked.

'A blackbird,' the firefighter answered. 'Or that could be soot from the chimney. Hard to tell.' He held it higher. 'See that cut on its foot? That's where the blood on your windowsill came from.'

Suddenly, it all made sense to her. 'Oh my God – it fell down the chimney? That was why the hearth was such a mess?'

The firefighter nodded. 'Then it flapped around your front room trying to find a way out.'

The tapping noise she'd heard; it was probably its beak against the glass. The rustling sound, its feathers. She wanted to laugh with relief. 'Is it OK?'

'Fine. The bleeding on its foot has stopped.'

Now she did laugh. A chuckle bubbled up from deep in her chest. She turned to Martin who was smiling right back. 'A bird. Can you bloody believe it?' She looked at the chimney stack and had the crazy impression it was eavesdropping on the conversation.

'Shall I let it go?' The firefighter was looking at her

expectantly.

'Please.'

He stepped back from them and placed the bird on the ground. As soon as his hands lifted, it instantly took flight. Keeping low, it arrowed straight for the mouth of the lane where deep shadow engulfed it.

'Drama over,' the firefighter said, brushing one palm against the other.

Laura lifted her hands. 'Thank you so much, it was very kind of you to come so quickly.'

'Our pleasure,' he replied, beginning to turn away.

'Oh, Laura,' Martin announced. 'This is Steve Maystock. Molly's father.'

The firefighter looked back at the vicar with a questioning smile.

'Laura was asking about Molly,' Martin explained, 'she saw her photo up at the church.'

Molly's father turned round properly but didn't look at her. 'I can only thank you and your congregation for all the hard work you've done. It's amazing.'

As he spoke, Laura's gaze was on him. His face was handsome, in a bony sort of way. He looked like a marathon runner. But she detected a hint of weariness there, too. The strain, no doubt, of caring for a child with a life-threatening condition. She wanted to reach out and touch him. Embrace him. She wanted to march back into the cottage and write him a cheque for whatever was needed to make Molly better. How could life be so unfair? She almost turned to Martin and demanded he answer that. Why was God so cruel? 'She's such a lovely little girl.'

He looked at her, pride making his eyes shine. 'Thank you, she is.'

It was no good: she couldn't fight the urge to say more. She just couldn't. 'We... my husband and I...' God, she thought, I sound like the queen now. She knew she was blushing. 'We've been talking to Martin about staging something at the church – a fundraising event for Molly.'

Her comment obviously took Martin by surprise. He blinked a couple of times before recovering his composure. 'I'm not sure if you realise, Steve, but Laura's husband is Owen Wilkinson, the –'

'I know who he is,' Steve cut in. 'He's the famous conductor.'

He looked, to Laura, like a boy who had been promised a treat by an unreliable adult. Too many disappointments to risk smiling. 'I appreciate anything you might do to help my girl.'

Might. There would be no might about it, she thought. 'I can tell you Owen is really very keen…He said to me this morning, the moment the concert he's involved in is out of the way, we'll start making arrangements with Martin here.'

Steve was moving backwards, nodding as he did so. 'Thank you. Thank you so much.'

A few seconds later, the fire engine began to swing round on an open section of field beyond the cottage. She heard the sound of a car engine from further down the lane. Owen's Audi emerged from the gloom as Martin began to speak. 'Sorry if I just put you on the spot there – I really didn't mean to. I only meant to introduce you to Molly's dad. That was all –'

'Don't apologise,' she said, climbing over the fence. 'I wanted to let him know we'll help.' Owen was getting out of his car, a look of confusion on his face. 'Just don't mention anything: not yet,' she added quietly, before turning to her husband with a smile. 'Darling! Panic's over. I've been a complete idiot.'

'It is?' He went to cross the track but had to step back to let the police car pass. The fire engine started to emit a loud beep as it began to reverse. Owen raised his voice. 'What on earth is going on?'

'A bird fell down the chimney. It had been flapping round the front room, knocking things over.'

'A bird? Jesus Christ –' He directed an apologetic

glance at Martin, who pretended not to notice. 'Bloody hell, Laura. I broke off rehearsals. I've just been flashed by at least three speed-cameras getting back here. Who knows how much that will have cost?'

Out of the corner of her eye, she saw Martin flinch. She was well aware that Owen never was the best at choosing the right comment. 'I'm sorry, I tried to ring you again when the police car arrived... but you didn't pick up.'

'Probably because I was racing along the sodding M60 trying to get here.' He had to pause as the fire engine rumbled past. She gave the faces looking down at her a wave. Owen ran his hands through his hair. He looked flustered. She knew he hated anything unexpected. 'Well...at least you are all right. A bird, you say?'

'Yes, a bird. It scared the life out of me when I heard it moving about in the snug.'

Now Owen's eyes were on the ski jacket she was wearing. 'Is that yours?'

'No – Martin kindly lent it to me when he arrived. I was standing out in the field shivering.'

'Right...of course.' He turned to the vicar. 'Thanks for taking care of her.'

'Absolutely no problem,' Martin replied, swinging a leg over the fence.

'Would you like to come inside for a cup of tea?' Laura asked. 'I think we all deserve one.'

'Got to dash, sorry,' Martin said. 'But listen – call in at Oldknow any time. Both of you.'

'Thanks,' she glanced at Owen who was now regarding the vicar with a dubious expression.

'Let me give you this.' She unzipped the ski jacket and handed it back. 'Very cosy.'

'Isn't it?' Martin draped it over one forearm and tipped his head. 'Great to meet you, Mr Wilkinson.'

'Yes. Likewise.'

Martin set off for his sports car and she saw Owen's

eyebrows lift at the sight of it.

'Let's get inside,' she said, linking an arm through his. 'It's freezing out here.'

CHAPTER 13

'I don't like him. "Got to dash." "Call in at Oldknow any time." What sort of a vicar speaks like that? And did you see his car? Bloody BMW? What are they paying vicars nowadays? A bit of humility wouldn't go amiss.'

She poured tea into a pair of mugs and put them on the table. 'Darling, he's only young. Better him than some florid-faced old bore with dandruff and an unhealthy liking for sherry. Isn't that your standard countryside vicar?'

'Not round here, it isn't,' Owen snorted, examining a digestive before taking a bite out of its side. A flurry of crumbs fell unnoticed into the folds of his jumper. 'How long has he been vicar of Oldknow?'

'Not long. He's still settling in. Like us.' She hoped desperately she could turn Owen's opinion of the man: it would make the organisation of Molly's fundraising event go far more smoothly. 'They found the remains of a child earlier; that bit they're excavating in the field by the church.'

'A child? Bones, you mean?'

'Only a skull. The top of one. They're searching around for more tomorrow.'

'Did they tell the police?'

Laura hadn't thought about that. 'Even when the remains are so old?'

'How old are they?'

'I don't know. It's an Iron Age hill fort.'

'I imagine the police will still want to look. Though, if the remains date back that far, they won't be bothered. But that's if.'

'You mean someone could have buried the body there more recently?'

'Who knows? That's why they'll need to inform the police. Anyway, I thought that vicar was an idiot. Suggesting I do an organ recital to raise funds. He reminds me of a young Tony Blair. All smiles and surface appearance. Not to be trusted.'

She wanted to say it was her idea about the organ recital. But once something was in Owen's head, it was hard to make him see things differently. 'It is in aid of a sick child, darling.'

'Is it? Not a little PR coup for him? A step on his way up the church ladder?'

How cynical of you, she thought. 'I believe he has the little girl's interests at heart.'

'We'll see.'

At least he's able to show an interest in children, she nearly retorted. 'I saw Dr Ford again this morning.'

'Did you?' His shoulders sagged and his voice lost its edge. 'Of course you did, sorry. How was it?'

She gave a smile. 'I think we have an explanation for the mysterious noises I've been hearing.'

'We have?'

'A viral infection of my inner ear. He said it should clear up on its own. A few weeks.'

'Really? A virus?'

'Yes,' she beamed. 'A virus.'

'Well, that's great news.' He said nothing more, but he didn't need to. It was obvious to Laura what he'd been wondering about the sounds: were they a presage of something more serious? Some kind of relapse to how she was before. The atmosphere in the room was noticeably lighter.

'Is that for me?' He reached for the A4 envelope with

72

Do Not Bend printed across the top.

'Yes. The postmark says it's from the Bridgewater Hall. Oh, there was another letter this morning. I opened it, assuming it was for me. But it was to the previous occupants of Lantern Cottage. Did you know they had a son? I'm sure the estate agent described them as a couple.'

Owen had got his envelope open. He slid out a glossy print from inside. 'Thought so,' he said happily. 'I asked for a copy of the posters they've put up all over the Bridgewater Hall. We could frame this. Hang it in the downstairs toilet.' He turned the notice round so she could see it.

A stock publicity shot of Owen conducting. She'd seen it so many times before. He really needed something more recent. The lettering announcing the event was refined, elegant. Running along the base of the sheet were logos from all the companies who'd sponsored it. The Cooperative Bank. McVitie's. Bruntwood. Astra Zeneca. Urban Splash. All businesses or companies with some kind of link to Manchester, she assumed. 'It looks wonderful.'

'Well,' Owen said. 'It will brighten up the loo. You were saying?'

'The last people who lived here. Did you know they had a son?'

'I don't even remember their names. Who we they again?'

'Edith and Roger Hall. The son is called William. This letter was about his transport to a respite centre near here. He must be disabled.'

'Sounds it. Did you return it to sender?'

'Of course. But I was sure the estate agent said the couple moved from here because they were getting too old to cope with going up and down the lane. Don't you remember?'

'Afraid not.' He tipped his head to the side. 'Well I never! Where did this come from? In a glass jar, too.' He'd spotted the Ovaltine and was out of his seat.

'The little shop in the village,' she answered. 'Not the supermarket, the other one.'

'Ovaltine,' he fondly rotated the jar. 'That takes me right back. I used to drink this as a boy.' He started to murmur a little song under his breath. Something about Ovaltinies.

She couldn't help but smile at the sight of him. Hair ruffled, shirt almost hanging out: in many ways, she thought, he still was a boy.

'Do you know?' he said, tapping a finger against the lid. 'I think I'll take a cup of this with me to bed.'

After he'd gone up, she sat at the kitchen table listening to the swish and rumble of the dishwasher. She looked at the clock. Not even ten. She didn't feel in the slightest bit tired. She contemplated seeing if there was anything on TV then realised the front room still needed to be cleaned. The firemen had tramped around in their boots, spreading soot all over the carpet.

She opened the laptop instead to check her emails. There was another one from the lady in America. Tamsin Harper. The subject line said, Viral ear infection. Probably saying how lucky I am that I don't have tinnitus, she thought. What had the woman said about hers? A hurricane blowing through a keyhole. How did people cope? She opened the message and began to read.

Hi Laura, I'm very happy for you. A viral infection! No doubt about it, that would be a nice resolution. I was wondering – did your doctor ask if the noises you hear are in one or both ears? (Unilateral or bilateral?) Did you check if there's any pattern to *when* you hear the noise? Has he referred you to an ENT specialist or consultant in audiovestibular medicine? There's only so much a doctor can tell by looking into your ear with an otoscope. Believe me, I've been there, done that! You didn't mention experiencing any discomfort with the noise. Normally I'd expect that with a middle-ear infection. Sorry to ask these questions, I hope you don't mind.

Laura stopped reading. Actually, she thought, I do. I do mind you asking all this. But another part of her was already thinking that Dr Ford hadn't asked those things. She returned to the message.

It's reasonable for you to expect a more thorough check-up. A full hearing test, X-ray, blood test, even a CT or MRI scan.

She had to stop reading again. What did the woman think this was: an episode of ER? Blood test? MRI scan? She was obviously labouring under the illusion everyone in the UK had private health care. Yeah, why not an MRI scan? Let's throw in some psychoanalysis and anything else that comes to mind, too. Silly woman. Laura closed the laptop without bothering to reply.

Right, she said to herself, taking the cleaning stuff from beneath the sink. In the front room she paused before the hearth to examine the mess of powdery marks.

They almost looked like they'd been put there by a brush. She supposed a bird's feathers were similar to a paintbrush. She imagined the marks were a message in a long-forgotten language. Hieroglyphics. Mayan code. Maybe something even older.

Could the sound of birdsong have been coming from the chimney? The thought had suddenly materialised in her head. Whatever the bird was, it might have built a nest up there. There could even be chicks; the noises they made would certainly be faint. Lacking in strength. Perhaps that's what she had been hearing. Except it was November. No chicks would be hatching now.

She considered how the chimney stack towered above

the roof. There would be room inside it for a nest, that was for sure. Several, probably.

Getting down on all fours, she poked her head into the hearth. Smoke-stained bricks angled in above her. The air felt cool. She craned her neck, twisting uncomfortably so she could see up the chimney itself. Blackness. No stars or glimmer of the night sky. Just complete and utter blackness. Like a physical entity, hanging there, silent and brooding. She was hit by the sudden sense that something was up there in the darkness, staring down at her. Shrinking away, she straightened to a kneeling position and regarded the fireplace. Her pulse had speeded up. The feeling of something being wrong persisted. Something what? Dangerous? Not dangerous. Just something…not right.

She stood, glad to move away from the dark opening and over to the window. She pulled on rubber gloves and sprayed the sill with disinfectant. A full hearing test. MRI scan. She couldn't help pondering over the American's latest message. Dr Ford had mentioned none of those things. Wouldn't a virus be accompanied by other symptoms? A headache at the least?

She began scrubbing at the droplets of dried blood and looked at the hearth once again. The thing needed a bloody good clean, too. All of it. Tomorrow, she decided, I'll search online for a chimney sweep. Get any birds' nests dislodged, along with anything else that might be trapped up there.

CHAPTER 14

Leaning to the side, she dropped the tissue into the toilet bowl and pressed the flush. No spots of blood or any other signs. Her nightie slipped back down as she stood. As she washed her hands, she looked in the mirror and examined the skin around her eyes. It looked tired. I feel tired, she told herself. Drained. Is this what getting old means?

The singing had broken out in the middle of the night. It had never happened in the middle of the night before. 3.07 was when it first came. A burst of notes, sometimes growing fainter, sometimes getting stronger. She had lain on her back listening to it, Owen fast asleep beside her. The certainty gradually grew. This noise is not in my head. She turned on her bedside lamp then lifted her hand to wake Owen; surely he'd hear it now, in the silence of the night? 'Owen! Owen! The birdsong is back. Owen!'

It was like trying to rouse an animal from hibernation. The pattern of his breathing changed first, followed by his head tilting back. His mouth opened slightly and tremors passed through the skin of his eyelids. The bird song warbled on.

She shook his shoulder harder. 'Owen, can you hear it?'

A hand appeared from beneath the duvet to wipe at the moist skin at the corner of his mouth. 'What?'

'The bird singing!'

The slack skin of an eyelid twitched more strongly, like

a cinema curtain about to rise. The singing stopped as it finally opened. 'Hear what?'

'Birdsong. Just now. Did you hear it?'

He cocked his head, eye already closing. 'I don't hear anything.'

'Not now. Just before.'

'No.' His voice was groggy.

'Never mind.'

His skull sank back against the pillow. 'Night.'

'Night.' Within seconds, his breathing had deepened and slowed. She reached over and turned her beside lamp off. About twenty minutes later, it started again. A quick burst, silence, another quick burst. Never long enough for her to try and rouse Owen again.

It seemed to be coming from somewhere so close, yet, at the same time, so very far away. Not in any room. The roof, maybe? Or the top of the chimney? It wasn't a nightingale, so which other birds sang at night? Did nightjars? She wondered if it was something exotic that had escaped from its owner's house. There must be dozens of foreign species that were happy to sing during the night. But how would it survive the cold of Britain in November?

At breakfast, she debated whether to say anything to Owen. He probably had no memory of her waking him. He was bent over his bowl, methodically working his way through some muesli. She knew his mind was on the concert. He was now completely in its shadow and would remain that way until it was over. He used the tip of a finger to prod some raisins on to his spoon. Raisins. 'I found an empty box of raisins in the garden,' she suddenly said. 'Next to the plant pots on the patio.'

He looked up, eyes refocusing as he travelled back from wherever his thoughts had taken him. 'Raisins?'

'Yes, a box of raisins. One of those little ones to go in a child's packed lunch. Snack-size.'

'I see.' He started to look back down and she knew its significance hadn't sunk in.

'We don't have anything like that. At least, I haven't bought any. Have you?'

The question elicited a half smile. 'Me? Darling, when do I have time to go shopping?'

'It seems strange, how it got there. It's not like it could have blown in from a neighbour's garden.'

He hunched a shoulder. 'Dropped by a rambler? Or mountain-bike rider. They sometimes come past, heading out to the moorland further up.'

'But in the back garden?'

'Sorry?'

'In the back garden? How would it get from the front lane into the back garden?'

He gave a sigh of exasperation. 'Well, what do you think? You obviously have a theory.'

His tone cut her. 'No… Not really. The only thing was if it's linked to the disturbances I've been hearing at night –'

'Ah, badgers. Yes, you're probably right. One could have carried it in its mouth from a bin somewhere else. Dropped it when it smelled the bird food.'

No, she thought. That's not what I meant. There were no teeth marks or drool on the box: it looked like it had fallen out of someone's pocket. Someone who was poking round our garden at night. 'I suppose so.'

He pushed his bowl to one side. 'Have you seen my car keys?' He glanced about, one hand checking his pockets. 'The bloody things.'

'On the fridge, where you left them last night.'

'Really?' He stepped to the side and plucked them from the top. Why he didn't just use one of the wall hooks, she could never understand.

'And sweetheart?'

He looked back at her, almost out of the kitchen door. 'Yes?'

'A kiss would be nice.'

'God, sorry.' Looking chastened, he came across and planed a quick peck on her cheek. 'This concert…'

'I know,' she replied, reaching up to wipe a fragment of cereal from the corner of his mouth. 'You didn't tell me if you sorted out the issues with the sopranos.'

He grimaced. 'I sent them home. I haven't time for people playing silly buggers.'

She looked down, trying to hide her concern. 'Sent them home?'

He jangled the keys about in his palm. 'That's right. We needed to work on the fourth movement anyway. They have no part in that, so I said they could clear off. Hopefully they'll use the time to study the passage and actually work out what I'm trying to achieve.'

'Oh. Are they due back in today?'

'Yes. But whether we'll revisit the start of the third movement is another thing. We'll see how things go this morning.'

Leaving an entire section of a choir hanging about. It was a risky move on Owen's part. She knew that he was trying to let them know who was boss. But the choir would have its pride. And he was just one, she thought. They are many. No wonder his stress levels seemed especially bad. 'Let me know what time to expect you home.'

'Of course. We'll speak later.' He headed for the door.

She turned her back on the kitchen window, of the view of him appearing round the side of the house and unlocking his car. Usually she liked to watch him setting off in the mornings; she would from their house in Richmond. But she was afraid the terrible thoughts would barge into her mind. Thoughts that had no place in her head.

The laptop's screen sprang to life. As the sound of Owen's car started up she contemplated the email icon on the desk top. Tamsin Harper and her questioning of Dr

Ford's prognosis. The woman, Laura thought, has a presence now, in my computer. I might not understand the science behind how she's in there – the technicalities by which her opinions are sent and received – but she's there all the same. And I let her in. I should never have joined that forum.

She moved the cursor to the internet browser and went online. After a second of thinking what to type, she decided on, Chimney Sweeps, Derbyshire.

A good half-dozen came up. Scanning the bit of text visible with each entry, she saw Pomerell & Son were based in nearby Glossop.

She brought up his site. Fully accredited with the Confederation of Chimney Sweeps. In business for over sixteen years. Sounded a good bet.

After having a shower and getting dressed she returned to the laptop and called the number on his contact screen.

'Andy Pomerell here.' He had a gentle voice. Probably somewhere in his late fifties.

'Hello, my name is Laura Wilkinson. I'm ringing to see if you could sweep our chimney.'

'Where are you, Laura?'

'We live near Oldknow. Just outside it.' She'd never had to give directions before; would he have heard of the lane? It was so tucked away... 'You turn off the B6104 road near a big mill. There are a few houses – not many – and you carry on until you see a building on the left. It's all boarded up, but I think it was a working men's club once. There is a sign on it. It's not a house, anyway. About thirty metres past that you need to look for a narrow lane –'

'What's the property called?'

She realised she was waffling. 'Lantern Cottage.'

'I know Lantern Cottage all right. Magnificent chimney you've got – on the original part of the property.'

'That's the one. Have you swept it before?'

'No. I've often passed it: I used to go mountain biking. Some good trails beyond your place. Nice couple used to live there.'

She felt herself sit forward. 'An elderly couple, the Halls?'

'Could have been. They bought me out a cup of tea once when I was changing a tyre.'

'And their son, William?' she stayed silent, waiting for an answer.

'Son?'

'A teenager?'

'Right you are.' His tone lifted. 'I'm busy rest of the week. Can it wait while Monday?'

'The earliest you could come is next Monday?'

'It is. Wood-burning stoves – I've never been so busy. Folk everywhere are wanting them fitted.'

She could try another chimney sweep, but anyone that busy must be doing something right. And he knew about the Halls. 'Monday will be fine.'

CHAPTER 15

The village high street was quiet. What little traffic that passed her was going in the opposite direction towards the A6 and Manchester. The modest car park opposite the GP practice had spaces, and after putting twenty pence in the machine at the entrance, she made her way back toward the estate agents, musing on the difference in parking charges between Oldknow and London.

The silver BMW owned by Mark Scott was not parked in its usual place at the side of the property. She peered at the windows, but the view into the office was obscured by displays featuring properties for sale: everything from cramped flats in the grim terrace opposite the mill to converted barns with indoor pools, paddocks and grazing land.

A young lady barely out of her teens looked up from her desk as Laura pushed open the front door. 'Hello there.'

'Morning,' Laura replied, glance going to Mark's work station. No sign of him. 'I don't suppose he's around?'

'Out inspecting properties,' she replied. 'Can I help?'

She took a quick breath in. 'I moved into a Lantern Cottage recently.'

She raised a finger. 'Mrs Wilkinson?'

'Yes.' Her smile was accompanied by a small shake of her head. 'Sorry, I'm still getting used to people knowing my name.'

She beamed back at Laura. 'I'm Becky.'

'Hello Becky, nice to meet you.' She couldn't imagine Becky negotiating prices or closing a sale: she seemed far too young. Perhaps she just did admin. 'The reason I popped by is because I could do with a forwarding address for the previous occupants of Lantern Cottage. We've been getting items for them in the post.' Well, a part of her said, just one. But you're not to know that.

Becky frowned. 'The sorting office up the road should be redirecting anything before it gets to you. I'm sure Mark would have made the necessary arrangements with Derek. He usually does.'

'Derek?'

'He's the manager there.'

Right, Laura thought. First-name terms. Because everyone knows everyone here. 'It's only the odd letter. The other day something arrived from the Primary Care Trust. Probably about their son, William?' She watched carefully for a reaction but Becky didn't even blink. 'It didn't seem right returning it to sender; it could have been urgent. After all, he has... health issues, doesn't he?'

She reached for a notepad. 'I'll check with Derek that the instruction is still in place. It may well have expired – they do after a certain number of weeks. And Lantern Cottage had been empty for a while before you moved in.'

'Do you have a forwarding address I could have?'

'Let me check the general files.' She went over to a cabinet and ran a finger along the middle shelf. 'Here we go, Lantern Cottage.'

Laura crossed to the girl's desk as the manila folder was laid down and opened. The first sheets were copies of the estate agent's profile for the property, complete with interior photos and asking price. Three hundred and ninety five thousand. Laura could still hardly believe they'd got it for fifty thousand less than that.

Photocopies of land registry deeds followed, along with the surveyor's report Owen had commissioned. 'Nothing on the Halls,' Becky said under her breath.

She came to the final sheet. Another photocopy. The graininess of the image made Laura suspect the original photo had been quite old. It was of a couple standing on the lane in front of the cottage. There was no extension at the end of the property. Was it the Halls? Laura leaned closer. The couple's clothing was from another century. The slightly-built man was wearing a collarless white shirt and what appeared to be tweed breeches. He stood with his arms crossed and feet apart, a serious expression on his face. What hair he had was swept back. Round, wire-framed glasses made Laura think of an SS officer. Someone who arranged executions with a cold, functional efficiency.

The woman was a bit further back, eyes downcast. She was a large woman: at least six inches taller than him. Her dress – a dark material that stretched from throat to ankle – puffed out at the hip, adding to her bulky appearance. Her hair was up in a bun so large, Laura guessed it would have stretched right down her back when untied. 'Who are those two?'

'No idea, from way back, I imagine. Funny how they never smiled for photographs in those days.' Becky closed the file and pointed in the direction of Mark's work station. 'The Hall's details will be in Mark's corner cabinet. He has the key, I'm afraid.'

'OK. Perhaps you could ask him to give me a call?'

'Will do. How are you finding it up there? Aren't the views lovely?'

'There are amazing, thanks. We're settling in very well.' She wondered whether to try again to get any information about William Hall. But the phone next to Becky began to ring.

Out on the high street, Laura crossed over to the convenience store next to the post office; she needed some milk. The rack of local postcards caught her eye. Bucolic views of farmland rising up to the purples of

Etherow moor. The Peak Forest Canal with a narrow boat nosing its way along. The flight of locks leading up to the old limekilns. A snow-shrouded Kinder Scout, black-faced sheep in the foreground. It really is a lovely place to live, she thought. And Lantern Cottage would be perfect if only it wasn't quite so set out on its own. The place just needed something to...

The answer came to her. Of course. It was so obvious. She stepped back outside and checked the notices in the post-office window. There was the photo of the kittens. Would she be too late?

Two hours later, she eased to a gentle halt outside the cottage. The passenger seat had been slid back as far as it would go, and in the enlarged footwell was a beige, plastic travel case. The kitten looked out nervously from the bars at the front. Laura was giddy with excitement.

There were two of them left, but this one – with dabs of white on its black and brown coat – appealed to Laura most. Fourteen weeks old, fully weaned and vaccinated. The thought of practical things like a litter tray, food, toys and a basket for her to sleep in only occurred to Laura after she said she'd take it.

After a quick trip to the nearest pet shop over in New Mills, she raced back to the place that was giving the kittens away and, after saying thank you far too many times, set off with her new companion.

'You sit tight,' she said. 'I'll take your things in first, then show you round your new home.' There was a milky quality to its eyes, almost as if the irises were still deciding on which colour to be. Laura realised the eyes of newborn babies were the same. The kitten's little face caused her chest to ache. 'I won't be long, OK?'

She removed the things from the boot and hurried to the front porch. The house had its usual aura of stillness. It was nowhere near to becoming a home, Laura realised. A cat would change that.

She unlocked the inner door and the burglar alarm immediately began to beep. After punching in the code, she carried the armful of items through to the kitchen and set them down in the corner. Once everything was sorted she went back outside and lifted the kitten from the car.

'Here we are,' she announced, raising the carry-case to face level and swivelling the front round. 'There is Manchester. The big, wide world. On that hill over there is Oldknow church.' She narrowed her eyes. They were huddled at the edge of the excavation – seven or eight of them.

'And this,' she said turning through one hundred and eighty degrees, 'is Lantern Cottage. Shall we go inside?'

She walked carefully, pointing her toes so her weight was smoothly transferred with each step. In the kitchen, she kept her spine straight, flexing at the knees so the carry-case descended smoothly to the floor. She knelt down next to it and opened the door. The kitten was cowering at the back, eyes wide and frightened. Deciding to leave it for a moment, Laura filled the kitten's bowl with milk from the fridge. Placing it on a tray, she crouched before the travel case once more.

'Come on,' she said quietly. 'It's all right. You can come out.'

The kitten didn't seem very keen to move. Laura scratched at the edge of the door and its frightened eyes moved to the noise. 'Don't you want to explore?'

A minute later and it still hadn't budged. Laura fetched the scrap of fur attached to a length of string and dangled it before the door. The kitten's eyes now tracked the lure, torso going into a crouch.

'What is it?' Laura whispered encouragingly as its tail began to twitch. 'What is it?'

Gradually it started edging forward, body low, bum in the air. Laura laid the piece of fur on the floor and jerked her hand so its tip moved about. The kitten readied itself then pounced, limbs awkward, mouth open. But she whipped the fur away and it looked about in bewilderment.

Using that technique, Laura lured it further away from the carry-case, across the kitchen, and into the front hall. The door to Owen's study was shut. It sniffed at the crack at the door's base, clearly aware there was something on the other side. By the time Laura had tempted it into the lounge, the kitten had tired of chasing the fur and began to happily nose around. Laura kept close, pointing out the plant, the coffee table, the TV.

It skirted round the hearth, eyes fixed warily on the dark opening until it was well clear. Laura noted its reaction with interest. The snug didn't seem to hold much attraction and soon it had completed a circuit of the two rooms and was back in the hallway at the foot of the stairs. It tilted its head to eye the steps rising steeply before it and then went very still.

'What is it?' Laura asked, looking up to the first floor.

It didn't seem to be looking at anything in particular. In fact, its head was slightly cocked, as if it was listening. Then it turned away from the stairs and made its way quickly back to the kitchen.

Quietly, Laura followed. It padded across the flagstones and stepped back into the travel case. Odd, Laura thought. Normally, cats couldn't stand being cooped up.

'You can't stay in there,' she whispered, crouching down to look inside. It was sitting at the back, calmly staring in Laura's direction. 'You've got a nice bed out here. Come on, Scaredy-mouse.' It didn't move so she extended a hand and gently clicked her fingers. It backed further into the corner.

Laura took a deep breath and stood. She looked round the kitchen. This wasn't right. Why wouldn't it come out? Over in the field by Oldknow church, the group were still gathered at the same spot. But now, among the tops and jackets worn by the archaeologists, was a yellow tabard. A policeman. They'd called in the police. The officer seemed to be addressing the group. Laura spotted a second one, standing near the graveyard wall. He was talking on his handset.

She glanced back at the travel case. The kitten seemed happy enough in there. Her food tray was empty – but Laura knew she wouldn't be long. 'Little mouse? I'm just popping out. There's milk in your bowl if you get thirsty. OK? I'll be back soon.'

As she stood, her eyes were dragged to the window. The two officers were now pacing about, heads lowered. As if searching for a lost item in the grass.

CHAPTER 16

God Save the Queen was belting out as the police car appeared further up the lane coming down from the church. Laura turned the volume down and squashed her little Clio into a passing spot, watching intently as they continued towards her. Neither of the two officers were the ones who'd attended her house the evening before.

Deep in conversation, they hardly bothered to break off and nod to her as they passed. They looked concerned, Laura thought, somewhat guilty that the knowledge gave her a slight thrill.

She parked next to the other vehicles by the church and, to her relief, found Martin Flowers in the church hall. He was sorting through a box of hymn books. 'Hi.'

He looked round and gave a broad smile. 'Hello there.'

She stepped inside, unsure what to say.

'Recovered from yesterday's drama?'

Briefly, she closed her eyes. 'I still feel foolish. Thanks so much for coming over.'

'Nonsense. Who wouldn't be unnerved by droplets of blood and a disturbance in their house?'

'I suppose so. I passed a police car as I drove up the lane.' That was disingenuous. She started again. 'Actually, I saw the officers in the field from my kitchen window. Were they... Is it something to do with...?'

He nodded, but in a casual way. 'Adrian was concerned about the lack of grave goods by the child's skeleton.'

'So they've uncovered more than just the skull?'

'A lot more. They were back here at the crack of dawn. It's all there, poor little lad. Or lass; they are unsure which.'

Like my dream, Laura thought. I can't tell if the figure in that is a boy or girl. 'What's the concern over grave goods?'

'According to Adrian, the child of an important person would be buried with some possessions. Things to help it in the afterlife: beads, coins. Offerings, basically. This just seems to be a skeleton, and a bit jumbled up, too. Not carefully laid to rest.'

Laura felt a sudden chill. 'Jumbled up?'

'Its position is odd – the legs are all bent. And it's twisted to the side.'

Laura could now see the figure in her dream; it also lay awkwardly. She felt a surge of dizziness and leaned back against the wall, both palms pressed against it. 'So they called the police because there were no grave goods?'

'No –' He paused, looking at her more closely. 'Are you OK?'

'Yes, why?'

'You look cold. Why don't you come away from the door?'

She entered the hall properly and sat down in a chair near to him. She could see that his expression had subtly changed. Now, she thought, he's scrutinising me. 'What were we saying?'

'Grave goods… or lack of them.'

'Yes.' He looked out the window. 'Here's Adrian now. You can ask him.'

She looked round and groaned. 'They'll be thinking I'm such a busybody, turning up here all that time.'

'No they won't. Actually, my guess is they quite like the attention. You're their very own groupie.' He winked at her as the outer door opened.

'Getting a bit nippy out there!' Adrian announced, giving his feet a vigorous brush on the doormat. 'That northerly wind. I'll not be surprised if it carries down snow soon –' He caught sight of her and his sentence dried up.

Behind him was the elderly lady who'd scolded him for being secretive about discovering the grave. She sent Laura a smile.

'Laura passed the patrol car on her way up here to discuss something with me,' Martin said, filling the silence.

She shot him a thankful glance.

'I was trying to explain about the absence of grave goods. How it caused a bit of confusion,' Martin added, picking up a box of hymn books. 'Maybe you could explain, I must pop over to the church.'

'That's right,' Adrian replied, rubbing his hands together and unzipping his fleece. 'It makes it harder to say with any certainty how old the skeleton is.' The door banged shut behind Martin. 'Grave goods would allow us to immediately place when it was from,' Adrian continued. 'Now we can't say for sure. The police need to be informed if there's any doubt.'

'Why might it have been buried without grave goods?' Laura asked.

'Perhaps,' the old lady chipped in, 'it wasn't a peacetime burial, after all. The fort may have been overrun by enemies. We might be finding many more bodies soon.' She seemed to be enjoying the airing of her macabre theory. 'Or – far less likely – the burial is recent.'

Her final comment made Laura turn towards the window. The dream I've been having…

'Don't look so worried,' Adrian smiled. 'I'd be astonished if the skeleton isn't from the Iron Age. We called the police just to be on the safe side.'

Laura crossed her legs. Part of her wanted to see the child's remains. She knew why. To work out if it matched the figure she'd been seeing in her dream.

'…area's heritage.'

She looked back. The elderly lady had just said something else. 'Sorry?'

'It's something else to add to the area's heritage. So much of the surroundings were shaped by the industrial revolution – the mills and canals. It's nice to have something pre-dating all that. Where you live – do you know there's a story to how it got its name?' There was a gleam in her eyes. Adrian looked uncomfortable.

'Lantern Cottage?' Laura asked. 'A light was hung on a hook on the side building. Above the hatch in the wall.'

'But,' she gave a mysterious smile and sat down. She was, Laura guessed, a teacher once. 'Why would a light be hung in there?'

'I sort of assumed it was a blacksmith's. That side building was his foundry.'

'No. Adrian, you know the details. Come on.' She was looking at him but nodding in Laura's direction.

Adrian crossed his arms. 'It's to do with the mines. Up past your property there used to be quite a few. There was a rich seam of coal there, once.'

That part of her address suddenly clicked: Coal Lane. Of course.

He looked ready to leave it at that but the lady prompted him with a rolling motion of her fingers. 'And?'

Adrian looked like he was in mild pain. Laura wondered if he was bursting to use the toilet. 'Miners would make their way up your lane. Before the sun even cleared the hills. Cartloads of coal were then transported back down to fuel the kilns – with the lime being shipped in along the Peak Forest Canal.'

'So why the lantern?' Laura asked, now thoroughly intrigued.

'It acted like a light in a shop window, I suppose. For the owners.'

Laura saw the photo from the estate agent's: the couple standing stiffly before the property. 'So if it wasn't a blacksmith's...'

'Birds. They used to rent out canaries for the miners.'

'Ca –' Her voice came out as a croak. She cleared her

throat. 'Canaries?'

'That's right. This was all before gas-detecting equipment. Canaries were the early-warning system in those days. They'd be served out in their cages through that hatch. Because it was dark, the lantern let the owners note down which miner had which bird, is my guess.'

'Canaries,' Laura whispered. The birdsong; it didn't sound like anything she'd ever heard in Britain. The unbroken stream of notes rising and falling for endless seconds. Was it canary song? 'When was this? How long ago?'

'Oh,' Adrian was now striding towards the toilets at the far end of the hall. 'Early eighteen-hundreds.'

CHAPTER 17

The light was blinking on the answerphone in the kitchen. It was the only sign of life in Lantern Cottage: the kitten certainly wasn't emerging from its travel case to greet Laura. She pressed the button and began to remove her coat.

'Hello, message for Laura Wilkinson. It's Mark Scott here. You called in earlier asking about a forwarding address for the Halls. Perhaps you could call me; it'll probably be best to tell you over the phone.'

She hung up her coat and pressed the callback button.

'Gasgrove Hepman, Becky speaking.'

'Hi Becky, it's Laura Wilkinson. I popped –'

'Mark's right here. Let me transfer you.'

She crouched down before the travel case.

'Laura? Hello, it's Mark.'

'Hello, Mark. Thanks for getting back to me.'

'No problem. You've been receiving post for the Halls?'

'Well…only one or two things.' Bending forward, she could see the kitten at the back of the case. Just sitting there, still as a rock. 'I thought if I could forward them on it would avoid delays.'

'Sadly, Mrs Hall passed away a few months ago.'

'Oh.' She knew the Halls were an older couple, but she didn't realise that old. Maybe having William so late in life had been a contributing factor in the lad's health problems.

'Her husband – Roger – didn't cope with his wife's

97

death so well. In fact that, and looking after William on his own, proved too much. He had a breakdown and is now in full-time medical care.'

She frowned. Mark Scott must be talking about psychiatric care. The breakdown was obviously severe. 'Gosh, that's terribly sad.'

'Was the letter for him? I have the name of the relative who has power of –'

'It was for the son, actually. William.'

'William? It was addressed to him?'

'Not to him specifically. I opened it not realising who it was for; it was from the Primary Care Trust. About his travel arrangements.'

'I see. That's obviously an admin error. Just return it to sender, if you could.'

'I already have.' She paused, wondering how to turn the conversation to William. 'What if I get any other bits and pieces for him –'

'I'll give you the address of this relative.'

'Why would it be an admin error about William's travel arrangements?'

'He doesn't need them any more. It's a very unfortunate situation, but he had to go into full-time care. A specialist facility.'

'He's disabled?'

'No. I mean, yes. He's not in a wheelchair. I don't know the correct terms, sorry. It's mental, not physical. He's like a young kid; he can't look after himself.'

She thought of the empty box of raisins from the garden. A snack for a young child. She realised she was staring at the kitten. It looked nervously back. 'So he had to move away from the area?'

'Not far. He's in a place called the Skylark Trust. He used to go several times a week; hence the travel arrangements. But it went to full time when Mr Hall became ill.'

She stood. The place Martin Flowers mentioned. The

one always needing volunteers. 'What a sad state of affairs.'

'I know. But the care he's receiving – and his dad, too – it was what they both needed.'

'OK. Thanks for explaining.'

'That's fine. As Becky mentioned, post should be getting diverted to this relative. But if it doesn't, have you got a pen?'

She jotted the address down: Norwich. Miles away. Once the estate agent hung up, she placed the phone on the side and looked across to the church. She sensed her abrupt departure had caused a few raised eyebrows, but she didn't care. Canaries had been bred in the cottage. She needed to know more.

Once the laptop booted up, she went on the internet and thought for a moment. An inner window appeared: new mail, including another from Tamsin Harper over in America.

She clicked on the message.

Hi Laura, I hope you're well. I don't want to pester, but I haven't heard back from you. Have you been experiencing any more episodes? Many in the medical profession – on both sides of the Atlantic – are poorly informed about tinnitus. I'd hate for your GP to have misdiagnosed you. If you want to share any concerns, please, please contact me whenever you want. Warmest wishes, Tamsin.

She clicked back on the internet and Googled, 'Lantern Cottage, canary breeder'. The old property listing by Gasgrove Hepman topped the screen. Nothing about canaries. She tried searching, 'Coal mining, Oldknow, Derbyshire.' A couple of historical websites. One detailed the Mellor family, who built the limekilns in Oldknow. They had also paid for branches off the Peak Forest Canal to be dug that led to the kilns. The other site talked about the family's mines, including Derbyshire record office diagrams and grid references of the various, now disused, shafts.

A bird landed on the windowsill. A robin. She realised she'd forgotten to restock the bird table that morning. Part of her wanted to carry on the internet search; part of her was uneasy about what it would unearth. She looked away from the screen. A viral infection of my ear is causing sound effects in my head, she told herself. That was the GP's diagnosis. Plain and simple.

Sighing, she got off the stool and walked over to the back door. The box of bird seed was on the shelf to the side. As she opened the door, she heard light movement near the travel case. The kitten was bolting across the flagstones. She shut the door just in time to prevent it from getting outside. It looked wildly about.

'Hey,' she said gently, 'what's up with you?'

It glanced up at her and meowed. A horribly mournful sound. Laura bent forward, wanting to stroke it; to reassure it. But the kitten shied back.

'OK,' Laura stated. 'That's OK. But you're not allowed out yet. Not for a few more days. Now let me feed these birds and I'll come straight back in.'

But as soon as the door began to open, it flew at it again. She swiftly closed the crack. This was the strangest cat she'd ever come across. 'You're not allowed.'

She wasn't sure how to get out now. Something told her if the kitten got into the garden it would never come back. It sniffed at the base of the door, turned round, and stalked back to its case. Bizarre. After closing its flimsy wire door, Laura slipped out into the garden.

Birds darted away to a safe distance. The lower part of the pole which supported the bird table had a few more scratch marks. Splinters of wood stuck out in places and she wondered whether the badgers had tried to chew into the wood with their teeth. Maybe to fell it like a beaver would a tree.

After sprinkling a fresh layer of food across the platform, she went back inside. The kitten was watching from behind its bars with baleful eyes. Laura opened the door to the travel case and waited. It didn't come out.

Laura looked through the kitchen window. The birds were tentatively closing in, sparrows leading the way with encouraging chirrups. A fat chaffinch landed on the highest point of a waist-high shrub. She was wondering whether it would be first to the table when a streak of silvery grey hurtled in from the side. The finch didn't even have time to spread its wings before talons picked it off. A few rapid wing-flaps and the bird of prey vanished. Laura stared at the scene in astonishment. Did I just see that? But for the few small feathers showing among the shrub's upper leaves, she would have been tempted to believe she hadn't.

Everything had seemed so lovely: then death struck and was gone. The other birds were nowhere to be seen. How long would it be before they dared come back? She needed them out there. Something else occurred to her: it could have been the kitten. If it had been out on the grass, would the hawk have taken it? She glanced at the travel case. It's not safe for you out there. Not yet, at least.

A few chirrups from outside. The sparrows were back! For some reason the sight of them filled her with intense relief. Life continued as, of course, it had to do. One let out a fresh burst of sound and Laura realised what she should have been searching for on the computer. Swiftly, she typed out two words: canary song.

A host of sites came up and she skimmed the text for one that mentioned audio files. The most promising-looking site was American, written by a breeder. The introduction described how canaries were first brought by Spanish sailors to Europe. Monks bred them, selling the males who became sought after for their exquisite singing. Popular song canaries were Spanish Timbrado, Malinois and American Singer.

A highlighted phrase further down jumped out. Canary in a coal mine – a person or thing that provides early warning of an impending crisis.

At the side of the screen was a menu. Her mouth felt dry as she clicked on the audio file for Spanish Timbrado. A small inner box opened with a time counter in the corner. The clip was twenty-six seconds long. She moved the cursor over the play button but didn't click on it. What if this song is the same? What if it's the one I've been hearing? What would that mean? The thought made her feel slightly sick. But she had to know. She clicked play.

Three seconds of silence ticked by. She was beginning to wonder if the machine's volume was turned down when, without warning, a sudden burst of notes filled the kitchen. Her vision immediately blurred. It was precisely what she'd been hearing. There was no difference, none whatsoever. She tried to blink back tears. The song billowed out, such incredible joy carried within it. She was crying. But they weren't tears of happiness. How can I be hearing canary song?

The clip came to an end and, silently, she continued to weep. Did it mean she was getting ill again? She didn't want to get ill again. She thought that part of her life was past. She didn't want to hear things. She didn't want to start seeing things again, either: water as milk, abandoned soft toys, lumps in the duvet concealing a slumbering baby. Do I want a baby? I don't, do I?

The kitten shifted in its case. Laura's head turned. Did I get it because some part of me – buried deep inside – still craves motherhood? Am I being guided by emotions I can't even feel? She screwed her eyes shut and wiped at her runny nose. What I've been hearing is canary song. I've heard it several times. And I heard it before knowing canaries were even bred here. How can that be?

She brought up Tamsin's email and typed a reply almost before she knew what she was doing.

I don't know what's happening. I can hear things and I don't know if they are real. I'm so very scared.

CHAPTER 18

By the time Owen's car pulled up outside she was confident she looked normal. Cooling gel had reduced the puffiness around her eyes and a few carefully applied touches of liner concealed any redness. She'd tied her hair up, but with several strands hanging down to distract attention away from her face.

She checked her emails again: nothing back from Tamsin. As the front door opened, she closed the laptop. When he walked into the kitchen she had a smile ready. A pasta bake was in the oven and it smelled good. He looked like someone who'd just given blood; pale and unsteady.

'What a day –' his eyes settled on the kitten's travel case, its basket and litter tray.

'I bought a kitten,' she announced cheerily. 'It's the sweetest –'

'A kitten.'

The comment was flat. Dead. It was not even a question.

'Yes, there was a notice in the post-office window. Free to a good home. I couldn't resist.'

'Free?' He dumped his leather satchel on the side. 'So they won't charge to take it back?'

The comment was so harsh, she didn't reply.

He looked at her with an ugly frown. 'What did you expect me to say?' He spread his palms. 'You decide to get a cat. Just like that. No discussion, nothing. Do I want a cat? You know I don't like the things. Never have.' He glanced dismissively at the travel case.

A flush of irritation rose about her ears. 'You're never here. It's just me, on my own, day after day. I got her for some company.'

He stared at her, but she refused to look away. He couldn't deny it. He slumped into a chair, turned his head and regarded the empty basket. 'But the concert is only three days off. I'll be around so much more after that.'

'It's not just company. This cottage: it needs livening up. An injection of...' She tested the air with her fingertips, '...I don't know. Energy.'

'Flowers didn't do the trick?'

She looked briefly at the bouquet of lilies. Waxy white petals were just beginning to force apart their green casing. She thought of the ones upstairs, stalks blackening, flower buds dead.

He thrust his feet out. 'OK. I take your point.'

His expression had softened and so hers did, too. 'Really?'

He nodded. 'Who's the homemaker here? Certainly not me. If you think that's what it takes...' He regarded the basket once more.

His sudden acquiescence surprised her. Did that mean he felt it, too? The cottage's coldness?

'Where is it, anyway?'

'She seems to prefer the travel case. She's in there.'

He leaned forward in his chair and tried to look inside. 'Nervous, is it?'

'Just getting used to her new surroundings.'

Earlier, she'd put a bottle of red on the table. He held it above the two glasses. 'Would you like one?'

'Please.' She got off the bar stool and reached for the oven gloves. 'Are you hungry?'

'Not massively.' He raised his glass toward the travel case. 'Cheers. You're not the only one suffering from nerves around here.'

Rehearsals still going badly then, she thought. If he hasn't resolved the issue with the choir, he's cutting it fine. She decided against asking for details. 'It was a child's skeleton, up near the church.'

He took a moment to answer. 'The archaeological dig?'

'Yes.' She placed a couple of spoonfuls of food on his plate. Cherry tomatoes and lumps of chorizo added colour to the pasta. 'They're all very excited.'

'I should think so. You went back, then?'

'I just popped across. The police were there – like you said.' She put the plate in front of him.

'This looks nice.' He used his fork like a plough, digging it in and turning the food over. 'Laura, I can understand if you're lonely. But soon, we'll have more time together.'

She took her wine and retreated to the breakfast bar, knowing he had more to say.

'What I mean is, you don't need to be getting involved with a bunch of old archaeologists and a trendy vicar. I know it's on your doorstep as such, but –'

'They're not old.'

'Aren't they? I had assumed they were retired – they're up there each day.'

'Why does being retired make them old? They're not geriatric.'

'I didn't mean…are any of them your age?'

Are you my age? She wanted to say it. Because they're the same bloody age as you! He looked at her and she saw a hint of discomfort in his eyes. Had he guessed what I was thinking?

'Why don't you come into Manchester with me tomorrow? Have a day out; there's the Art Gallery on Whitworth Street. Pre-Raphaelite paintings. All the museums. You could catch the tram out to Salford Quays and look around the Lowry. There's probably an afternoon performance on in the theatre there.'

She imagined herself in Manchester. It made her realise

how isolated she'd become. He's right, she thought. I should push out; explore. Not linger here on my own.

'Especially with that stuff yesterday – you deserve a day out after that scare.'

She thought how great it would be just to drift around, have a coffee, watch the world go by. But what about the cat? She looked over at her travel case. Would it be OK to just leave her here all day on her own?

'It'll be all right.' He'd followed the direction of her gaze. 'It's not a dog. Cats are happy on their own.'

'I don't know,' she murmured. 'The little thing's still so unsettled. You know, some kind of bird of prey swooped down earlier and took this little finch?' She clicked her fingers. 'Gone. Just like that.'

'Where?'

'Right outside the window. Near the bird table.' He looked at the black panes.

'A sparrowhawk, I should think. They're surprisingly common round here.'

'Would it attack a small cat?'

He shook his head. 'Doubt it. Have a think about tomorrow. There's this great restaurant up the road from the college. Middle Eastern – really fresh ingredients. I'll treat you to lunch.'

She gave him a half-smile. 'I'll think about it. I spoke to a chimney sweep, by the way. About clearing any birds' nests blocking that chimney in the lounge.'

'Can he come round?'

'Yes. But not until Monday.'

'Monday?' His voice had taken on a distant quality. 'The concert will be over by then.'

'You won't know what to do with yourself.'

'You should ask if he can put those anti-bird cowls on.'

'Exactly what I thought.' She watched as he finished off his meal.

'That was lovely, darling, thank you.' He put his fork down. Looking inquisitively at the travel case, he reached for his wine. Then he tipped his head to the side and said in a shrill, cockney accent, 'I wish to complain about this kitten what I purchased.'

Monty Python. She couldn't stop the laughter erupting. It gushed out, rocking her in her seat.

Owen's eyes were twinkling as he looked at her. 'It's been a while since I've heard one of your belly-busters.'

He's right again, she thought. I haven't been laughing enough. It feels so good to just laugh.

CHAPTER 19

As usual, Owen was immediately asleep. She envied him that ability. No matter how stressed he was, contact with a pillow sent him unconscious in seconds. Anaesthetic couldn't work much better, she thought, settling down for a long wait.

She lay on her side and tried to clear her mind. Exactly why she chose not to tell Owen about the fact it was canary song was still unclear to her. He's got enough on, she reasoned, with the concert. But she knew that wasn't entirely why she kept quiet.

To tell him she'd identified the noise – and that, in the century before last, a canary breeder had lived in this house…he'd worry. Who wouldn't? He'd see it as symptoms, she knew he would. The creeping tendrils of her illness taking hold once more.

But she didn't feel ill. Not like before. When things got out of control before, she didn't know that's what was happening. Everything had been totally real; the smell of talcum powder, the sense of her baby just out of sight, sleeping in the next room. This time, a calm, rational part of her was looking on from the outside. She knew that to hear a canary singing wasn't right. But she couldn't change the fact she'd heard it.

She opened her eyes, thinking Tamsin might have got her email. It was tempting to go downstairs and check. Owen wouldn't wake up: not now. It would be three in the afternoon in San Francisco by now. Tamsin was bound to have –

Something soft banged against a window. The noise had come from downstairs. Turning her head, she stared at the timber beam just visible above her. Rattling, like the handles of the patio doors were being tested. She lifted her head clear of the pillow: did I really hear that? A cough. Light showed at the edges of the curtains. The exterior security light! Now she knew the sounds were real. Quickly, she climbed out of bed and lifted the corner of the curtain. The halogen lamp bathed the garden in a bright glow, but nothing was out there.

She heard the cough again, followed by a word, quietly spoken. Someone was directly below, trying to get in. Only by opening the window and looking down, would she be able to see the person.

Should she wake Owen first? There wasn't time; he'd take a few seconds to come round. Instead, she turned on his bedside lamp and then reached for the window. A good aggressive shout. Hopefully that would scare them off.

But before her fingers curled round the handle, she heard the kitchen door start to creak. Oh Jesus, did I lock it? When I came in from the garden, did I lock it? 'Owen!' she hissed. 'Owen, wake up!'

He turned his head, eyes still closed.

'Owen! Someone is in the house!'

Now he started to blink, eyes bleary and unfocused. She opened the window and looked down. The kitchen door was wide open. Her chest felt like it was collapsing. The kitchen window went bright as a light turned on. She glimpsed a hand bang the door shut. 'Someone's in the kitchen! Owen, call the police. Call them!'

He sat up and reached for the phone at his side of the bed. 'Are you sure, Laura? Did you –'

There was a metallic clatter as the cutlery drawer was opened too fast. Knives. Owen's eyes widened and he started pressing the nine button.

She moved to the bedroom doorway and turned an ear to the stairs. She could hear a faint humming, a toneless series of notes repeated over and over. The Teletubbies theme tune?

Behind her, Owen whispered into the phone, 'Police.'

The person was bumping around, making no attempt to keep quiet. His casualness terrified her.

Owen spoke quietly. 'Lantern Cottage, Coal Lane, Oldknow. There's an intruder in our house. Downstairs. The kitchen. Yes we are. OK, thank you. We will.'

Now the downstairs hall lit up. 'Lock yourself in the bathroom,' Owen whispered as he pushed past. 'The keys to the Audi are in the kitchen!' he called down in a tremulous voice. 'My wallet is in there too!'

She looked at his outline, illuminated by the light shining up from below. He was peeping over the banister, pyjamas hanging off his thin frame. She realised she was stronger than him. Faster, too. She twirled round, entered her studio and grabbed the three-kilo dumbbells off the rack.

At the top of the stairs she yelled down, 'Get out of this house! If you set foot on these stairs I'll cave your fucking skull in, so help me God!'

A shadow appeared in the corridor. Heavy footsteps approached from the kitchen. Her breath dwindled as a youth came into view. Seventeen? Thick black hair in a side parting. A shapeless shirt and trousers failed to hide his bulky form. Muddy slippers were on his feet. There was something not right about the way he stared up. No one spoke. He seemed mildly surprised to see them looking down.

'Did you hear me?' Laura snarled. 'Get out of –' Thick fingers were struggling to remove a raisin from the little box in his hand. The same type of box she'd found in the garden.

'Mummy?' His front teeth stuck out when he spoke.

'Oh my God,' Owen said very quietly. 'Is he disturbed?'

Not disturbed, she thought. Confused. He's confused.

The person looked round, eyes criss-crossing the ceiling. 'Twee-pies leap.' He raised a forefinger to his wet lips. 'Shhhh!' Then he shuffled into the front room. A second later the television went on.

She turned to Owen, a barbell still clutched tightly in each hand. 'I know who he is. He's called William and he used to live here.'

CHAPTER 20

'Nighty-night, big fellow.' The policeman nodded amiably at William as a carer from the Skylark Trust guided him out of the front door.

'Nigh', nigh',' he mumbled, batting a big hand up and down.

They were lined up in the front hall, as if seeing him off on holiday.

'Night, William.' Laura managed a smile even though her heart was still thudding away.

The front door shut and the officer turned to her. 'Not having much luck, are you?'

It was the same officer who'd called when the bird had become trapped in the house: his tone was light-hearted.

'I need a drink,' Laura replied. Some of the vodka in the freezer would go down nicely, she thought, but it'll only keep me awake. 'Anyone for a cup of tea?'

He shook his head and the remaining staff member from the Skylark Trust did the same. She still looked mortified at what had happened. 'I really cannot apologise enough, Mr and Mrs Wilkinson. As I said, he's totally harmless; but you weren't to know –'

Laura held up a hand. 'Really, it's fine. The poor lad was just confused.'

The staff member looked dubiously from her to Owen. Laura guessed she was afraid they would press charges or make an official complaint.

'He just wanted to watch telly,' she added casually, trying to placate the woman. 'Didn't he, Owen?'

He adjusted the belt of his dressing gown. She could see his hands were still unsteady. 'That's right.'

'Sounds like William,' the staff member said. 'He'll watch it for hours if we let him.'

Owen coughed. 'Tell me, has he done this kind of thing before?'

She gave a vigorous shake of her head. 'Never. It's totally out of character. I mean, he's walked a good four miles down country lanes to get here. It's incredible, really.'

Laura chose not to mention the empty raisin box she'd found in the garden the other day. 'How old is he? In terms of mental ability.'

The staff member crossed her hands in front of her. Laura knew the question placed her in an awkward position; the information was probably confidential. But he had just broken into their house.

'William has a mental age of around five. But there are other issues, too.' The staff member cast an uncomfortable glance in the policeman's direction.

He also looked eager to know.

Her fingers tapped a couple of times. 'William registers on the autistic spectrum and, as is often the case, has other issues alongside that condition: co-morbidity, as it's known.'

'Like what?' The officer asked, thumbs now hooked into the shoulder seams of his stab-proof vest.

'Mild dyspraxia. And probably ADHD. But, as I'd like to stress, he's not in any way violent. Obviously he needs full-time care and we provide that for him.'

Not, Laura thought, at a sufficient level to stop him wandering about at night.

'I will be making a report and, I imagine, his sleeping arrangements will be reviewed in light of this. Once again, I am so sorry this happened. I work nights – I'm on duty from eight each evening. Call any time after that and I'll be happy to answer any other questions you might have.' She handed Laura a card and looked expectantly at them.

'Mr and Mrs Wilkinson?' The officer asked. 'Are you happy with…'

Before Owen could reply, Laura stepped forward. 'Perfectly. It was an unfortunate mistake. No one is hurt, everyone is safe, let's leave things at that.'

The staff member's relief was palpable and the police officer inclined his head. Laura realised she'd probably just saved him a pile of paperwork, too.

'We'll be off, then.' The officer allowed the staff member to go first, speaking over his shoulder as he followed. 'Really, you should set your burglar alarm at night.' He tapped the panel by the front door. 'Just activate the ground floor. You have motion sensors throughout.' He pointed to the little blinking box set into the corner of the ceiling.

'We'd prefer not to feel prisoners in our own home,' Owen replied a little harshly.

'Besides,' Laura cut in, her tone more pleasant. 'We've got a cat – so it would set –' The kitten. I'd forgotten all about it. She turned round and hurried back to the kitchen.

The little thing was still in the travel case, backed into the far end, eyes wide and anxious. Bloody hell, Laura thought. It'll never come out now.

As cars pulled slowly away outside, she opened a bag of treats and sprinkled a few inside the door of the travel case. 'Come on, Scaredy-mouse. Have you even used your litter tray yet? Mummy thinks you haven't.'

'Very magnanimous of you,' Owen announced behind her.

She knew he wasn't talking about giving the kitten some little fish shapes. 'Was there any point in kicking up a fuss?' She sat back on her heels. 'Really?'

He ran his hands through his hair. A familiar gesture when he was stressed or tired. 'No, I suppose not. That staff member knew she was lucky: I could see it in her

115

face.'

'Exactly. And the police will have logged it. That's automatic when you call them, isn't it?'

'Yes, you're right.'

She leaned forward to look into the travel case again. 'Come on little thing, mummy is here. Won't you come out?'

'How were you so sure it was the son of the couple who lived here?'

The box of raisins in his hand, Laura almost said. Evidently, Owen hadn't even noticed them. 'Sorry?' she replied, playing for time.

'You knew it was William. How?'

'Oh.' She sat back on her heels once more. She didn't want to admit what she'd been getting up to trying to find out about William. Owen would only worry. 'After we got that letter about travel arrangements, I happened to pass the estate agent in the village. So I asked for details of the previous occupants. He mentioned a teenage son who's in care because he can't look after himself. At the facility up the road…it just clicked.'

Owen stared down at her for a moment longer. 'I see.' His gaze shifted to the clock. 'Shit – it's after midnight. Are you coming up?'

'In a minute. I need a camomile tea first. You go.'

'OK.' He came over, leaned down and placed a kiss on top of her head. 'What a night.'

She reached up and squeezed his hand. 'One thing after another, isn't it?'

'Seems to be.' He set off for the stairs. 'Kitchen door locked?'

'Kitchen door locked.'

'Kitten OK?'

'Far as I can see.'

'Night, then.'

'Night.'

She flicked the kettle on and, once the ceiling started to

creak above her, quietly opened the laptop. The screen sprang to life and she saw a new message waiting. Thank God! Tamsin had got back.

You poor thing, Laura. Here's me sending you a huge hug. Don't worry, OK? You mustn't worry. Oh gosh, it's horrible what you're going through. It's worrying, distressing, even frightening – all those things. But you must listen to me, OK?

Don't let your T control you.

Show the dammed thing who's boss. Many doctors will tell you that nothing can be done about tinnitus. Just forget about it, they'll say. And although they're ignorant, they happen to be right. You must try not to let it affect you.

The kettle clicked off, but she didn't care about a drink. This woman, she thought. This lovely woman living half-way round the world, I only care about what she has to say.

I've seen so many people about my T. I let it drive me indoors and cut me off from the world. I let it put worry creases in my face. I've been poked and prodded and put through so much in hospitals. But it was a fellow sufferer who said to me that there is only one person who can truly do something about your tinnitus – and that is you. Laura, you'll have to find ways to live with your T. Make the best of your situation. The more you can force yourself to forget about it, the less you'll notice it and the easier you'll be able to cope, believe me.

Laura wanted to cheer. She was right. She was so bloody right. It's canary song. So bloody what? A little bird singing. Big deal. Laura climbed off the stool. Sod the tea, she thought, I'm having a proper drink. Frost made the neck of the vodka bottle stick against her fingers. She closed the freezer, grabbed a shot glass off the shelf and filled it with liquid made lazy by the cold. Bloody marvellous, she thought, knocking it back. Bloody marvellous. She refilled it then turned to her laptop. This woman who I have never even met is absolutely right. Her attitude is what I need. Bless her, bless her.

I'm signing off now, OK? But contact me any time. There's a lot more about your symptoms I would like to know. Birdsong is quite rare, you know? You need to get more advice. (Personally, I think your current doctor sucks.) Make use of your wonderful health service: book an appointment with a consultant at your local hospital's ENT department. Demand answers. Let me know how it goes and don't worry. You'll survive this, just like me and millions of others have. All my love, Tamsin.

Laura felt light-headed. There were tears in her eyes as she typed an answer.

Tamsin, your words are a tonic to me. As if by magic, they appear on my screen and transform my spirits.

She knew she was gushing but didn't care.

In Britain we call it vim. I think you use the word chutzpah? It's your chutzpah that I'm drinking in now. I was being cowed by this horrible condition. But no more. Now I'm fighting back. Thank you, Tamsin. I will get a second opinion, and I will be demanding a referral to an ENT consultant. Thank you with all my heart, Laura.

After pressing send, she sat back and took in a huge breath. She felt so alive. If it was light outside, she thought, I'd put on some trainers and go running over the hills. Run for miles.

The card from the staff member at the Skylark Trust was by the computer. William. Her mind switched to him as she raised her glass and took a contemplative sip. Why, she thought, didn't I remind Owen about the box of raisins in the garden? Why did I also keep it back from the staff member? She pursed her lips: stop fooling yourself. You know why. You kept that quiet to smooth everything over. To minimise the fuss. She thought of William again, standing at the bottom of the stairs, looking around and then holding his finger to his lips. It was conspiratorial. Like the gesture would make sense. And right before that, he had said something. She couldn't make out what, but he had said something. She wanted to know. Lifting the card, she examined the address printed in the corner. Tomorrow, she decided, I'll try and find out.

CHAPTER 21

'You're sure, now?' It was the third time Owen had asked.

She nodded her head. 'I feel exhausted, darling. I don't think I really got back to sleep. Maybe after your concert? We could have a day together in town then.'

He glanced at the clock on the wall, satchel in hand.

You need to go now, she thought. Or you'll hit the morning rush on the A6.

'Besides,' she added. 'It's really not fair on the kitten. It's still too young to be left alone. Not for an entire day.'

He sent an unsympathetic glance towards the far corner. Its food had disappeared in the night and the litter tray had been used, but it was back in the travel case when they came downstairs.

'So your daily schedule's now dictated by a small animal?' His tone was light-hearted. Just.

'No.' Smiling pleasantly, she sat on the bar stool and waved towards the door with her fingers. 'Go on! You'll be late.'

He turned to the window immediately behind her. She knew where he was looking. The church. 'So what will you do today?'

'I don't know. Probably go back to bed for a bit. And I need to get some shopping. There's that big Waitrose near Cheadle.'

'You won't go back to the church, will you? I don't think staring into the grave of a dead child is…it's not a healthy thing to do.'

'No, I won't go over there. OK?'

He started to go then turned back to her. 'I…I meant to ask. How's your hearing been with this viral infection? Have you…?' He left the question unfinished.

You mean have I been hearing more birdsong, she thought. 'It's been fine, darling. There's no discomfort. I'd never have guessed I even had a virus, to be honest.'

'Good.' He smiled briefly. 'I feel like I've dragged you up here to simply abandon you.'

'Owen, don't be silly. We both know the score. You concentrate on making the performance perfect.'

He nodded. 'I'd better go.'

A few seconds later he appeared beyond the kitchen window. She could see him out of the corner of her eye but didn't want to look properly. That might make the horrible thoughts start. He was standing by his car, one arm raised. Damn it, he was waving goodbye. Trying to look relaxed, she glanced up and waved back.

Last night, he was pathetic. The sight of those thin arms, all the muscle wasted. So weak, so helpless. He couldn't defend you, the useless man, he's a failure, a sad excuse, an invalid. He won't last much longer and soon you'll be alone, alone and childless –

She ducked from his sight and slapped herself hard across the face. The voice died away and she looked across at the kitten. It was watching her from the shadows.

Once she was sure Owen's car had disappeared from view, she got up and looked over at the church. No sign of anyone in the field. She rested her forehead on the heels of her hands. What is happening to me? The dream came back after she returned to bed. The same figure, bent knees jutting out, a forearm jammed behind its head. She could remember puzzling over its posture in her sleep – part of her brain analysing images being produced by a separate part of her mind. Strange.

She'd come to some sort of conclusion but now, in the

cold light of day, it eluded her. A vague impression of realisation. Something about how the figure was lying.

Her mind switched to the website about canaries. How bizarre tinnitus could manifest itself as birdsong. Did other people just hear random birdsong? Or did they also hear a specific bird? Tamsin would know. She checked the clock. 7.43. About midnight, her time.

There was no reply to her last email. Laura cringed slightly as she read what she'd typed. It was so effusive. But with good reason. I shouldn't feel embarrassed, she thought, beginning a new message.

Hi, Tamsin. Me again. It's almost 8 in the morning and my husband's gone to work. On my own once more, as usual. Well, not totally, as it happens. I got a kitten! Dear little thing, but still very nervous. Currently, she prefers her travel case to the (very expensive) basket I bought her.

Thank you again for your encouraging words. They really gave me a boost. I remember reading that stress can sometimes trigger tinnitus. And tinnitus causes stress. A vicious circle. So I'll try to keep my emotions in control.

Also, I wanted to ask you about the birdsong I hear. It definitely is a canary. Don't ask me why it's a canary — until I heard an audio clip of one on the internet yesterday, I couldn't have said what canary song sounds like.

Do other sufferers hear song from specific birds? You mentioned other people sometimes hear snatches of music. Are they songs they are familiar with? Ones they could name?

All this makes me think of a science quote someone once came out with, something about the fact we, as humans, have only mapped a fraction of the oceans' depths – but how our brains work is even more of a mystery. (Excuse my atrocious paraphrasing.)

Anyway, time to see if I can coax this kitten further than the kitchen. Love, Laura.

The message went on its way to America and she closed the laptop. 'Scaredy-mouse?' she called softly. 'Come on. You can't hide in there forever.'

She got down on all fours and crawled across the flagstone floor, face ducked low. It was in there, curled up. But its eyes were open, regarding Laura intently. 'Mummy wants to play. Come on little thing. Won't you play with me?'

It sat up and cocked its head. Now in front of the little door, Laura made kissing noises. 'I know you've been out. Your food bowl's empty.' The bit of fur on a string; that did the trick yesterday. She retrieved it from the hooks near the back door. Back at the travel case, she lowered the scrap down and started making it tremble by shaking her hand.

The kitten's eyes widened.

By dragging it along the floor, Laura enticed it out of the travel case, across the kitchen and then along the corridor to the front hall. Funny, she thought, how they just can't resist the urge to catch things. Once again, it sniffed at the bottom of the door into Owen's study, before it crossed to the foot of the stairs. It sat down, eyes raised to the first floor, tip of its tail twitching.

'Come on,' Laura said, cupping a hand under its belly and lifting it up. 'I'll carry you. Must seem like the north face of the Eiger from down there.'

At the top, she pointed to the right. 'The spare room. Just boxes in there for now.'

Stroking the top of the kitten's head, she set off along the corridor. 'Bathroom's this one. That's mine and Owen's room opposite.' They got to the little step down into the room above the snug: the one she'd converted into an exercise studio. She saw with dismay the lilies were now totally dead. Not just dead, almost rotting. The leaves had withered and the stalks buckled. Oval flower-heads pointed down at the windowsill and the water in the glass vase had turned brown.

Laura turned away. 'Here's where I do my exercises. That's a Swiss ball, yoga mat, my dumbbells – also anti-burglar devices, nowadays.' She stepped closer to the single, framed photo on the wall above the dumbbell rack. 'Can you see me? Look, there I am, at the edge of the stage.'

She studied the black-and-white image before adding, in a quieter voice, 'It's what I used to be. All day I'd spend...' But the words were too heavy to get out. Like pebbles, weighing on her tongue. She had to turn her back on the picture. 'And that's you over there.' She pointed at the floor-to-ceiling mirrors. The kitten seemed oblivious to its reflection. 'It is, that's you.' Laura moved closer so it could see itself nestled in the crook of her arm. 'That's –'

Canary song suddenly filled the room and the cat's body flexed as her claws sank into Laura's skin.

She gasped with pain and dropped the kitten to the floor. It landed on all four feet, back impossibly arched. A low guttural moan escaped it as it glared malevolently at itself. The canary song continued and the little animal backed away from the mirror, now hissing, needle-like teeth bared.

Laura looked on in fear and confusion. The singing seemed louder than ever before. In a flash, the cat was out of the door and she heard it race down the stairs. The singing stopped. Laura caught sight of herself. Her hand was clapped over her mouth, face drained of all colour. Pinpricks of red were already showing through the pale blue sleeve of her cashmere jumper. But there was no pain; she felt nothing other than an overwhelming desire to throw up. She ran for the bathroom as her stomach muscles began to convulse.

Wiping the last of the sick from her chin, she picked out a fresh ball of cotton wool and examined the punctures in the skin of her forearm. The kitten's claws had gone right in. Lucky it was so small, Laura thought – an adult cat could have caused a nasty wound.

Dabbing at the holes, she glanced at herself in the bathroom mirror. She looked dazed and bewildered. What had just happened? Everything had occurred so quickly. She'd been moving closer to the mirror, lifting the kitten slightly so it could see itself. The canary song had been so much louder. But also something else: clearer. Like whatever was making the noise had been close. Very close. What had happened next changed everything: the kitten had heard it, too.

The implications of that were enough to make Laura feel sick all over again. If it had heard the singing, she thought, the noise is not in my head. It was definitely no symptom of an ear infection, the onset of tinnitus or, worse, her illness recurring. It was coming from somewhere within the house.

She smoothed antiseptic cream on the wounds, replaying what had just taken place, trying to be sure of the sequence. The kitten had been definitely looking at the mirror when it suddenly bolted. But had it begun to move before the noise started? She strained to recall exactly what had happened, when. Me holding her up a bit, stepping forward and saying something. Something like, look – that's you. Then pointing with my free hand. Which had happened first – the sound ringing out or the kitten catching sight of its reflection?

Laura's mind jumped forward to when the kitten

landed on the floor. There was no doubt it was reacting to its reflection by then: it was facing the mirror, back bent up, fur standing on end. So had the reflection spooked it? The little thing had probably never seen a mirror before. How silly to thrust it in front of one.

She set off down the stairs. 'Mouse? It's OK, Mouse. Where are you?' She found it in the kitchen. Back in the travel case, cowering at the far end of it. Like it wanted to go home. 'What made you jump like that?' She looked into its huge eyes. 'Did you…was it something you…' This is ridiculous, Laura thought. I'm trying to question a cat. 'OK, little thing. You stay in there. It's OK. If that's what you want, stay there.'

She went to the shelf, emptied a handful of the fish treats into her palm and returned to the travel case. Crouching, she put one hand inside to sprinkle the biscuits on the blanket. The only movement was the kitten's tail, writhing about like a severed portion of snake. 'Mouse? I have to go out now. There's milk in your bowl if you get thirsty. OK? I'll be back soon, I promise.'

She let the rest of the biscuits fall on the blanket. The one its mother had given birth on. The smell would be a source of comfort for the kitten, according to the breeder. 'All right, Mouse? I'll be back soon.'

She was half-way across the room, car keys in her hand, when it let out the tiniest little meow. Laura stopped and looked back. The sound was so forlorn. 'You know what, Mouse?' She glanced about. 'I'm not leaving you here on your own. You're bloody well coming with me, that's what you're doing.'

CHAPTER 22

The drive over to the Skylark Trust took them through rolling countryside, the purple hills of the Peak District a brooding presence in the distance. *Pretty Vacant* was playing on the CD and Laura had happily sung along to most of it before she realised the loud music was probably freaking Mouse out.

'Sorry.' She switched to Classic FM and immediately recognised *The Lark Ascending* by Vaughan Williams. A lot more soothing for the kitten, she imagined, as the violin notes wavered and soared.

'Do you think William really walked along this country lane back to Lantern Cottage?' she asked. 'It wouldn't have been that hard, I suppose. Just a case of not taking any turn-off until you reached the main road back into Oldknow. A child could manage it, especially one in the body of a young man.'

Mouse was moving around more. She came to the door of the travel case and looked about as if the world wasn't quite so intimidating.

'What I need to know is why he goes off on his midnight walks. Something's driving him back to the place where he once lived. Perhaps he doesn't realise the Skylark Trust is his new home.' She cast another quick glance down at the kitten. 'Like a cat finding its way back to its previous house.'

A short while later a sign jutting out of the hedgerow let her know the centre was about to come up on her left.

She took the next turning and followed the little road down to a cluster of stone buildings. A brand new minibus was parked in the car park. On its side were the words, Skylark Trust, with the silhouette of a little bird floating above them.

Laura parked next to it and turned the radio off. She sat for a moment and studied the entrance. A ramp led up to it, handrails on each side. She realised every building was single storey. Wheelchair access. A dull ache started in her spine as she imagined the deformities some of the poor things inside must suffer from. Shifting uncomfortably in her seat, she looked down at Mouse. 'You seem happier. I'll be back before long.'

She wound down her window a little to let in air and was about to climb out when both entrance doors swung open at identical speed. A young girl stepped into the sunlight and Laura recognised her instantly as Molly Maystock. She was beautiful; more so than in the photos on the collection boxes. Her hair was lovely – long, straight and perfect for tying into plaits. Or putting up in a bun. Often, that was Laura's favourite part of a performance. Not the actual dancing – with all the pressure to achieve a flawless performance – but just sitting backstage, listening to the orchestra tuning their instruments while a stylist arranged her hair. Those were the memories she cherished most.

In time, she'd learned how to do hair herself; swirls, braids, folds. She imagined visiting Molly at her house. Spend hours together, brushing each other's hair and then arranging it different ways. That would be such fun.

Her dad appeared behind her and she took his hand. Arms gently swinging, they set off slowly down the ramp toward an old blue car on the other side of the car park.

Half way across, she had to stop. Laura watched her shoulders rise and fall a few times, her father beside her, obviously battling the temptation to support her. Then she gave a nod and they continued across to their vehicle. It wasn't fair, Laura thought. Why should such a precious little thing have to suffer like that?

Once they'd left, she slipped out of her own car. There was a sign in front of the entrance. Childish lettering and a series of arrows. Hydrotherapy pool. Jump-about gym. Multi-sensory centre. Nature trail. Activity centre. Residential units.

As soon as she stepped onto the ramp the front doors began to part. In the foyer was a large cage. Inside it was a parrot with blue, green and red feathers. It broke off from its preening to examine Laura.

'Good morning,' someone said.

The accent was unmistakably African. Laura turned to the front desk and saw a black lady smiling at her. It dawned on her that she hadn't seen a single non-white face in Oldknow. 'Morning, my name's Laura Wilkinson.'

'Morning, Laura.'

'Hi.' She paused then smiled. 'Sorry, I probably should have rung before arriving. I was speaking to the vicar at Oldknow, Martin Flowers – I live near the church – about setting up a dance therapy class here.'

'Martin? He's been wonderful to us.'

'Yes – he couldn't praise the centre highly enough. I've just moved here. I lived in London before and used to be with the Royal Ballet.'

The woman's face was beaming. 'The way you moved as you came through the doors. Such grace!'

Laura blushed. 'Thank you. I have experience of teaching dance to children and Martin wondered if I might be interested in taking a class here. He said you're always on the lookout for volunteers.'

'Always, always, always. Let me see, who should you speak to?' She started looking at a list of names.

'Actually, would it be possible just to have a look round? I don't expect you to arrange anything with me right now. But it would be wonderful if someone could show me what facilities you have here.'

'I will get someone for you, no problem. There is a studio over in the activity centre. It has big mirrors.'

'It looks to be an amazing place.'

'It certainly is. Please, one moment. I will make a call. Your name is Laura?'

'Yes.'

She picked up the phone. Laura's nerves were jangling. She felt light-headed. I'm not being dishonest, she reasoned with herself. It would be good to set up a dance class here. She turned round and saw the parrot observing her. A wave of illogical dread surged into her stomach. What if it asks me something? Something embarrassing. Aren't you a naughty girl? Making up lies.

The bird took a series of sideways steps along the wooden pole until it was just on the other side of the bars. Laura noticed a little sign at the base of its cage. Marty the Macaw. Well, Marty, I wish you'd stop bloody staring at me.

The inner door opened and a staff member in dark blue trousers and a white tunic stepped out. Laura was relieved it wasn't the one who'd been at her house the previous night.

'Laura? My name's Denise. You'd like to have a look round?'

'Hello, yes. If it's no trouble.'

None at all. Felicity says you're a ballet dancer?'

Felicity was still beaming from behind her monitor. 'Was. More years ago than I'd like to admit. But I took a music and movement class down in London until recently.'

'For children with disabilities?'

She hesitated. Princesses-in-training. 'Not really. But Martin said there are carers who could...'

'Yes. The staffing levels are brilliant. Let me take you over to the Activity Centre.'

The front doors opened and she followed Denise back down the ramp.

'We'll also take a look in the hydrotherapy pool.

There's a session going on now.'

From somewhere high above notes started raining down. Laura looked up and was about to comment on the beautiful sound when the words stuck in her throat. Could Denise hear it, too?

'It's a skylark,' she commented, smiling across. 'Was that what you were wondering? I can never spot them, but it's up there somewhere.'

Laura almost laughed with relief. 'This place is idyllic.'

Denise nodded. 'To be honest, we could have called it the Curlew Trust, Tawny Owl Trust, Cuckoo...Swallow...Woodpecker...Heron – it's like a bird sanctuary out here.'

'I get a fair few in my garden. Finches, sparrows...that sort.'

'Where do you live?'

Laura realised that the other woman might well have heard about the incident involving William. 'Just outside Old – wow, is that the hydrotherapy pool?'

'It is.'

Through the misty plate-glass windows of what looked like a converted barn, Laura could see a pool about twenty metres long. Denise took her up another ramp and into a corridor with a smooth plastic floor. A large window overlooked the main room.

'We'll stay out here to save removing our shoes and socks. The water is kept very warm and those hoists are set into rails at the side of the pool. They can be moved up and down its entire length.'

A child was in a harness that dangled from one of the metal arms. A therapist was moving the legs of the boy out in slow circular movements while another kept his head from slipping below the water. A girl – maybe ten – was being lifted from a chunky-looking wheelchair. The helpers started strapping her into the harness below a hoist on the other side. Her legs were like two withered roots and, hating herself for it, Laura had to look away. 'Great for mobility, I imagine.'

'Absolutely. Especially for children who are normally confined to wheelchairs. The water supports their weight and allows such freedom of movement.'

The child from Laura's dream flashed up in her mind. The way it seemed somehow suspended in space. Almost like it was floating.

'The Activity Centre is next. We'll go this way.'

She led Laura along a corridor lined with images of children. Some had been photographed being wheeled round the gardens. Others were in the gym, sitting on trampolines or propped in a shallow pit of foam cubes – or simply splayed out on a big mat, arms and legs akimbo. But they were all smiling and laughing. Laura slowed down to look more closely at their happy faces. Maybe, she thought for the first time, I could teach here. If I could just get over how their bodies make me feel. Surely that was possible?

'There are various rooms here, but I think this one would be best for what you have in mind.' She showed Laura into a deserted studio. Laura immediately saw it had a sprung wooden floor. Mirrors ran down one side. Exercise mats were neatly piled up in the far corner and there were speakers among the halogen lights set into the ceiling.

'This place is incredible. How on earth has it all been funded?'

'Mainly through some very generous donors and very dedicated fundraisers.'

'Amazing.' Laura raised her eyebrows. 'And do children actually live here? I noticed a sign saying Residential Units.'

'There are rooms for ten children or young adults who need round-the-clock care. Most stay for short periods – mainly to provide some respite for their families or carers. Four, currently, live with us full time.'

Including William, Laura thought. 'Could...could I see the living facilities? If this is anything to go by...'

'Of course. They're over this way. Does the studio look like it would be of use? If not, the gym has a soft floor and runners in the ceiling for children who need to be – '

'No – the studio would be perfect.'

'Good.' Her stride broke as she looked at Laura. 'Can I ask; what was it like to be a ballerina? You did it professionally, is that right?'

'I did, yes.' The question was one Laura didn't look forward to. Many women dreamed, as young girls, of being ballerinas. Few understood the endless gruelling work required to actually become one. Or the fierce competition to win through. The rivalries and alliances that constantly shifted. She gave her stock answer. 'It was everything I'd hoped it would be – and more.'

'I bet,' Denise said a little breathlessly.

Laura knew she was picturing the spotlight beaming down, bouquets of flowers, rapturous applause.

'But not something,' she added, 'that you can do – or would want to do – forever.' The comment, she'd learned over the years, worked well. It closed the gap between fantasy and reality. Brought everything back down to earth and made the person she was talking to realise Laura was human, too.

Denise nodded. 'Yes – you hear stories about the wear and tear on your joints. Though you're in terrific shape, if you don't mind me saying.'

'Thanks. It leaves you with good body awareness, that's for sure. I can't go long without exercising.'

Denise showed her through the doors of the residential unit. There were cheery murals on the walls, plants in large pots. 'This building has its own catering unit. There is a communal living area for activities and an outside play area at the back.'

Laura heard a television. William liked to watch the television. 'What about somewhere just to relax?'

'The TV lounge. We also find computer games can work quite well – especially for the children with autism.'

135

Denise opened the door to her left and Laura immediately saw him. He was in a large chair directly in front of the TV. A couple of other children in wheelchairs were playing on a computer game, staff members at their sides. On the other side of the room, a young girl was being held upright by some kind of frame on wheels. Her head was swaying to and fro and she grinned in their direction, eyes magnified by the thickness of her glasses. One hand began to flap weakly.

'Rosie, hi!' Denise exclaimed, before turning to Laura. 'Come and meet Rosie.'

As they got closer, the girl's hand flapped more quickly and a string of saliva stretched from her chin. Laura kept her smile fixed in place as Denise knelt down and produced a tissue. 'Rosie, this is Laura.'

The girl's eyes were glittering with delight. Laura wondered how often anyone came to visit. Rosie's head started to wobble with effort as one arm rose slightly higher. Laura realised she wanted to shake hands. She bent forward, readying herself to snub out any urge to back away. But, to her surprise, it didn't come. She realised the joyful sparkle in the girl's eyes was making her smile in return. Genuinely smile. She took her hand. 'Hi Rosie, it's really nice to meet you.'

She made a kind of humming noise. Happy.

'So, Rosie,' Denise announced. 'Are we going for a walk in a bit, you and me?'

The girl let go of Laura's hand and wrenched her head round to look at Denise.

Laura saw her chance. Edging away from them, she began a slow and casual circle of the room, studying the paintings on the walls, keeping William in the periphery of her vision all the while. Denise was now holding Rosie's hand as the girl started to speak in agonisingly slow syllables.

Laura stopped at William's chair. 'Hello,' she whispered. 'I've brought you some raisins.'

CHAPTER 23

He looked up briefly, eyes dropping to where her breasts jutted from beneath her thin jumper. His bottom lip was glistening and she thought, for one uncomfortable moment, he was ogling. But she realised the look in his eyes wasn't lustful; it was more disturbing than that. It was the look of a hungry infant. He certainly didn't show any sign of remembering her as he finally turned back to the television.

She slid the nearest chair round so it was angled towards him. He watched warily from the corner of his eye. 'Do you like these?' she asked, removing the box of raisins she'd bought earlier in the village shop.

His front teeth emerged as a grin spread. ''Sins!'

'Here you are.'

He reached for them eagerly, almost knocking the box from her outstretched fingers.

'Your name is William, isn't it?' She kept her voice quiet and friendly.

Stubby fingers were fumbling to open the small box. The bottom edge of it was pressing down into the blubbery swell of his belly. He resorted to ripping the top flap off. A couple of raisins were prised out and shoved into his mouth.

Laura could see Denise glancing inquisitively in her direction. She gave a reassuring wave and pointed to William. Making friends, she mouthed.

Denise raised a thumb before turning to Rosie. Laura looked back at William. 'What else do you like?' He was chewing away, eyes fixed on the telly. A cartoon was playing. 'Do you like the telly?'

He nodded. 'Telly.'

'That's good. And is it nice living here?'

He made no reply and she sensed he was using the television as a way of not engaging. 'Did you like where you lived before?'

A forefinger dug more raisins out from where they were lumped together in the little box. He palmed them into his mouth.

'Was it nice living in Lantern Cottage?'

His eyes moved to her for a moment. The name had meant something to him. If only, she thought, I could turn the damn telly off. 'The house up the steep lane? With the great big chimney?'

'Chimey,' he muttered, eyes glued to the screen. 'Big.'

'That's right. I live there now. You came to visit us last night. Do you remember?'

He frowned slightly. His eyes were back on her, but she could tell he wasn't really seeing her. 'My be'room. Big chimey.'

Of course, Laura thought. The room that's now my exercise studio had childish wallpaper when we moved in. She remembered seeing racing cars and rockets, many obliterated by clumsy crayon scrawl. What must it have been like for his parents: having a child whose body grew up, but whose mind never did? The chimney was behind the wall now covered by her mirrors. She thought of the way the kitten bolted from the room as the canary song materialised from thin air. 'Do you like birds, William?'

'Birdy,' he nodded. 'Birdy sings.'

Her heart jolted. She leaned forward, elbows on her knees. 'Did you hear a birdy singing?' she asked quietly. 'In your bedroom?'

His frown deepened and he looked away. 'Twee-pie.'

'What was that? I didn't hear.'

Hesitantly, he mumbled into his chest. 'Twee-pies leap.'

Twee-pies leap, she thought. That's what he'd said at the bottom of the stairs! Twee-pies leap. What did it mean? 'William, did you hear a bird singing in your bedroom?'

'Twee-pie,' he repeated more loudly, digging at the raisins. 'Not leap?' He sounded scared.

She couldn't make sense of his reply. Denise was now standing up. She took a step in their direction but Rosie clutched at the hem of her top. She bent forward to stroke the side of the girl's face. Laura knew she didn't have long. 'Did your mummy and daddy also hear a bird singing?'

He looked about. 'Mummy? Where mummy?'

Damn it, Laura cursed, I shouldn't have mentioned his mum. He obviously doesn't understand she's dead. 'William, was the bird you heard inside the house?'

He raised himself up in his chair, head twisting around. The empty box fell to the floor. Oh no, she realised, he's looking for his mum. He thinks she's come to visit.

'Twee-pies leap, William. What's twee-pies leap?'

A hand went up and he rubbed a knuckle hard against one eyebrow. 'Twee-pie!'

The word was said with aggression. Denise looked round sharply.

'What is twee-pies?' Laura asked.

'Twee-pie! Twee-pie!' he suddenly yelled.

Pie, not pies. He raised a hand and, for a moment, she thought he was going to hit her. But it swept past her face. He thrust a finger at the television. 'Twee-pie! Leave twee-pie 'lone!' He was on his feet, bellowing. 'Leave twee-pie 'lone!'

Denise ran across, as did the staff members from near the computers.

'William?' Denise called. 'It's OK, William.' Her eyes bounced to Laura for a moment.

'Leave twee-pie alone? Who is twee-pie?' Laura demanded. 'Who? Tell me.'

'William, hush now, hush now.' Denise put one hand on his shoulder.

'Who is twee-pie?' Laura tried again.

Denise shot an infuriated glance at her. 'Stop asking him that question, will you?'

'William, tell me who twee-pie is!'

He let out a roar of anguish. 'Don't move twee-pie! Bad person come! Bad person!'

One of the other staff members started pulling Laura away. 'You need to come with me.' His tone was harsh.

As Laura was directed roughly toward the doors, Rosie started to wail. William collapsed back in his chair, hands clapped over his ears as he began to groan. Laura glimpsed the television screen just past him. The cartoon was still playing. A black-and-white cat was creeping theatrically along a curtain rail. Perched on the end was a canary with an enormous head. Tweetie Pie. William had been pointing at Tweetie Pie.

CHAPTER 24

Laura wanted to curl up in a ball; the way they were all looking at her was awful. Appalled, bemused, outraged. Behind her, the parrot let out a low, rumbling squawk of disapproval. Who's a naughty girl, then?

The woman who'd been doing most of the speaking so far was, Laura gathered, the duty manager. Next to her was Denise. She was the one who looked most outraged. The staff member who'd led William away from Lantern Cottage had also appeared, summoned from her bed, judging from her puffy-eyed appearance.

'I'm sorry.' Laura's hands were clasped before her. 'I had no idea he would get so agitated.'

'You asked him about his recently deceased mother,' the duty manager replied. 'Exactly what did you expect?'

'I didn't mean to...' There was no point trying to explain herself. 'I'm sorry.'

'And you deceived us. It's tempting to call the police.'

'I didn't deceive you. I can teach dance. I'd like to –' 'That's definitely not going to happen now, she realised. It was written large across all their faces. 'I'd better go.'

'Yes, you had.' The duty manager looked at the staff member who'd taken William back to his room. 'How is he now?'

'He's OK. I made him some hot chocolate. He's gone to sleep.'

Sleep, Laura thought. Twee-pies leap. That's what William said at the bottom of the stairs. Tweetie Pie's asleep. He'd pressed his forefinger to his lips. Don't wake up Tweetie Pie; that's what he meant!

'Good.' The duty manager turned to Laura once more. 'Why did you do it?'

Otherwise, Laura thought, the bad person would come. She started to lift a hand, the effort almost too much. 'Because...he said something to me when he was in our house. I needed to know what it was.'

The woman looked mystified by her answer. 'So you trick your way in here and demand that a very vulnerable person explains himself to you? He has the mind of a young child! What you did was disgraceful.'

They were all glaring at her. She bowed her head. 'It wasn't the first time he's been back.'

That took the wind out of the duty-manager's sails. 'Pardon?'

Laura nodded. 'He's been out to the cottage before. I found a box of the raisins he likes in our garden. Plant pots have been moved. I've heard him coughing out there, in the night.'

The duty-manager looked at the lady who worked the night shift. 'Louise?'

'That's ridiculous,' Louise stated, looking at Laura. 'She didn't make that claim when I came to collect him.'

The duty manager shook her head. Her voice now had a pitying tone. 'I'm sorry. It's best you go. Please leave.'

Laura saw it was futile. They don't want to listen to me. She retreated towards the doors which sprang open behind her. Sunlight flooded the floor at her feet. 'Please tell him I'm sorry.' She turned round and stepped out into the brightness beyond.

'He was talking about Tweetie Pie! It's a canary from an old cartoon. From about the same time as Tom and Jerry. It may have been the same guy who did them. Fred Quimby, I think. The little bird had this catch-phrase. "I tawt I taw a puddy tat. I did! I did! I did" He had a lisp, you see. William was definitely talking about a canary.'

Scaredy-mouse sat behind the bars of its travel case. Its eyes looked at Laura in such an understanding way. She wanted to stop and give it a grateful hug. But she needed to get back.

'You heard it, too. I'm beginning to think you did. Up in my studio? That's William's old bedroom, you know. When we were in front of the mirror, you heard it singing, didn't you?'

She went over the encounter once more, trying to screen out the parts where poor William got distressed. He'd mentioned the chimney: he'd said to leave Tweetie Pie alone. Not to move Tweetie Pie. Something about a bad person coming, if you did. His dad? Did his dad used to beat him? Perhaps if William disturbed the canary and caused it to start singing. She could imagine William – a young boy – being fascinated by a little bird singing. But, for a grown-up, the noise would have been infuriating. Look at me, she thought. I've only been in the cottage a few weeks and it's already driving me up the wall.

The turn-off for Lantern Cottage appeared and the car passed into shadow as it laboured up the steep slope. They emerged on flatter ground and the first thing she saw was that chimney, thrusting up against the cloudy sky. So like a silhouette. And the part near the top where it widened out: that was big enough...it hit her with such clarity she had to stop the car. Her hands, still gripping the wheel, were trembling. Her foot slipped off the clutch and the car gave a sudden lurch and stalled. She pictured the figure from her dream; the strange way it was positioned. Realisation dawned.

The body wasn't lying on its side. It was upright – in a shaft! Wedged; somewhere dark and cramped and cold. Just short of the opening. She couldn't tear her eyes from the chimney stack. Oh my God, was there a child's body in there? Trapped, one arm behind its head, knees bent out and twisted.

Fingers shaking, she managed to restart the car and park beside the cottage. As she got out, she was acutely aware of the chimney looming over her. It gave her the same feeling as when a man she didn't know stared at her in the street, ugly thoughts so obviously in his head. Keeping her eyes averted, she removed Scaredy-mouse from the passenger foot well and hurried up to the front door, thankful that the eave of the porch hid her from the chimney's view.

As soon as the front door opened the burglar alarm began to beep. She entered the numbers, carried Scaredy-mouse down to the kitchen and put the case in the corner, noticing the kitten was pressed against the far end once more.

She crossed to the cellar door. As usual, the temperature quickly dropped as she descended the steep stone stairs. The energy-efficient bulbs were so slow to reach full brightness; dead leaves rustled as she reached the bottom step. Dreading seeing a toad on the floor, she scanned the shelves for Owen's toolbox. There it was, above their walking boots. She grabbed it and hurried back up to the kitchen, slamming the door shut behind her. That place was so, so horrible.

Almost back out into the front hall, she remembered Scaredy-mouse. 'Hey.' She crossed over to its case and undid the front door. 'I'll be upstairs, OK? You come up, if you want.'

At the bottom of the stairs she realised she still had her shoes on. Kicking them off, she continued up in her tights. The first-floor corridor seemed longer than usual. The door into her studio at the far end was open. She strode purposefully up to it and took the shallow step down. Blackness had now spread through the lilies.

Turning round, she stared at the mirrors. The shaft of the chimney was behind them. This was where the original cottage used to end, before the snug and this room above it – William's old bedroom – had been added. She recalled giving the decorators their instructions: strip back the walls to the bare plaster and fill in any bits that need it. The paint was to be a shade by Fired Earth, a lovely subtle green to impart a sense of peace and calm. The floorboards needed to be sanded and varnished and the window replaced with a double-glazed one.

She stood before the end mirror; the one Scaredy-mouse had spat at when the canary started to sing. The thick screws attaching it to the wall were the cross-haired ones.

She unclipped the lid of Owen's toolbox and searched for a screwdriver with the correct tip. By standing on her Swiss ball she was able to reach the screws in the upper corners. Each movement caused the ball to wobble and she had to use all the strength in her abdominal muscles and legs to maintain balance. The yellow-handled screwdriver felt good in her hands and, within seconds, the first screw was out.

It fell to the floor and bounced across the boards. She repositioned the Swiss ball, stood back up on it and started on the opposite corner. Within seconds that screw dropped to the floor, too. The next two were a quarter of the way down. She rolled the ball away and removed them while standing. When the two at knee height come out, the mirror started to lean forward ever so slightly and she realised only the screws in the bottom two corners now attached it to the wall.

Slapping a palm against the shiny surface, she got on her knees and unscrewed the final pair. Keeping a hand against the glass, she stood back up, locked her core, braced her knees and pulled gently at the huge rectangle of glass. It came away from the wall with a slight tearing sound. Oh my God, she said to herself, it weighs a ton.

Gripping each edge tight, a cheek pressed against the cold surface, she managed to tip it onto one corner, then started trying to lower it lengthways along the bottom of the neighbouring mirrors. Its lower edge was about eighteen inches from the floorboards when she knew it was too heavy. The fingers of her left hand were curled round its lower edge; they'd be trapped when it came into contact with the floor. She attempted to straighten it back up, but couldn't. Idiot, she said to herself: I should have rolled up some towels and placed them across the boards. Too late now. Her left hip felt like it was being jammed up into her bottom rib as the mirror dragged her shoulder lower. She was going to have to drop it.

She snatched the fingers of her left hand away and jumped back. The mirror hit the floor with a mighty thud, big enough to shake the entire room. A crack immediately raced across it and both pieces started toppling towards her. She lunged for the larger of the two, just managing to push it back against the wall. As it connected heavily with the mirrors behind – sending a mass of cracks zig-zagging across them - the other part of the mirror hit the floor and shattered. A tide of silver shards glided across the smooth floor. Both of her hands were in her hair, tips of her fingers pressed into her scalp. She looked with horror at the fragments surrounding her stockinged feet. Shit. Shit, shit and double shit.

Lifting her eyes, she could now see the portion of wall that had been hidden behind the mirror. The decorators had stripped the old wallpaper all right. But they hadn't bothered painting the bare plaster. Bloody cheek. They'd simply painted to just past the pencil lines marking where the mirrors were going to be. The older, yellowing plaster behind was pitted and cracked in places. They hadn't even bothered skimming over it properly.

A patch down near the bottom caught her eye. It was a different shade to the rest. Whiter – which meant newer. The only spot the decorators had actually gone to the trouble of filling in. But some of it had come off and there was now a small opening at the base of the wall. She stepped towards it and a searing pain lanced the bottom of her left foot.

CHAPTER 25

Mouth open in a silent gasp, Laura looked down. The broken glass, she thought. I've just crunched my foot into a load of broken glass. Idiot! She lifted it up. Blood was already soaking through her gossamer-thin tights. Careful to keep her balance, she cupped the foot in one hand and plucked the needle-like pieces from where they protruded from her sole. She could feel warm blood pooling in her palm. Shaking it off, she looked at the sea of silvery fragments spread around her.

One good stride, she thought. That would get me into the corridor and on to carpet. She sank down on her right leg, the one she could always get a bit more height with, and sprang for the doorway. For a glorious instant she was flying again – just as she used to up on stage. She barely had time to close her eyes and relish the sensation before the ball of her right foot connected with the edge of the step. She stumbled forward, momentum taking her across the corridor. Fending off the wall with both hands, she jogged to the bathroom, yanked a few feet of toilet tissue off the roll and wound it round her bleeding foot.

There was a dustpan and brush in the spare bedroom. By hopping, she was able to retrieve it and return to the studio. Down on her knees, she used the brush to push the broken glass back across the floor. Once the area before the exposed section of wall was clear, she examined it more closely.

The fresh plaster at its edges had been laid on thick. Using the end of the screwdriver, she chipped away until it was all on the floor. Older plaster now formed the rim of the opening. She could see bristly bits sticking out of it. Horsehair and even pieces of straw, by the look of it.

The brick behind the plaster was old; the same type as those which formed the outer walls of the cottage. That made sense, she thought This was the end of the building once, prior to the extension she was now in being added.

The groove between two of the bricks was especially deep and she managed to get her fingertips in. By tugging at the upper brick, it shifted slightly and she realised the mortar hadn't crumbled away: someone had been picking at it. There was now a gap between the two bricks – about the same width as a finger. Laura brought her face closer and, as soon as the smell coming from the opening touched her nostrils, she was overcome by emotion. A bitter-sweet yearning for something from long ago. Her childhood, the memory too indistinct to pinpoint. Where, she thought, have I smelled this smell? It was musty and stale. Clothing from a dressing-up box that hadn't been used in years? Curtains from a room whose windows were never opened? Not my house. Somewhere else. Somewhere I spent time as a little girl.

She gripped the higher brick by both ends and started wiggling it from side to side. More mortar started to come loose. By pushing and pulling, the amount it shifted slowly increased. But it was hard work. After a couple of minutes the muscles in her forearms were burning. She sat back and blew at some loose hair hanging over her eyes. There was a hammer in Owen's toolbox. Using the screwdriver as a chisel, she tapped away at the mortar. That was better. She tried the brick again and this time it began to slide out. The smell increased in strength.

Before removing it completely, her fingers became still. What, she wondered, would she find behind it? Could there really be a child's body trapped there? Not at this level: it was only at the mid-point of the chimney here. The thing stood taller than the roof by a good eight feet. This would be the point where the shaft flared out. She didn't know why, but she felt sure the point where any corpse was would be higher. After all, the body in her dream was near to some kind of an opening. The top of a chimney?

Clenching her jaw, she pulled the brick clear and placed it on the floor. No moths or spiders or woodlice cascaded out. She noticed the surface of the brick that had been facing inward was covered by a thin, brittle layer of something very much like pale cement. Tentatively, she lowered her face to look in the gap she'd created.

There was a cavity beyond. Black as coal. She stared into it, wondering how big the space was. If it was the chimney, it would be big enough to wave an arm around inside. I should remove more bricks, she decided. Then I can poke my entire head in. She pictured looking down: light would be visible from the living-room hearth directly below. And, she thought, if I lie on my back, I might be able to see a circle of sky up above.

She picked up the hammer and screwdriver and smashed away the mortar from the brick, immediately below. Loosening this one was far easier, and within minutes, she'd eased it from the wall.

Strange, she thought. I can see the end of a plank of wood. There's some kind of floor in there. How could there be a floor half way up a chimney? She sat back and looked from left to right. Where she was kneeling was too far over. The shaft of the chimney would be in the centre of the room; she was just inside the door. Perhaps the planks were the same ones that formed the floor of her and Owen's room.

That seemed to fit; there was a step down into the studio and the opening she'd made was at the height of that step. So she wouldn't be able to look up the chimney after all. All she'd broken through to was a cavity beside the chimney shaft. The gap between what was once the outer wall and her bedroom.

She studied the opening again. Enough light was getting in to reveal that the cement-like layer also covered the wooden planks. She reached out a finger and tapped it. Rock-hard. How big was this cavity? Did it stretch right up to the roof? She rummaged through the toolbox for a torch. There had been a big one down in the cellar, on the shelf right next to the toolbox. Damn it, she thought. Why didn't I think to bring it up?

As she put her hand into the opening and started patting about, a sharp bang shook the floorboards.

CHAPTER 26

Laura stepped back out into the corridor. Oh no, she realised, there's blood all over the place. Drips of it ran the entire length of the carpet. There was a blotchy handprint on the wall. Lifting her foot, she checked the tissue. Every bit of it was bright red, no white at all. Sodden fragments hung down. Now she was upright, the sole of her foot had begun a vicious throb. Whoever was at the front door knocked again.

'Hang on!' she called down. With both hands on the banister, she hopped down the stairs and looked through the hallway window. A grimy-looking man somewhere in his fifties was out there, facing the front door. His clothes were stiff with dirt and could see his hair was in a similar state. Some kind of tramp? Did he want food? She certainly wasn't answering the door when it was only her in the house.

She started to duck down but he suddenly turned. 'Mrs Wilkinson?'

Straightening up, she nodded. He held an imaginary phone to his ear and over-emphasised his words. 'I rang earlier. Left you a message?'

A message? She hadn't noticed a message. But then again, she thought, I didn't check the answerphone before rushing upstairs. Her foot continued to throb. 'Two minutes.'

She hopped down to the kitchen and hit the play

button as she removed the first-aid kit from the cupboard near the back door. Sitting on the flagstone floor allowed her to see into the travel case; Scaredy-mouse was still in there, tail twitching once more. 'Sorry, that was me upstairs. Did I frighten you?'

The message began to play as she pulled blood-soaked tissue from her foot. 'Mrs Wilkinson, it's Andy Pomerell, the chimney sweep.'

She looked up. The chimney sweep. He'd met Edith and Roger Hall, who lived here last. He might know something about William. His message continued to play.

'It's…let me see, nine-fifty on Friday. My last appointment of the morning has just had to cancel, so I could fit you in then. Call me back if that…actually, tell you what, I'll stop by. I'm only down in the village, so it's not far out of my way. Call me if you won't be in, otherwise, see you shortly before lunch.'

She nodded to herself, binding her foot tightly with bandage. 'Did you hear, Scaredy-mouse? We're going to find out what's up that horrible great chimney. Isn't that good?'

After securing the bandage in place with a length of sticking plaster, she got up and gently slid her feet into her sheepskin slippers. From the kitchen window she could see his work van parked behind her car. Ladders were attached to its roof.

Careful to keep her weight off her left foot, she limped back down the corridor and opened the front door. 'Sorry to keep you waiting. I had a little accident.'

His mouth was slightly open. He looked concerned. 'Are you OK?'

'Yes. I sliced my foot open. On some glass, that's all.'

'Oh.' He held a finger against his cheek. 'It's from your foot?'

'What?'

'The blood.'

'There's blood on my face?'

'And your hands. And all over your top.' His glance dropped to her feet and rebounded back up. 'You're sure you're all right?'

'Yes, fine. I came straight down the stairs, you see. Didn't think to look in a mirror. Even though that's what I cut my foot on!' She let out a short laugh. 'Seven years' bad luck.'

'Right.' He still looked alarmed.

'You met the Halls, then? Who used to live here?'

'The Halls? Oh, yes. Well, not met. They just bought me out a cup of tea one time.' He jabbed a thumb over his shoulder. 'When I was out on the lane changing a tyre. Few years back, that was.'

'Did you meet their son, William? Did they say anything about him?'

'Their son? No...can't say they did.' He was frowning slightly.

'You didn't talk to him?'

'No. Just the old couple.'

She stared off into space. He wasn't even aware they had a son. She looked back at him, disappointed. Could he be lying?

He stepped back. 'Do...do you want me to come back another time? Give you a chance to clean yourself up?'

'What? No, stay. The chimney...'

He looked up at it. 'Birds have got in, have they?'

'It seems so. Could you check nothing is blocking it?'

'No problem. I'll get my brushes from the van.'

She watched as he slid the side door back and removed a couple of folded sheets, several lengths of pole and a bucket with a load of brush-heads sticking out.

'Don't worry about mess,' he said over his shoulder. 'I'll screen off your hearth with a sheet and tape up the edges. No soot gets out.'

After leading him through to the lounge, she pointed across to the fireplace. 'There it is. A bird fell down it the other day. There was a fair amount of soot dislodged.'

153

'Is it painful?' He was looking down at her feet again.

She realised she'd crooked her knee and raised the heel of her left foot to reduce the pressure on its sole. 'It'll be OK.'

He crossed the room, got down on one knee, ducked his head into the hearth and shone a torch up.

She crossed her arms. 'What can you see?'

'This hasn't been swept in years.'

'Is it blocked? Can you see if anything's blocking it?'

'Something's up there, yes.' He brought his head back out and sent her a smile. 'Don't look so worried. I'll have it cleared in no time.'

She tried to smile back. 'It's a large chimney, isn't it?'

'Needs to be – it's quite exposed up here in winter.' He detached strips from a roll of gaffer tape and lay them sticky-side-up across the hearth tiles.

'How would they have cleaned it back then?' She laughed. It sounded shrill. Not natural. 'Send a child up, or something?'

He grinned as he started taping a dust sheet round the edge of the hearth. In the middle of the sheet was a hole with a square of material hanging over it. Like the flap in a pair of long-johns, she thought. For cowboys to pooh through.

'In Mary Poppins films, maybe. The practice was a lot less widespread than people think.' With the sheet in place he got to his feet. 'Now, I'll bring the hoover in. It's a big noisy thing. Industrial. You might prefer to be in the kitchen.'

'Can...can I watch?'

He seemed mildly surprised. 'Well, there's not a lot to see. The suction nozzle from the hoover goes through this flap in the middle. Then I feed the brush through and direct it up the chimney. Like all the best magic shows, you won't see how it works.'

'Oh. But you'll come and tell me if you hit anything, won't you? Anything...big. I'll be in the kitchen.'

He was giving her another curious look. 'If that's what you want.'

Back in the kitchen, she wondered what to do. Scaredy-mouse was still in its case. The sound of the chimney sweep's vacuum certainly wasn't going to help matters. Laura opened the laptop and checked her emails. Tamsin had got back.

Hi Laura, great to hear you're feeling a little better. My T has been bugging me on and off for three days now. I got some good sleep last night but at five o'clock this morning it came roaring right back. It's like living on an airbase at times! I'm so glad you're getting a second opinion. Don't let them give you the brush-off!

Go arrange that booking with a consultant too. Yes, stress = tinnitus = stress. It can turn into a vicious circle if you let it. Try not to worry. Tinnitus is simply the perception of sound being generated by your brain. You need to remember we hear with our brain, not our ears. The bit of your brain that processes and filters noise has just gone a bit kooky.

Did you know that when there is absolutely nothing to hear whatsoever, the brain will generate noises for you? They proved this by putting a bunch of medical students in a soundproof room and asking each to note down what they heard. Over ninety percent described all sorts of stuff even though the room was completely silent! It was all being created by their brains.

As for hearing canary song – weird! Real canary song? That's a new one to me. And you're sure you've never heard a canary singing at some point in your past? Maybe it's a forgotten childhood memory that's decided to resurface. This one guy I corresponded with, he'd hear birdsong. Like a flock, he said, all singing together. Often at night (how he knew it wasn't real) then during the day – while driving, when he was on the golf range, in his office. It got so bad he had to give up work for a while.

Laura stared at her words, dimly aware that the chimney sweep's vacuum had started to grate and whine. I don't hear a nameless flock of birds singing en masse, she thought. I hear just one. But that's not what was making her feel frightened again. It was the part of the sentence, 'while driving, when he was on the golf range, in his office'. She realised there was only one place she'd ever heard the canary singing: Lantern Cottage. Never in the garden, never in the car, never anywhere but inside the house.

She'd just finished typing a reply when she heard a cough from behind her. The chimney sweep was standing in the doorway, holding up a large dustbin liner. 'That's the last of it. Three I've filled up.'

The bag was bulging. From the way he was holding it up, whatever was inside couldn't weigh much. 'You've filled three sacks?'

'Yes. Birds' nests. Generations of them. Like an aviary that chimney was.'

She closed the lid of the laptop. 'You said you'd tell me!'

The smile fell from his face. 'They just kept coming down. One after the other. Sorry.'

She climbed off the bar stool, wincing as her bad foot made contact with the floor. 'Is...was there only birds' nests?'

'And soot. Clouds of soot. I had to change that bag in the hoover twice as well. That's another first for a single chimney.'

'Is the chimney now clear? Nothing else is up there?'

His eyes dropped for a moment. She guessed her hands

had been fluttering. 'Clean as a whistle.'

She crossed her arms. This wasn't right. 'How can you be sure? Can you see right up it now? Why are you looking like that? It's a reasonable question, isn't it?'

He blinked. 'I can't see sky, if that's what you mean. It slopes in near the top. But the brushes can pass through it now, no problem.'

'Pass through it? You can feel them poking out the top?'

'Yes.' He sounded troubled. 'Why?'

She couldn't say what she was thinking. He'd have seen a child's skeleton, surely, if it had tumbled down into the hearth. She glanced at the sack again. Just birds' nests, she thought. Should I ask him to open the bag so I can check? She couldn't quite believe it was only nests up there. She'd felt so sure—

'I'll do a smoke test; to check it's drawing properly. I'm sure it will be.'

She went to brush her hair back and saw the dried blood, like a coating of rust, on her fingers. She'd forgotten to wash it off. 'Smoke test?'

'Takes all of a minute.'

She trailed him to the front door. He placed the sack outside, next to a couple of others. They looked very full, too.

'You should be sitting down.' He pointed at her foot.

'It's OK.'

The hearth was back to normal, all traces of the dust sheets and gaffer tape gone. He removed a coil of what looked like compressed cardboard from his pocket. 'This gives off a thick plume of smoke. It'll soon fill the chimney and, all being well, come pouring out the top.'

She thought of the opening she'd created upstairs. If it connects to the chimney, she thought, some smoke should seep out into my studio. 'I'll be upstairs. Tell me when it's lit.' She turned about and started hopping for the door.

She was a bit out of breath by the time she got to the

top of the stairs. Going as fast as she could, she headed to the room at the end of the corridor and knelt at the hole.

'It's lit now!'

His voice came from two directions: up the stairs and, more faintly, from the opening in the wall before her. She stared at the hole. No smoke came out. Not a wisp. But she could just see something in there. All but hidden by the darkness. The corner of something. A small box?

'Drawing fine, it is!' he shouted. 'Checking outside to see if it's coming from chimney's top.'

She heard the front door open. What was it in there? She started to reach in. What if it's an ancient trap? For mice or rats. Fearing it might snap down on her fingers, she poked the screwdriver into the opening instead. She heard the scrape of wood on the concrete layer. The object could move, so it wasn't connected to the floorboards. A box? The base was wooden but she could now just see a row of thin bars. A cage! It was a small cage. About the same size as a half-brick.

She put the screwdriver aside and gingerly reached a hand in. Pinching a corner bar between a finger and thumb, she started dragging it closer to the light. There was something inside it. Something dead. She let go. A pale, furry little lump. A hamster? No, it had feathers, not fur. She reached back in and tilted the cage to get it through the small opening. The object inside weighed nothing. It rolled over, two tiny feet scrunched into balls. A bird, feathers a faded yellow.

The chimney sweep called up. 'Smoke's coming out top at a good old rate!'

She couldn't take her eyes off the tiny corpse. It looked like it had been there for years. Decades.

'Mrs Wilkinson? Smoke's drawing fine! Little Tiddles nipped outside. Is that OK?'

She turned her head to the open door. 'Tiddles?'

'The cat. It went out the front door.'

Scaredy-mouse! She'd escaped.

CHAPTER 27

'Laura? Laura!' Owen called. 'Where are you?'

She felt too weak to muster a reply. The tears had come so suddenly and then they just wouldn't stop. She hadn't cried so uncontrollably since...being taken into hospital. 'Here.'

The word was no more than a whisper. The poor chimney sweep, she thought. He didn't want to take my money. He'd got all his equipment back into the van so fast and was about to drive away when she'd come back out of the cottage with a cheque.

'I'm sorry it's so wet,' she'd said, thrusting the tear-stained piece of paper through his window.

'Really, there's no need. I feel so bad about your cat.'

'No, you must take it.'

Reluctantly, he'd laid it across his dashboard and looked at her. 'You're sure you're OK?'

'Yes.' She'd crossed her arms and scanned the fields once again. 'She's so small. It's dangerous out here. Birds – those ones that attack other birds...'

'And your husband is definitely on the way home?'

She'd nodded.

'Why don't you go inside? Make a cup of tea and put your foot up. The cat will reappear once it's hungry, I bet you.'

Where could Scaredy-mouse have gone? They'd scoured the lane in both directions. She'd gone round the garden calling its name. But the kitten had vanished. Or was hiding.

'Laura? Oh, Jesus, Laura.'

She looked up. Owen was standing in the kitchen doorway, arms hanging at his sides. 'She got out. Now she's lost.'

'We...we'll find her.' Slowly, cautiously, he approached. 'Come on, you can't sit there. Let's get you up.'

I must look silly, she realised. Sitting in the cat's basket, stroking one of her little toys, my bad foot stretched out before me. 'I needed to sit on the floor. Because of my foot. The flagstones were too cold.'

'Yes, you said on the phone you'd cut it. How?'

'A mirror broke upstairs. I trod on some glass.'

'Laura, there's blood all over you. Let's get you cleaned up.'

'Can you check the fields at the back? What if she strays over to where the badgers live? She might go down one of their burrows. They can be very aggressive can't they, badgers?'

He crouched down beside her, hooking a hand under one of her arms. 'Come on.'

He sat her down on a kitchen chair and slid another one over. 'This foot?'

She gave a nod and he placed her left foot on it. She was still clutching Scaredy-mouse's toy.

'Right, first things first, let's get this blood off you.' After wetting a tea-towel, he came back over and started dabbing at her forehead, then her nose. He moved to her right cheek. It was everywhere.

'There's dust and all sorts in your hair,' he muttered, now starting on her fingers. 'What on earth were you doing?'

'I wanted to see behind the mirror. The bit Scaredy-mouse hissed at when the canary last started to sing.'

He raised his eyes and looked at her for a moment. Then he lowered his head and continued to work at her fingers. 'You've been hearing the noise again?'

'Yes. I forgot to say, it's canary song. I looked it up on the internet.'

'How often have you been hearing it?'

'A bit. I think Scaredy-mouse heard it too, you see. Which...which means if she did, it's not just in my head, is it?' She wasn't sure he'd understood: he didn't say anything. 'Owen?'

He continued to wipe at her fingers. She stared at the top of his head. There were freckles visible on the bit where his hair had started to thin. Or were they those other things, she thought. Liver spots. One was the shape of Ireland, where we went for our fifth wedding anniversary. The Emerald Isle. I liked it there, except the fields weren't as green as I expected. 'So I tried to get the mirror off to see what was behind it. But it fell and some of it smashed. I found a hole in the plaster that the decorators had tried to cover up. The bricks behind it were quite loose. There's a funny smell in there, from when I was a little girl. Owen, there's a dead canary. It was in the wall. A canary!'

'You've removed some bricks from the wall?' he asked, head still bowed. His voice sounded a bit odd, like he needed to clear his throat.

'Two bricks. A canary, Owen. What I've been hearing ever since we moved in.'

His shoulders sagged and she felt his breath on the back of her hand as he let out a sigh.

'Go and see for yourself. It's true. I can't explain it, but it's true.' When he looked up at her, she could see his eyes were moist. She didn't like his expression. It reminded her of before. 'Go and look before you start to judge me! I'm not making this up!'

'OK, OK, I'll look – after I've seen to your foot.' He reached down and eased the slipper off. There was a fair amount of blood inside. 'Christ, Laura.'

'I was in a rush. I didn't do a good job with the first-aid

kit.'

He examined the bandage. 'Do you think it's still bleeding under there? Maybe we should get you to hospital.'

'Don't be silly, they'll be busy enough. It's only a cut foot. Owen, why would there be a canary in the wall?'

He closed his eyes for a second. 'Let me take a look.'

While he was upstairs, her eyes strayed to the laptop. She'd sent Tamsin another message. Or was it two? It was after the chimney sweep left. She knew she'd mentioned the hole in the wall. Would Tamsin have seen it by now? The woman had said her tinnitus was bad. Laura doubted she'd have gone out. She was still contemplating whether to haul herself over to the laptop to check when she heard Owen coming down the stairs. When he reappeared he looked a little pale. And confused. The cage had a hook on the top and it was hanging from his finger. The canary was inside.

'See? Do you see now?'

He stopped in the middle of the room and looked at her. 'This was in the wall cavity?'

'Yes!'

'Where you removed the bricks, it was in there?'

'Yes!'

He walked over to the back door, unbolted it and placed the cage outside. 'The studio is an utter mess. Blood everywhere.'

'What shall we do with it?'

He slid a chair out, sat down, glanced toward the door and shook his head. 'I don't know, but I don't want it in the house.'

'When do you think it was placed there?'

'The body is desiccated.' He shrugged. 'Years.'

'Owen, this cottage was once owned by a couple who bred canaries. They handed them out to miners through that hatch in the shed wall.'

'How do you know that?'

'One of the archaeologists up at the church told me.'

'I see.'

'Don't you think it must be from that time?'

'I suppose so.'

'But why put one in the wall?'

'Perhaps some kind of superstitious thing? Didn't they used to bury a black cat in the foundations of a house to bring it luck?'

'I don't know. I keep thinking of that saying, a canary in a coal mine. A sign that something bad is about to happen.'

His eyes locked on hers. 'Do you feel like something bad is about to happen?'

The question instantly jarred her. All he had to do, she thought bitterly, was add my name to the end of it and he could have been a psychiatrist. They loved that way of turning your comments back on you. 'Owen, I'm fine. Shaken, upset, confused; but I know what's what. I know what's real.' She looked meaningfully at the back door. 'That cage out there, it's real.'

He dropped his head and started picking at a thumbnail. She could tell that husk of a bird had thrown him. Its existence could not be denied. 'I'm worried, Laura. So much of this...' He looked despairingly about the room. 'It's so similar to what happened before. Can't you see that?'

Her stomach turned over. She found it so hard to talk about when she became ill. The memories were so vague, for a start. 'It's not the same,' she murmured, hearing uncertainty in her reply.

'Walking into the kitchen earlier. Seeing you over there in the corner...'

'The dream; that's the same. Or almost. A child, trapped in a tunnel.' She avoided mentioning her fears about the chimney. 'I don't know why it's started. I don't want a baby. I did once, but not now.'

He glanced at the soft toy in her hand. 'Why did you

buy that kitten?'

'Scaredy-mouse?' Her laugh was over in a second. 'I told you: because I was lonely. Am lonely.'

'Lonely?'

'Yes. I told you; in here on my own for so much of the day.'

He nodded. 'I know. I'm sorry. You call yourself mummy when you speak to it. Did you know that?'

'Do I? But that's normal.'

'Is it?'

'Yes. People always say they're a pet's mummy or daddy.'

'Do they?'

'Yes. Bloody hell, Owen, it isn't a substitute baby, for crying out loud!' She dropped the cuddly toy on the table.

The sound of a vehicle came from outside. Looking past Owen's shoulder, she saw a car through the kitchen window. It pulled to a halt. 'I wonder who that is?'

'Mmm?' He was blank-faced.

'In the car.'

A guilty look twisted his face. His head half-turned but he didn't look round properly.

'Owen?'

His lips bunched in regret. 'I'm sorry. It's my fault, I know it is. This damned concert.' He looked so sad. 'I rang him earlier, when I was upstairs. I don't know how to deal with this. I'm sorry, Laura.'

'Who?'

'Robert.'

'Robert who?'

'Robert Ford.'

The car door shut and she saw him looking through the window at her. No, she thought. The doctor. Owen's called that bloody doctor.

CHAPTER 28

'You had no right! None!'

Owen looked totally forlorn, caught between answering her or the front door. The bell sounded again. 'Laura, at the very least, your foot needs seeing to.'

'You didn't call him about my foot. You bastard! You bastard!'

'Laura, please. Let's just...' He made downward movements with both hands and then went to let his old schoolfriend in.

She had so much emotion welling up, no words would come out. She felt betrayed. Conspired against. Afraid.

She knew about the process Owen had now set in motion. She'd been through it before. She refused to go through it again. She could hear them exchanging quiet words in the porch. The fact it was her they were talking about was so demeaning. Already, she thought, roles were being assigned. Mine, if I'm not careful, will become that of a mental patient. She grabbed the toy off the table and lobbed it back into the cat basket.

Dr Ford stepped into the kitchen a few seconds later. There was a mixture of wariness and concern on his face as he looked over. She didn't believe the concern was genuine. Owen was skulking behind him, as well he might. The shit.

'Hello,' she smiled warmly. 'Sorry not to get up. My foot...' She gestured at it with one hand. 'Silly accident. All my fault.'

Dr Ford shrugged in an understanding sort of way. 'You stay put, Laura. Please.'

Owen had circled round him to approach the kettle. 'Tea or coffee, anyone?'

That's right, she thought. Try and normalise this, Owen. Make it all friendly and civilised, your attempt at getting me confined to a psychiatric ward. 'I'm fine, thanks, darling.'

'Robert?'

'No,' he replied, still looking in her direction. 'Thank you.'

Well that's a relief, she thought. No drink: perhaps he's not settling down for a long visit. Perhaps he'll bugger off really soon.

'Owen says you opened it up on some broken glass?' His gaze was now on her foot as he came over, black medical bag in one hand.

'Yes, thanks so much for coming out. I was trying to move a mirror and completely misjudged the weight of it. Over it toppled. Bits of glass shot everywhere! Seven years' bad luck, damn it.' She flashed him a smile which he returned, though his eyes remained serious. 'Please.' She gestured to the chair where Owen had been sitting.

Dr Ford lowered himself onto it. 'May I take a look?'

'If you don't mind.'

He bent forward and started to remove the blood-stiffened bandage.

'Owen?' she said loudly. The hand he was using to stir his coffee visibly jolted. Good, she thought. I'm glad that made you jump. Pity you didn't burn yourself. 'Would you bring a bowl over? Something to put these dressings in.'

'Of course, yes.'

As he began to peel the bandage away, Dr Ford cleared his throat. 'Owen said you've been feeling a bit down.'

Ah, she thought, subtle. Slip the question in while doing something else. The casual approach. He kept looking at her foot and she could see those ear hairs of his sticking out. Someone really needed to pluck them. 'I wouldn't say down. As you pointed out when I came to see you, it's not easy moving somewhere new. Settling in has been a bit hard. Especially with Owen in Manchester so much.'

'Have you met many people – locally, I mean?'

'There's a group. I met them when I drove over to introduce myself to the vicar; he's very pleasant.'

'The Reverend Flowers? He just took over from Tim Dobby.'

'The previous reverend?'

'Yes.' Dr Ford glanced at Owen. 'How long was Dobby in charge? Forty years?'

Owen tilted his head and narrowed his eyes. 'I don't know. When I was in the choir up there, Reginald Burridge was vicar. He made way for Dobby just after I enrolled at the RNCM. That was in 1968.'

'So I'm right; over forty years,' Dr Ford replied. The last of the bandage came off and he examined her foot. 'One nasty slice. The wound has closed, though. No fresh bleeding.'

'That's a relief. It probably looked worse than it was.'

He undid the clasps of his carry case. 'I'll clean it up and see if we can make some Steri-Strips stick. So, you've found being alone here somewhat unsettling?'

She thought: you still haven't looked properly at me yet. Nought of out ten for bedside manner. 'Yes, I suppose I have.'

'Obviously, Laura, you became quite unwell a few years ago.' Finally, he risked a glance in her direction, but it lasted less than a second. He touched a ball of cotton wool to the neck of a small bottle then pressed it against her foot. It felt wonderfully cool. 'Would you say you're experiencing similar thoughts and feelings now?'

'No, not really.' She made sure the denial didn't sound too vehement. He looked up and studied her closely as she spoke. Now, she thought, I have to be very careful. 'I can see why Owen might have thought that was the case. The kitten escaping – that was, is, distressing for me. The little thing's too small to be outside. I'd had an accident with the mirror upstairs, cut myself, dripped blood all over the place. Owen, bless him,' she sent him an affectionate smile, 'was alarmed. And no wonder, too.'

Dr Ford nodded, now tearing open a pack of Steri-Strips. 'You mentioned, when you came to see me, that you've been hearing things.'

'Oh, the birdsong?' That's an easy one, she thought. 'Yes, but that's a result of the viral infection you diagnosed, isn't it?' She sat back. Game, set and match to me.

She watched calmly as he tried to detach a strip from the backing paper. 'I received a call earlier on about a patient of mine.' He fixed her with that stare of his. 'He resides out at the Skylark Trust. William Hall?'

Oh shit. Thank God Owen was putting the milk back in the fridge, she thought. He won't have seen the look on my face. I should have realised there was a chance Dr Ford would be William's GP. Stupid, stupid, stupid!

'You travelled out there earlier today?' the doctor asked innocently.

Owen was looking round. He was frowning. Laura knew she was trapped.

'Laura?' Dr Ford repeated gently.

She showed a palm to Owen. 'I was going to mention it – when I got the chance.'

He looked aghast. 'The youth who broke in here last night?'

'Yes.'

'Who lived here? You went to see him?'

'Yes.'

'Why?'

She shrugged, mind racing for an acceptable explanation. 'I felt so concerned for him. The poor lad, he looked so lost and confused.' Owen took her comment in. It seemed her answer might suffice. But then Dr Ford spoke again.

'William was left quite disturbed by your visit, Laura. You were asking him about birds. About a bird singing.'

Owen's face sagged. He looked seasick. She sighed, half-closing her eyes. 'I know this looks odd. When I mentioned it to William, he seemed aware of it. I think he's heard it, too.'

'William, you understand, has some quite complex issues —'

'I know that,' she couldn't help snapping. 'But deafness isn't one of them.'

'No...but his mental age is very immature.'

'He mentioned a bird singing to me.'

'The birdsong you think you can hear?' Owen whispered.

The way he said 'think' angered her. 'Yes, darling, the song that I think I can hear. The one that belongs to a canary.' She let her eyes move to the back door.

Dr Ford was still fumbling about with the packet. She almost asked him to pass it over, but then he managed to detach one. 'The staff felt you had gained access to William under a false pretext.'

'That's not true! I am interested in setting up a dance therapy class. Or I was. They won't want me now.'

He applied a strip to her foot. 'I must say, Laura, I'm concerned.'

'You really needn't be.'

'Laura, you're doing a very good job hiding it, but it's plain to me that you're agitated. Seeing you here today — you're not the same person who came to see me at the practice. Your appearance would strongly reinforce that impression.'

'My appearance? How do you mean?' I know what he's doing, she thought. He's STAR testing me according to some scale of mental health. Not sure which one, but that doesn't matter. They're all roughly the same.'

'Your ability to...OK, when did you last wash your hair?'

'I've been doing DIY! If my hair is untidy or there's dust in it, I do apologise. I was planning to have a bath later on, if that helps.'

He drew in breath. 'I'm worried that – being here, alone – is not beneficial to you.'

'I live here.'

He applied another two strips and sat back. 'There. Owen says you'd not be prepared to consider any sort of medication to help address –'

'I won't take pills.' The fact he'd already raised the issue with Owen angered her further. 'Have you even read my medical notes?'

'Yes, I have.'

'Good. So you'll know how strongly I feel about chemical coshes. I've lost months of my life to those already. Months.'

'Very well. Then how about we discuss a change of scene for you? That would be good. Somewhere you can properly rest and recuperate, where you'll have professionally trained people to –'

Her finger jabbed at him. 'I will not be admitted to a psychiatric ward.'

'Laura, I think it will really help. Just until Owen can be here with you –'

'You mean, until after his performance? Pack me off so he has no unwelcome distractions? So you can sit there in the audience, telling people he's an old school mate of yours, ever-so-civilised, knowing I'm locked-up in a mental unit somewhere?' She saw them exchange a glance. 'Owen?' Tears were in her eyes. 'How could you do this to me?'

'Darling.' Owen looked close to crying, too. 'We're trying to help you here.'

'Really? Really?' She couldn't believe they'd hatched

this plan. Anger surged up. The two of them, she thought, behind my back. The pair of shits.

'Laura,' Dr Ford crossed his legs, voice slow and even. So calm. So pacifying. 'Let's all pause a moment to —'

'No, let's not fucking pause. Let's make this very clear, instead. I am not willing to enter into any form of psychiatric care. And if you have me placed in it, I will view that as a breach of my human rights.'

The two words caused his lips to part slightly. Nothing came out.

'Yes, that's right, Doctor. I've read up about this. Things aren't so easy as they once were, are they? If you put me in care, I will sue you when I get back out. Do you understand?'

Silence. Like a wire, tightening.

He sent a look at Owen before addressing her. 'It's your decision, yes.'

She could have slammed a fist down on the table, but knew he'd only make a note of it. Instead, she kept quiet as he closed his case and stood. Only when he got to the door did she speak again. 'And Dr Ford? If you're so concerned about personal appearance, why don't you pluck those ridiculous ear hairs of yours?'

Owen looked mortified as he followed the doctor out.

CHAPTER 29

Something broke her sleep. She lay still and listened. A wet pattering sound, seeping slyly into the bedroom. She opened her eyes and stared fearfully up at the ceiling. It should have been dark but it wasn't. She could see the outline of the lampshade, and above that, the shadowy roof beam. Was the security light on again? Was that it? A dull clatter had her reaching out for Owen.

Her hand came down on cold mattress and her heart beat even faster. He's not there. I'm alone. She looked to her side to make sure. Light was showing at the edges of the curtains. But it was not the security light. Daylight. She realised the sound she could hear was the shower running. Owen was in the shower.

Her head sank back against the pillow and she let out a long sigh. It was the best night's sleep she had since moving in. For once, she wasn't the first awake. The clock on Owen's beside table said seven fifty-one. Amazing. She so rarely slept past seven. She sat up, her sense of disorientation being swept aside by a happy feeling. The miraculous result of a proper night's rest. She threw the duvet back.

When Owen appeared in the kitchen all the breakfast things were out. She pressed the plunger down on the cafetière, humming a tune to herself.

'Morning.' His greeting was more like a question. 'I

thought I'd let you sleep in.'

'When do I ever wake after you?' she asked brightly. 'Never.'

'No...it was a bit odd. You were dead to the world when I went for my shower.' He looked at the kitchen table.

'Sit down, the toast will be getting cold. Coffee?'

'Yes, thanks. Um...this is very nice.'

She smiled. 'Amazing what ten hours' decent sleep can do.'

'How does your foot feel?'

'Much, much better.'

'Any sign of the kitten?'

'No.' She turned to the window overlooking the back garden. 'I checked the bowl of food you put out. All of it has gone – maybe it was her.'

'Let's hope so.' He continued to gaze at her. 'You're...you're feeling fine, I take it?'

'I know! Isn't it odd? I feel absolutely amazing. So refreshed.' He shook his head slightly. 'What?'

'I was really concerned how you'd be this morning. I admit it. But look at you: right as rain.'

She poured a couple of coffees. 'Did you sleep well?'

'You know me.' He was buttering a piece of toast, glancing in her direction with each stroke of the knife. 'So am I forgiven?'

The business with Dr Ford, she thought. 'Of course you are.' After the doctor had left, they'd stayed in the kitchen and talked. Her fury had grown steadily fainter as she'd begun to see things from Owen's perspective. He had been scared, that was all. Afraid she'd had some kind of relapse.

Once she'd accepted that he'd acted out of concern, it had been easy to divert her anger at Dr Ford. She knew it was a bit naughty to take it all out on him. But the man's attitude was so awful. Eventually, after much prompting on her part, Owen had conceded the doctor lacked tact.

He'd even smiled faintly when she'd mentioned her parting comment about the ear hairs. Ford's face! It had been such a picture as he'd beaten his hasty retreat.

But she also knew that, throughout their conciliation of sorts, one area had been skirted around. The canary. Neither of them had told Dr Ford about it, even when the opportunity had presented itself. Neither of them, it seemed, was prepared to raise it after the man had left, either. She knew why Owen had avoided the subject. He had enough to be dealing with.

Before going up to bed, she'd announced that she was going outside for a last look for Mouse. But Owen had insisted he do it. So she'd watched through the windows as the torch beam probed the garden's dark corners. She'd even limped down to the front door, stood there and called for a while. There'd been a definite bite in the breeze blowing up the valley. She'd remembered the team leader's words at the archaeology site. Snow would be arriving soon.

Up in their room, she remembered lying back, wondering how long it would take to drop off. Would the thought of Scaredy-mouse out there torment her through the night? Would the dream come back or – worse – the sound of canary song? Next thing, it was morning.

Owen was midway through a bite of toast. 'So,' she announced. 'Feeling confident?'

'Confident?'

'Saturday; last day of rehearsals. Performance tomorrow.'

His eyelids fluttered. 'Yes, last day.'

'Has the start of the third movement clicked with those sopranos?'

'*Pianissimo possibile*,' he sighed. 'How many times can I spell it out?'

Obviously not, then, she thought. 'Firm but fair, that's all you can be.'

He didn't look convinced and they sat in silence for a

few minutes. She couldn't stop glancing at her laptop. The previous night, when Owen had been searching outside for Scaredy-mouse, she'd quickly checked her messages. Tamsin hadn't replied, but she would have done so by this morning, Laura felt certain.

Owen gave a cough. 'Will you be all right, Laura? I can't tell you how much it bothers me – '

'Relax. I'm going to put my walking boots on, go out and find that kitten – even if it means roaming the hills all day. I won't even be in here – I'll be out there, breathing fresh air and stretching my legs.'

'With your injured foot?'

'It's no problem. The cut was so fine, you can hardly see it now. I don't think those stick-on things were even necessary.'

He nodded uneasily. 'And when this performance is over, we'll clear things up. Properly.' He glanced at the ceiling.

Did he mean we'll discuss the canary's corpse, she wondered, or sweep up the mess I made while discovering it? She waved a hand. 'Of course. What time do you think you might be home?'

'Well,' he pushed back from the table. 'I don't want to carry on too long. No point at this stage. Early evening, hopefully?'

If everything goes smoothly, she thought. If all the orchestra and the choir obediently follow your directions. 'It'll be brilliant, darling. I know it will.'

'I'll phone, OK? Lunchtime or just after.'

'OK.'

'Right.' He tapped both forefingers on the edge of the table and stood. 'Once more into the breach.'

'For Queen and Country,' she smiled.

'For glory,' he grinned back.

'For England,' she announced in a dramatic voice.

'And for us!'

They were both chuckling as she got to her feet and

held her arms out. She saw how things would soon be. They'd start doing the things they'd dreamed of while down in London. Walking in the Peak District. Day trips to Windermere, Snowdonia, the sand dunes at Formby. A visit to the Tate in Liverpool. The Yorkshire Sculpture Park. Shopping in Chester. It would be good. Life would soon be good.

Owen stepped round the table and his arms encircled her. She closed her eyes and let her cheek rest on his collarbone. Just to be hugged like this, she thought. It's so —

Canary song cut off her thoughts.

Her eyes snapped open. A torrent of notes rising and falling. At last! At last, it's happened with Owen close by.

'Laura?' Confusion was colouring his voice.

He's heard it too, she thought. Thank God, he's finally heard it! It's not just me. The sense of relief caused her to whimper.

'What's the matter?' He drew back and looked into her eyes. 'You jolted.'

The singing continued, but absolutely nothing was registering on his face. He's not hearing a thing, she realised with dismay. How can he not hear it? She wanted to wail. She wanted to drop to the stone-cold floor and wail.

'Laura, what's the matter?'

She blinked back tears. 'My foot. The edge of a flagstone...'

He stepped away and looked down. 'The wound hasn't opened up again?'

'I don't know.' A long, high note was hanging in the air as she sat down. 'I don't think so.' She removed her slipper and the note fractured into a chaotic jumble once more. 'Have...have the stitches held?'

He leaned forward. She looked over his bowed head, trying to locate the sound. Where are you? It seemed slightly muffled. What had Owen done with the dead canary? Was it still in its cage outside the back door?

He gently eased her foot back down. 'Looks fine, but go easy on it, won't you?'

'Easy. Yes, of course.'

He straightened up and looked about as the song trickled to a halt. 'Now, what did I do with those damned car keys?'

CHAPTER 30

Owen's car was still in view, but she didn't care. She opened the laptop, fingers drumming impatiently against her thighs as it went through its machinations. Bloody thing, bloody thing, why is it so slow?

The Audi revved and she looked up. A tap turned and the stream of thoughts started to flow. There he goes, the pathetic excuse for a man. Look at his white hair, the way it sticks out. The feel of his arms just now, so thin and feeble. Age is gnawing at his body. Soon, he'll be–

'Shut up!' She looked about the room. 'Just shut up!'

She remembered that Owen had placed the cage outside the previous evening. Ignoring the voice, she opened the back door and looked left and right. No sign of it. He must have thrown it in the bin. Doesn't matter, she thought. I found it hidden in the wall and I know I just heard singing.

Back at the laptop, she saw the screen had settled down. She went to her emails. Tamsin had replied.

Hi, Laura. Golly, I don't know where to start. This is odd. Really odd. It's so upsetting for you – I can tell that from your messages.

Let's deal with the first one you sent – where you told me that you only ever hear canary song when you're in your new home. You guess it's happened to you over a dozen times now. Laura, I don't think you've got tinnitus. Tinnitus is not specific to one place. OK, people often become aware of it when they're in bed. But that's because things are peaceful and quiet and the brain has a chance to register faint noises.

You've been hearing it during the day and at night. Plus, you think the kitten might have heard it, right? It reacted to something in your studio.

Probably its reflection, Laura said to herself. If the noise was real – if it was outside my head – Owen would have heard it just now. But he didn't. So it's been going on in my mind all along. How can she say it isn't tinnitus?

Now, your second message. A dead canary in a cage? That's been bricked up behind a wall? That's creepy. Laura, I only wish I could actually be there with you. It must be so distressing. What can I say? If it's not tinnitus, something else is generating that noise in your house. Or someone. I'm worried for you, Laura. The part of your message was a bit muddled where you mentioned being ill before. I'm guessing some kind of breakdown? What's happening to you now, I think, is destabilizing you. Can you think of anyone who might want to do that? Does your new home have neighbors? Were the last people forced to move out because the bank foreclosed on them? Maybe it's worth thinking things over to see if someone is behind this.

And last thing, Laura, I don't think you should stay in the house. It's plain to me this noise is coming from inside it. Why risk upsetting yourself more by being there? Have you a good friend nearby? Someone who has a spare bed you can use? PLEASE let me know what you decide. Be strong, Laura. You're a special person. You'll

beat this, Tamsin.

Laura stared at the screen. There were no neighbours. It couldn't be the previous occupants – Mrs Hall was dead, Mr Hall was confined to a hospital somewhere and William...he was just a child. Which meant...which meant that it could only be...

She reached for the keyboard and began to type.

The only person who could be doing this to me is my husband.

She hit send and checked over her shoulder, almost expecting him to be there. The room was empty. She thought about her husband. Could it be him? Was he pretending not to hear the canary song just now? Why would he do that? Why torture her?

The ring of the phone made her shoulders flinch. She couldn't face answering it. She didn't want to speak to anyone. Not now. The answerphone message clicked in and she cocked her head.

'Hi Laura, it's Martin Flowers. I'm en route to Chester. Church business I won't bore you with. I wanted to speak to you – I don't suppose you're there?' He waited for a second. 'No. I asked a member of my congregation about the Halls, who lived in Lantern Cottage before you.' He coughed in a needless sort of way. 'I wanted you to hear this from me, Laura. They weren't quite as old as I thought. In fact, Mrs Hall was only fifty-three when she died. Laura, I'm afraid she committed suicide. Not in the cottage, in the canal. Weighed her pockets down with stones and stepped into the water. It's generally believed the stress of caring for William drove her to it. Sadly, all that pressure was then transferred to the husband, Roger. He wasn't able to manage – that and losing his wife, I suppose.' He sighed. 'Unfortunately, he was admitted to hospital where he's still receiving psychiatric care. That's why William is being looked after out at the Skylark Trust. I hope you got all that. Please call me if you'd like to talk further. Otherwise, I'll see you soon. OK, bye.'

The phone clicked and silence returned. Laura didn't move. Suicide. And the husband in psychiatric care. The bloody estate agent hadn't said a thing about Mrs Hall killing herself. No one said a thing about that. Did Owen know, too?

She felt dirty and sly as she analysed how things were between them. Searching for signs of deceit. Picking over his behaviour. The move up here, she thought: that was all him. He wanted to spend the end of his career working in the place where it originally started. Who, she thought, do I know here? No one.

Her mind was now whirring. This focus on his career, she thought, it was always something I just accepted. Part of being married to someone at the very top of their profession. We've had to move all over the place for his career. Stints in Germany, France, Austria. A year in New York. No wonder my friends melted away over the years. All I've ever done is trail after Owen. Things could have been so different, if only we'd had a family. But that was another thing decided by him. First through his physical failings, then through his mental ones. Hiding from the issue, refusing to even discuss seeing a doctor. But he's happy to involve one if it's about me. Oh yes. Then he's only too bloody keen to call in medical help. And now it's all too late for me. My chance has slipped by and I'm too old. Not physically able. Infertile.

The voice in her head started to join in, shrill words speeding up. He's a selfish, useless man. He's always been selfish. He's never really cared about you, never, he doesn't love you, if he loved you, he'd have let you have a baby, children, they're the most precious thing of all, they're the point of everything and he couldn't even give you a child!

Rather than shut the thoughts out, she let them continue. There was truth in them. The voice was speaking the truth. She climbed woodenly off the stool and left the kitchen. The door to Owen's study was shut, as usual. So rare that she went in his study, wherever it was they'd lived. Searching for dirty cups; that was the main reason. There may as well be a sign saying 'Keep Out'.

Feeling like a trespasser, she turned the handle and looked inside. Framed posters lined the walls. Posters advertising his performances. Other people had photos of their children in frames. He had his performances. They were his children.

She considered the one and only ballet-related picture in the entire house. Tucked away in my studio, she thought. Of the hundreds of images I could have selected of me on stage, I chose that particular one. And Owen, in all these years, has never understood its true significance. He thinks it's something I look on with pride! A fond memento of when I used to dance. That's how bloody clueless he is.

Dotted among the hundreds of CDs lining the shelves were his collection of miniature instruments. Gourds the size of grapefruits topped by goatskin. A gnarled bit of wood with a few strings stretched between the curved ends. A row of metal fingers that lifted just clear of a dark brown base. A harmonica. A penny whistle. His guitar propped in the corner. Toys, she thought. The only toys he's ever allowed were for himself. It's all been about himself.

When did I become an embarrassment to him? An encumbrance to his career? Something he has to factor in before deciding his next move. He really does despise me.

She screwed her eyes shut. It didn't make sense. We had plans, the two of us had plans. Owen is obsessed, yes. But his is a world of music. He deals in beauty. There isn't a spiteful bone in his body.

She began to examine the words running down the

spines of his CDs. His collection of classical music was so huge it was ridiculous. But he also liked music from far-flung places. Music from other eras; sea shanties, tribal songs, monks chanting. He liked more ambient noises, too. Sounds from nature; recordings of thunder, lions roaring, surf breaking. Birds singing?

Rows and rows of CDs were simply marked with letters. WP – 18". OP (South Africa). GH – HL. ASI (1997). There were dozens of them. Hundreds. Did any contain canary song? It would take days to go through them all.

A piece of paper was half-hanging over the edge of his bin. She picked it out and unfolded it. Something he'd printed from the internet. It looked technical. A graph, the axis marked with dB and Hz. A subheading read: 'Range of Human Hearing'.

Hz was cycles per second. He'd underlined a bit about 8000 Hz being at the upper range of human hearing. Noises above that included the whine from cathode-ray TVs, dog whistles, bats and some types of birdsong. He'd placed a question mark by the word birdsong. Why? Why had he done that?

Thinking of how the canary song was always so faint, she refolded the piece of paper and put it back exactly where it had been. The room felt leached of all warmth. She crossed her arms and looked out of the window. The sky was a pale grey. The wind moaned and she remembered Scaredy-mouse was out there somewhere. Tamsin was right, the cottage wasn't a good place to be.

She looked at the expanse of wall visible between Owen's framed posters. She ran her eyes across the ceiling. There was a hairline crack in the plaster and she pictured the structure of the building beneath its outer layer. The bricks and beams, joists and joints. Its skeleton. There was something about it. Something brooding. As if it was listening and waiting, biding its time. The urge became overwhelming: she had to get out.

CHAPTER 31

Standing on the front step was a lot chillier, but she didn't mind. Once the zip of her coat was done up, she tucked the bottoms of her jeans into the thick wool of her socks and then slid her gloves on.

The cold breeze swept through her hair and she thought about going back inside to find a hat. But the burglar alarm was on and the prospect of those silent rooms made her shudder.

Tentatively, she stepped down on to the lane, easing her weight onto her injured foot. It felt fine, to her surprise. Her walking boots fitted snugly and she'd laced them extra tightly to stop her foot from sliding about. It seemed to have worked.

She skirted round the cottage, pausing to look at the shed extension with its shoulder-high hatch. She could imagine the little cages being handed through it to a queue of miners, waiting where she now stood. Wouldn't Owen have known what it was for? He'd lived in the nearby village all his life.

As she rounded the next corner a couple of blue tits fled towards the fields. The bird table had been picked clean, as had the bowl of cat biscuits on the back lawn. She took the packet of fish shapes from her pocket and shook them. 'Mouse! Where are you, Mouse!'

The only noise was wind blowing across her ears. She made her way along the back fence looking for any sign of the kitten. The chicken wire Owen had tacked onto the lowermost struts of the fence were bent up in one place. The grass below had been worn into a smooth channel that led out into the field. The badgers.

She continued to the end of the garden where a row of stumps stuck out of bare earth. The vegetable patch, annihilated by the creatures. Like a famine had fallen on the land. Next to it, Owen had placed the big plastic compost bin. To its left was a gate leading back to the lane. She trudged out, eyes on the grass verge and ditch as she shook the packet of treats. 'Mouse!' Some sections had become overgrown with brambles and she used a stick to try and part the thorny tangle.

Behind it was the dry-stone wall. Edith Hall had used stones like those to kill herself. Laura wondered how long it was before her body was discovered. Did it bob up, eventually? Or did they drag the brown water, snagging her corpse with a hook?

After about fifty metres there was a gap in wall. Mouse could have got through that, she thought. She climbed over the collapsed stones and followed the edge of the field to where it fell away into the next valley. The canal was down there; the one they used for transporting limestone; the one Edith Hall had drowned herself in. She made her way down and stared into the brackish, still water. Dead leaves lay on its surface and, in places, the bank had started to crumble. She stepped closer to the edge, wondering what Edith Hall had felt as she'd stepped into the water. Had it been cold against her skin? Made her shudder? Or was she beyond feeling by then? Beyond tasting the silty water as it flooded into her nose and mouth and eyes?

If Mouse had fallen in here, her body would never be found. She followed the towpath for a while, calling for the kitten every now and again, before giving up and following it the other way until it connected with another branch of canal. The sign at the junction pointed in three directions. Oldknow two miles to the right, New Mills five miles to the left and Whaley Bridge six miles in the direction she'd come.

She retraced her steps once more. As she walked slowly along, she thought about the sheet of paper in Owen's study. Now, clear of the confines of the cottage, she didn't think it could have been him. How could it be? It wasn't possible. It meant hiding a loudspeaker somewhere in the house. Setting off the song somehow on a timer or something – since she'd often heard it when Owen was out.

No, she concluded, it wasn't my husband. Why would he do such a terrible thing? Now she felt a keen sense of shame for even allowing such suspicions to take hold. Is it the house, she wondered, planting these dark thoughts in my head? She thought about all the times she'd stood rooted to the spot, waiting for the silence to be broken by birdsong. All the time, she realised, it was as if the cottage was also listening. To me. The two of us, straining to hear what the other one was up to.

She reached the point where she'd joined the towpath and started climbing the grassy incline. Halfway up, she spotted a shallow mound and altered direction towards it. A large circular stone had been laid flat at the top of the faint slope. It was covered in dried sheep droppings. There was something almost sacrificial about it. Perhaps the farmer used it as a platform at shearing time. She called again, 'Mouse!'

Standing there, she realised the tip of Lantern Cottage's chimney was peeping over the brow. Watching. She stuck two fingers up at it. Something tiny and cold made contact with her cheek. She turned into the wind and spotted a couple of flakes drifting towards her. The layer of white cloud above was utterly motionless. An upside-down landscape, she thought, spotlessly clean and pure. Not like here. She climbed the remainder of the slope, refusing to look at the looming chimney as she made her way to the garden fence. At the bit where the chicken wire had been forced up she stopped. From this angle, she could see a faint furrow leading off right across the field. The comings and goings of the badgers. This, she realised, could have been where Scaredy-mouse got out. The furrow led straight toward a copse of trees.

She got to them a couple of minutes later and studied the ground. The grass was patchy beneath the trees, becoming practically non-existent round the trunks themselves. Where the badgers lived was obvious; the holes they'd dug into the slope were massive. One or two looked almost large enough to crawl inside. Would I fit, she wondered? Like Alice, heading down, down into another world?

The thought of the bristly, stump-legged creatures lurking within put a swift halt to her daydream. How many of them lived down in the tunnels? What if Scaredy-mouse had followed the trail like she'd done? The dark holes looked menacing. But to a young cat – cold and frightened – they might have represented shelter. Somewhere out of the wind. The poor thing wouldn't have known what lurked inside. Oh God, it would have been attacked, surely. She thought about the deep gouges on the base of the bird table. Claws like six-inch nails.

'Mouse,' she called in a muted voice from the edge of the copse. She shook her bag of treats again. 'Mouse, Mouse, Mouse.'

The burrows stared back. Spiders' eyes, clustered and close. Nothing moved. Feeling like she was creeping into an enemy encampment, she trod stealthily between the trees and knelt at the entrance of the largest one. Weak daylight shining in revealed the sides of a remarkably smooth tunnel, just a few strands of tree roots sticking down from the roof. There was a musky, feral smell as she leaned her face in, shook the packet and called out softly. 'Mouse, are you in there?'

For some reason she almost expected an echo to come

bouncing back. But the dense earth simply absorbed her voice like a sponge. The only sound was the church bell ringing from across the valley. The initial chimes finished and she readied herself to count the ones that marked the hour. She was expecting twelve of them, but they stopped after just two. She sat back. Two? That couldn't be right. She checked her watch and saw that it was. Two o'clock? How long, she wondered, had I followed the canal for? A couple of hours had vanished without trace.

With a last look into the burrow, she stood and peered through the trees. The church was visible. She was able to make out the hands on the clock tower. The big one pointed straight up, so it was something o'clock. The little one pointed to the two. Dots of colour were in the field. They were digging about again.

She turned her back on the badger's entrance and looked at the cottage. She could see the extension housing the snug and, above it, her studio. The chimney jutted up above the main roof and, yet again, she was struck by how like a figure it was. The window to her studio was also visible and she contemplated how the canary song was always so loud in there. Who'd built the extension? When had it been tacked onto the original cottage? Were they responsible for hiding the cage in the wall?

She stared across at Oldknow church. Adrian Moore, the excavation leader, would know. He knew all about the canary breeder, after all. She recalled his previous reluctance to engage with her. What else might he have been keeping quiet about?

CHAPTER 32

Once in the car, she'd realised how cold she'd become. She turned the temperature gauge up and sat there for a while with the engine running. Warm air began to permeate the inside of the vehicle. It would be nice to just put some music on, she thought. Ease the seat back and sit here for a while.

But she couldn't do that. She needed to speak with Adrian Moore.

Oldknow High Street was quiet, as usual. Waiting at the lights to change on the deserted junction, she looked idly off to the left, where the smattering of shops led up to the GP's practice.

She flinched. A black Audi was emerging slowly from the car park. The man at the wheel had a shock of white hair. Owen. His car turned left, heading towards High Lane and the A6. He wasn't at rehearsals at all. He wasn't in Manchester, he'd been right here visiting Dr Ford.

The traffic lights were still on red as she snapped her indicator down and turned onto the High Street. Owen's Audi was powering up the hill and she tried to follow him. But his car was moving too fast. She pulled over, deciding to ring his mobile instead. The thing wasn't in her coat. Damn it! She could see it by the laptop in the kitchen, where she'd left it. His brake lights shone for a brief instant as he reached a bend in the road. The car disappeared.

It had been about her, that much was obvious. Secret discussions, behind her back. They were making plans, working out what options were available to them. The sense of betrayal was so acute she had to lean forward and clutch her stomach. Forehead resting against the wheel, she sat there breathing through her mouth, waiting for the pain to subside. How could he lie like that? Everything he'd said earlier about being right as rain, about clearing things up properly. All of it false.

She climbed out of the car, closed her eyes, put her feet shoulder width apart and took several slow, deep breaths. In through the nose, out through the mouth. How she calmed herself before stepping out onto the empty stage, that spotlight glaring down like the eye of God. The old trick still worked. Her heart rate steadied and the waves of dizziness cleared. Now she felt anger.

The door to the surgery swung back faster than she'd meant it to. The receptionist behind the counter looked irritated as it hit the wall with a bang. Not slowing down, she marched down the corridor toward Dr Ford's room. His door opened and he stepped out, attention on the file in his hand.

'Lee Perkins?'

A man in jeans and a sweatshirt started rising to his feet.

'What were you doing just now?' There was such rage in her voice it took her by surprise.

Dr Ford's head came up and he just blinked as she closed the gap between them.

'I saw his car leaving just now.'

He turned his head. 'Mr Perkins, sorry. Could I..?'

The man was swiftly retaking his seat. 'No problem.'

Dr Ford stepped back and motioned her in. 'Mrs Wilkinson, there's really no need to be upset.'

'No need? How dare you discuss me with him?'

He closed the door behind her. 'Please, sit down.'

'I will not sit down! I'm making a complaint about this.

I want you to be punished for this!'

'Mrs Wilkinson, try to be calm. Can I get you a hot drink?'

'A hot drink?' She knew she was shouting but she didn't care.

'You look cold. You're shaking.'

She glimpsed herself in the mirror on the wall above his sink. Oh my God, she thought, I look...wild. The wind in the fields had blown her hair all over the place. Her face was pale, except for two bright crimson blotches on each cheek. 'I do not want a drink– '

'Have you eaten today, Laura?' He lifted a hand as if to usher her towards a chair. 'Let's get you something to eat. A snack.'

She stepped away from him. 'Don't tell me what to do!' She could see he was trying to take control of the situation. 'This is about you, not me. I will not allow you and my husband to hatch plans about me, do you hear?'

He nodded, hand still out, showing her his palm as he backed away. 'OK. That's fine. I'm sitting down, Laura. I won't come near you. Won't you sit down too, so we can talk?'

'I will not. What did you two decide about me? What plan have you made?'

His eyes went to his desk and he adjusted the mouse on his mat. Mouse, she thought. I've lost Mouse. Eaten by the badgers. Torn to shreds. She glanced at the window. My poor Mouse.

'Mrs Wilkinson, there is no plan.'

'Rubbish!'

He went to say something else then changed his mind. Sitting back, he closed his eyes and then spoke. 'Mrs Wilkinson, I don't think I'm the best person for you to be seeing right now. Would you mind if I called in the practice nurse? Perhaps you'd feel more comfortable with someone else. Just until you, until things are...more settled.'

'You're evading my question. He was here just now.'

She looked for any sign of her medical notes on his desk. Clever. He must have filed them away. But there was something on his screen. He saw where she was trying to look and closed it down.

'Mrs Wilkinson, I would never discuss a patient with someone else.'

'I heard it again. This morning. We were in the kitchen and I could hear it, plain as day.'

His face changed. The sympathetic tilt of his eyebrows adjusted and he looked at her intently. 'The birdsong?'

'Yes.'

'You heard the bird singing?'

'Yes, I heard the canary singing.' She looked at him. He squirmed as she did. Why, she thought, is he so concerned about it being birdsong? Of course, she realised: William heard it, too. William is another of his patients. 'I'm not the only one, am I?'

He frowned. 'Mrs Wilk– '

'William – he knows about it, doesn't he?'

'I cannot discuss another patient with you.'

'God damn you! You'll discuss me with Owen!'

'Laura, I have not– '

'Stop lying to me! I just saw him. This morning, when it was singing, Owen was oblivious to it. Or is that just what he wanted me to think? Getting warm, am I?'

'Warm?'

'Closer to the truth?'

'I'm sorry – I don't follow you.'

'Oh come on, we both know there's birdsong in that cottage. Or maybe the recording of one. Playing on a speaker hidden somewhere.' She narrowed her eyes. 'Is that what Owen's up to?'

Dr Ford dipped his chin slightly, eyes still on her. 'You think Owen is the cause of what you can hear?'

'You tell me.'

'Laura, you must talk to your husband about this. I can assure you, he is not plotting against– '

'Bullshit. You wait until I get my hands on him. You just bloody wait, I'm going to– ' She realised her mistake. She shouldn't have said that. Made a threat. She crossed her arms.

Dr Ford was now sitting forward, hands clasped between his knees. 'Go on, Laura.'

'It doesn't matter.'

'You were saying something about your husband. How you were going to...'

'I don't want to talk about it.'

'What would you like to do to Owen?'

No chance, she thought. He won't lead me down this path. He knows I'm angry. More than angry. He's trying to trick me into saying I'm angry with Owen. That I want to hurt him. He can only section me if I'm a danger.

'What if you discuss your thoughts with one of my colleagues, then? Or someone from social services? Would you prefer that?'

'I'm not discussing it with anyone. I have to go.'

'Laura, I really think you should stay here.' He began getting to his feet.

'Don't come near me!' It came out as a shriek. Her finger pointed at his face. 'Keep back!'

His hand was up again as he sank back into his chair. 'OK, OK. But please stay here, Laura. Don't...don't go back to the cottage.'

There'd been something in his voice. 'Why?'

He looked away for a second. 'You're very distressed. At least sit in the nurse's station until you– '

'It's not the end of this.' Keeping her eyes on him, she reached behind and scrabbled for the door handle, not wanting to give him the chance of grabbing her.

He sat with a sorrowful expression as she stepped back into the corridor, slammed his door and started running for the way out. He's hiding things from me, she thought. Everyone is. Only one person can give me the answers I need. Adrian Moore.

CHAPTER 33

She couldn't see a red BMW among the few cars parked at Oldknow church. Which meant Martin Flowers must be still in Chester. Thank God, Laura thought. My visit to the Skylark Trust must have got back to him by now. He'll be just as appalled as everyone else.

One of the beech trees at the edge of the graveyard was creaking in the wind. Dead leaves were tumbling across the path. They made little scratchy noises as they passed her feet.

She gazed out across the Cheshire Plain and saw the horizon was misty and blurred. Snow, maybe, sweeping in from the Irish Sea. It was now certainly cold enough.

At the far end of the graveyard, she looked over the wall. Adrian was there with five others. The pit was larger now and they were all inside it, totally engrossed in their work. To the side of the rim was a folded tarpaulin, weighed down by several chunks of stone.

She climbed through the gap in the wall and silently made her way over. I said to Owen I wouldn't do this, she told herself. Go looking at the remains of a dead child. But now, standing at the edge, she couldn't help it.

There were a lot fewer bones than she'd imagined. The skull, then a modest pile of vertebrae and collapsed ribs. The pelvis was off to the side, as was what appeared to be a femur.

It's not it, she realised, with a mixture of confusion and

relief. It's not the body from my dream. No arm bone was trapped behind the head. First the chimney had nothing to do with it, now this. All my stupid fears, she thought, are turning out to be false.

She circled the rim to see what the nearest pair of archaeologists were doing. Brushing away at a U-shaped bit of bone. It was embedded with small teeth. Adrian and the other three were kneeling next to more bits of skeleton. The thin bones looked like little branches half-submerged in the dark earth.

The child wasn't the only one. More people had died here.

'Adrian?' Someone said.

He glanced at the person who'd spoken, who pointed at Laura. Adrian craned his head back and, for a long second, they just looked at each other.

'How many?' Her question caused all work to stop.

Adrian put his brush down. 'We've found four so far, maybe five. Hard to tell. There are animal bones here, too. Not as deep as the human remains, so probably more recent. We're trying to work it out.'

She hugged herself against the cruel wind. 'How did they die?'

'We don't know. Perhaps they were killed. One skull has certainly been crushed.'

'Are they all children?'

'We're not sure about two of them.'

'How long have they been here?'

He climbed to his feet, grimacing as he did so. 'A long time. One had some beads near the hand: we're sure they're Iron Age. Carry on everyone, we'll lose the light soon.'

One by one their heads went back down. Only Adrian continued to watch her.

'Sorry,' she said, pushing a clump of hair back. It will, she thought, take hours of brushing to clear these tangles. 'I'm interrupting you.' She looked across at Lantern

Cottage. It squatted there on the opposite slope of the valley. Vile toad.

He adjusted the sleeve of his fleece. 'Are you looking for the vicar?'

'No. I was looking for you.'

He nodded as if he suspected that already. 'Shall we go inside? I'll make us a drink.'

As they walked to the church hall a handful of fat snowflakes drifted past. They touched down silently in the long grass. Advance parachutists of a much larger invasion.

Inside, Adrian said nothing as he prepared their drinks. She observed the snow starting to come down in fits and starts. Things looked in the balance – sometimes it almost stopped, but then it picked up in intensity.

'Milk and sugar?' he asked from the kitchen doorway.

'Just milk, thanks.' She felt remarkably calm. Like finally learning your marks for an exam. You couldn't sway the result, so why let things get to you?

He brought the drinks over and sat on the opposite side of the table. 'You look cold.'

'Yes.' She'd stuffed each hand up the opposite sleeve and her forearms were pressed against her stomach. 'I was out walking.'

'Over near your house?'

She nodded.

'Are you OK, Laura?'

He hadn't used her Christian name before. She hadn't been sure if he even knew it. She pursed her lips. 'Not really.'

'No.'

'How much do you know about Lantern Cottage?'

He looked into her eyes. She could see him preparing an answer. Which meant he was deciding which details to filter out. She didn't want to be told half a story. She needed everything. 'I know about the Halls. I know what happened to the parents. I know about William. I've been...hearing things. Sometimes a bird sings in the cottage.'

His eyes slid away from hers. She saw movement in his throat as he swallowed.

'It's a canary,' she continued. 'I'm certain about that.'

He made eye contact for a moment and then stared into his tea. 'A canary?'

'Yes. You told me the cottage was once owned by a man who bred them.'

'I did.' He brushed the rim of his cup with a fingertip. Dirt was packed under the nail.

'Apart from the Halls, who else has lived in that cottage? The original part has been added to. There's the conservatory and the extension. Do you know who built them?'

'Just previous people. No one of any note.'

'I found a birdcage hidden in the wall.'

He dragged his eyes back to her face. 'Where?'

'To the side of the chimney shaft. Up on the first floor.'

'A birdcage?'

'With a dead canary inside. It had been hidden there a long time ago. Who built the extension at that end of the house? I found the cage when I was in there, removing some bricks in what used to be the outer wall.'

'I don't know.'

'But you do know something. You're not telling me something.' She removed a hand from her sleeve and placed it on his wrist. 'That's why we're sitting here, isn't it? Please tell me.'

He looked across at the exhibition stand on the other side of the hall. 'It's a tragic story. You say a canary...' He quietly mouthed the words. Like they were a crossword clue that baffled him.

'Yes. Why? Is that important?'

Slowly, his eyes returned to hers. 'The man who bred canaries – he was one of the last people to be hanged at Strangeways prison in Manchester.'

Her hand slipped off his wrist. It retreated, like a frightened animal, across the table. She heard William's hoarse yell once more. The bad person will come. The old photo in the estate agent's. That man with the wire-framed glasses and harsh face. Adrian's voice was distant and the troubled look hadn't left his face. 'He was convicted of killing his wife.'

'When?'

'1865. He strangled her, put her body in a cart, wheeled it to the limekilns and placed it inside.'

'The ones down the road?'

'Yes, there's a path. Not used much nowadays, apart from the odd mountain biker. It cuts across the valley. A stone bridge goes over the Goyt and then you follow it up the other side. He only confessed to it a week after killing her; there was nothing left of her by then but ash.'

Her hand was clamped over her mouth. She peeled it away. 'Why?'

'He refused to say. He was a very quiet sort, shy, devoted to his birds. Maybe too devoted, who knows? They say he wept whenever one of them died.'

'So he didn't ever explain why he killed her?'

'No, he never did. She was, by all accounts, a large woman. Larger than him. Some say domineering – that she had a tongue on her.'

She mulled over the comment. Domineering. A tongue on her. Grounds, in time gone by, for a husband to use violence. She could see her in the photo, standing slightly behind the husband. Master of the house. 'That's why he killed her?'

'Who knows? But...there was something else, from that time.'

'What?'

The cry of the wind outside lifted and a mass of ticks sounded on the window. She looked toward it; dusk was beginning to fall and the air was now thick with fat swirling flakes. Another gust of wind. More buffeted the glass.

'I should get back out. We need to put the tarpaulin in place,' he said distractedly.

'What else was there?'

He wrinkled his nose. 'Just before he killed her, a child from the village vanished.'

Everything seemed to go very still. His face was the only thing she saw, as if he was looking at her down a long, dark, pipe. 'A child?'

'Yes, a boy. Six years old, he was.'

The words thudded into her brain and she knew that whatever he was about to say would explain everything. She stared at him as he drew in a long breath.

'The canary breeder didn't admit to killing him, but he used to let children look at his birds. He'd take them into the shed, the one with that hatch, and let the kids pet them. They didn't have any children of their own...'

He couldn't keep the look of disgust from his face as he pushed the bench back and stood. 'Most people thought he killed the lad. Certainly, no one shed a tear when he went to the gallows. Why he killed his wife? Maybe she found out what he'd been...doing. To the youngsters.' He came round the table and laid a hand on her shoulder.

She kept looking straight ahead. It was all she could do. 'What about the boy's body?'

'Never found. Probably also went into the kiln.' His hand left her shoulder.

He reached for his cup and she heard a glottal clicking as he gulped. She thought of rope cutting into windpipe.

'Sorry to be the one to tell you all that, I really am.'

Once he'd gone, she dug her hands through her hair, thoughts flying around. The boy was never found. The cavity in the wall, where the canary had been hidden. How far did it go? Far enough to hide a small boy's body?

CHAPTER 34

The beeping from the burglar alarm cut out and silence reasserted itself. Her hand hovered before the buttons, forefinger still extended. She listened. More than listened. Tested. For sounds. For smells. For anything that might indicate something amiss.

The house gave nothing up. It seemed impervious to her presence. As she'd driven up the lane, power lines bowing back and forth in the gathering gale, the building had slowly taken shape through the haze of swirling snow. First the front corner, then the first-floor windows and, finally, the chimney.

Reaching the cottage, she'd pressed the brakes too hard. Or maybe the layer of snow had been thicker than she'd realised: the car had gone into a slow skid, only stopping when the front wheels went over the edge of the top step. Stone had ground loudly against the vehicle's underside. The vibrations through her feet had felt like a dying shiver: sure enough, the car had refused to start again. It would be a long walk back down the lane.

She flicked the hall lights on and was about to set off up the stairs when she did hear something; a single beep from the kitchen. The answerphone. Did Owen keep to his promise and ring at lunchtime?

The number five was flashing on the display. Five new messages. A red light was also blinking on her mobile. She started with the landline. The electronic voice told her the first message was received today at 2.19.

'Mrs Wilkinson, it's Dr Ford here. I'm really sorry you felt the need to rush off like that. I think it's very important that we talk. Please call me as soon as you get this message.'

The next one was from 2.34. 'Mrs Wilkinson, it's Dr Ford. I left you a message about fifteen minutes ago asking you to call me. I'm going to pop up to Lantern Cottage with a nurse, just for a chat. See you shortly, I hope.'

The next message came in at 2.45. 'Mrs Wilkinson, Dr Ford here. I'm having trouble locating you; there was no sign of anyone when I called by just now. I hope you don't mind, but I'm going to try contacting your husband to see if you're with him. Please call me.'

Owen next, at 3.17. 'Laura? Sorry I didn't call you earlier. Darling, no one can get hold of you. I've just tried your mobile and left you a message there. Please call me the instant you get this.'

Owen again at 3.49. She looked at the clock. Only seven minutes ago. 'Laura, I'm coming home. It's about twenty to four. I should be there by half-past at the latest. Call me, please.'

Thirty minutes, she thought. He'd be back in thirty minutes. Was that good? She wasn't sure. Whether he was on her side or not, she wanted to get to the bottom of it all before he arrived.

The missed call on her mobile showed up as from Owen's phone. She decided to listen to it later, turning to the laptop instead. The screen lit up to reveal a mass of messages from Tamsin.

She started at the bottom.

Laura, I'm online right now. Don't worry what time it is, get in touch. Let me know you're all right. I'm worried for you! Tamsin.

The next one was the same, as was the one after that. She

scrolled to the most recent, received just eleven minutes ago. Tamsin was repeating the message over and over.

Laura clicked on the latest one and typed a reply.

Tamsin, it's me. Sorry to take so long, I've been out looking for Mouse, my kitten. A man with good local knowledge has just told me a murderer once lived in my house. He killed his wife and a young boy from the village, it seems. I think the boy's body is hidden upstairs, in the same cavity as where I found the canary. I'm going to find out.

She pressed send and removed her jacket. The windows were now almost black. Just visible beyond them, she could make out the continuous movement of snowflakes. They were swarming in the wind, settling on every surface.

The laptop beeped and she saw Tamsin had replied already. She really is there, Laura thought. Half the world away, waiting at her machine. Bless her. She clicked on her reply.

Get out! Laura, just get out of there. Please!

Soon, Laura thought, hanging her jacket on the back of the chair. I will soon. At the top of the stairs she looked along the corridor. The door into her studio was shut, closed by Owen the night before. After he'd gone in there to examine the hole in the wall. Spots of her blood were visible on the carpet as she walked down the corridor. Like Hansel's trail of breadcrumbs, she thought. Leading me along.

At the door, she paused and waited. On cue, the singing started. She knew it would. It was very faint and soon stopped. Just a short burst of notes. But as she began to turn the handle it started again, another burst, this one longer and more confident. As if it was warming up.

The light went on and she surveyed the room. No

205

wonder Owen had shut the door – it was a complete mess. Broken glass formed a tidemark halfway across the floor. Smears of dried blood were all over the place. The lilies had started to putrefy, mushy stalks and blackened flower-heads melting into the windowsill.

She turned to the wall opposite the mirrors and looked at the framed photo there. It had been taken in the seconds following her last-ever performance. Everyone on stage, standing behind the curtain after it had dropped for the final time. That curious, between moment. No longer in performance mode, but not offstage and out of costume, either. The adrenaline was still there; everyone's eyes were shining. But shoulders had lowered, smiles were more natural.

Most of the dancers were grouped round the principals. Some were clapping them, several were embracing. Laura was standing apart, looking off into the wings. All those years ago, she thought, and I can remember precisely what I was thinking about at that second. The exit.

A month before, the Director had taken her aside to say that she would never make it further than first soloist. Her career could go no higher. Owen was waiting for her decision on his proposal of marriage. She'd walked straight off that stage, accepted, and never danced again. It had been, she'd decided, the perfect time to move on. Start a family. Become a mother. Blinking away tears, she saw the hammer was laid across the top of Owen's toolbox. Next to it was the opening.

The singing picked up in strength, the pitch of the notes rising higher, before falling away. She knew that the wall contained the answer. She was totally certain of that as she approached the gap in the bricks. He hid you in here, didn't he? You poor little boy. This is where he put you.

It was obvious; she'd been looking at the wrong side of the wall. When the canary breeder had concealed the boy's corpse, this room didn't even exist. He would have broken into the other side of the wall in the room where Owen and she now slept. If anything, when the extension had been built, the paint and plaster had just added fresh layers to the tomb, sealing it more tightly.

The canary sounded almost jubilant. Everything was fitting into place. It had been trying to lead her here all along. Kneeling, she looked for the torch so she could shine it through the gap. She'd forgotten to bring it up from the cellar. Peering into the opening, she could see the cavity must be almost two feet wide. The smell was a lot stronger, and suddenly she saw a bedroom. Her grandmother's bedroom. Such a large room, with its own sink in the corner. Chest-high vases holding green plants. Palms. The enormous bed with its quilted eiderdown, and at the foot of it a wooden box with carved sides. Her blanket box: that was the smell! As a little girl, Laura would climb in when playing hide-and-seek with distant cousins. Inside it were rarely-used sheets and covers. Lacework items, shawls, bonnets, tablecloths. Faded things from a bygone era.

The inner surface of the cavity's far wall had also been coated in the same brittle layer. Pressing her cheek against the crumbling edge and closing one eye, she could just make out the first few inches of floor to the left. Something was there.

Could she see cloth? Was it a sack? It seemed quite bulky. That far in, it must be leaning against the bricks that formed the chimney stack itself. The canary song was soaring, notes being held for seconds at a time. 'I know, I know,' she whispered. 'We're nearly there. I'll get him out, I will.'

She reached her arm in. The edge of the opening was digging into her shoulder. Whatever was in there, it could only be millimetres beyond the tips of her fingers. She strained with all her might and the nail of her middle finger caught on the edge of something hard. By completely emptying her lungs, she was able to extend her hand a fraction further. It felt like the end of a leather shoe. She hooked her nail into what must have been stitching and tried to drag it forward. But something prevented it from moving.

Owen's hammer was right next to her. She withdrew her arm and picked it up. Screwing her eyes almost shut, she swung at an exposed brick. The head of the hammer made a satisfyingly loud thud and the brick shifted a little. She swung again and the end of the brick fractured. Another swing and pieces of it fell to the floor. She turned the hammer round and used the twin spikes to rut at the connecting mortar. It was soon falling out and she knew a couple more blows would loosen two, if not three bricks. Then, she thought, the hole will be big enough to get my entire head in.

She turned the hammer round and swung once more. The loud crack of metal connecting with brick seemed to echo with a deeper, heavier thud. The brick was half out as she struck it again. This time two thuds come back. She stopped mid-swing and listened. Another thud and another. It was coming from downstairs. Someone was kicking at a door. The accent of the impacts lifted as wood started to splinter and come apart. Someone was smashing the kitchen door in! She could hear its bolt rattling with each blow. The canary song was now so loud it seemed to fill her head. She came out into the corridor. The thuds were quickening: one, two, one, two, one two. She heard animal grunts and, for a wild moment, imagined a huge badger butting the wood with its head. Then she heard the door crash inward. Keeping hold of the hammer, she ran into the bedroom, grabbed the phone and dialled 999.

CHAPTER 35

'Where birdy! Where birdy!'

She was peeping down through the banisters as William lumbered into view. He stood in the front hall, chest heaving in and out. There was snow in his hair and one slipper was missing. It looked like he'd run all the way.

The canary song rolled on, waves of it seeming to emanate from the walls around them.

'Where birdy!' he roared again, hands now slapping at his ears.

He hadn't seen her as he staggered into the lounge. She didn't reveal her presence. There was such strength in his shoulders and arms; all that power, governed by such an immature brain.

He carried on yelling as he blundered about below. She heard the table go over, the crash of ornaments breaking. She knew this was her chance to flee the cottage. But he could hear the canary too. She was no longer the only one. She couldn't leave him.

When he reappeared, he was crying with frustration. 'Where birdy!'

'William.'

His head came up and he looked at her with bloodshot eyes. He was terrified. 'Birdy moved? Where birdy?'

She approached the top step. 'It's OK, William. Shush now. I'm coming down.'

'Where birdy?' He moaned the words. 'Where put it?'

She laid the hammer on the carpet of the landing and started to descend the stairs. 'William– '

'Where! Must put back!'

'The birdy from in the wall? The birdy in the little cage?'

'Yes, yes.' Drool was coming off his chin. 'Where it?'

She was now halfway down. 'William, did you make that hole?'

His head bounced up and down. 'Yes. You moved birdy?'

'What else is in there, William?'

He slammed a hand down on the banister and the whole thing shook. 'Must put back! Now! Now!'

'Put the canary back? Why?'

He placed a foot on the stairs and she retreated up a step in response. He was glaring at her now, like she'd stolen his most favourite thing in the world. She glanced quickly back at the hammer. Could I get to it before he grabbed me?

'Where birdy? Where?'

I don't know, she thought. I don't know where it is. Owen put it outside the back door, but I don't know what he did with it after that. Did he throw it in the bin? He said something about getting rid of it.

He took another step, then his eyes roved about as if he'd heard something apart from the groan of the wind outside. 'Bad person come.' He raised a hand to his mouth, knuckles pressing against the underside of his nose, fingers tentacling at her. 'Put birdy back or bad person come. Poke with fingers, poke, poke!'

Poke fingers? What did he mean?

'Put back before bad person!' He was pleading with her now.

'I...I'm not sure where it is. My husband – he put birdy outside.'

'Birdy outside?'

'Yes, outside. In the dustbins, I think. Or the compost

heap, maybe.'

He whirled round and started for the kitchen, shoulder catching on the corner and causing him to stagger. 'Must hurry. Quick, quick, hurry!'

She was still at the halfway point of the stairs, unsure of what to do. She knew William shouldn't be outside in his state. He wasn't even wearing a coat. But the song was so insistent. It kept going, gnawing at her attention. William would return soon with the cage. He'd want to shove it back through the gap. For all Laura knew, he'd want to replace the bricks, too. She needed to get the child out before he did.

She turned about, retrieved the hammer and set off along the corridor.

Back at the opening, she heard hollow bangs as the bins were tipped over on the patio. The wind must have caught one of them – it began a hollow rumble as the gale rolled it about. Layered with the noise were William's anguished mutterings.

Her first hammer blow dislodged the partially broken brick. The next swing turned the one above it forty-five degrees. She smashed at the corner sticking out and it vanished into the cavity. The next blow caused a group of three to collapse.

That must be seven gone now, she thought. Enough for me to climb through, if I wanted. The hammer hit the floorboards and she stretched her arm back into the dark hole. It was a shoe! She could feel the laces. The poor little boy's shoe. She patted her fingers to the side and felt another. She nudged it with a knuckle. It wasn't empty; it would have moved, otherwise. The poor child, hidden in here for years. Decades, all alone.

Gritting her teeth, she felt a little higher. The shoes seemed quite big for a boy. There was felt-like material shrouding their upper parts. Then other cloth that wasn't as smooth. She tried pulling and the edge of it came away like tissue: she tested it between her finger and thumb. It felt like it had tiny holes in it. Ones eaten away by moths, or something worse? Mice?

As she withdrew her arm, the halogen lights above dimmed for a moment. In the storm outside she could hear William shouting. The cage couldn't have been in any of the bins.

She looked down at the long strip of material in her hand. It was stained a brownish yellow but she knew it would have originally been white or cream. The intricate arrangement of holes must have taken ages. She was wondering why a young boy would have been wearing a lace undergarment when the lights flickered once more and then went out completely.

CHAPTER 36

It was as if blackness had flooded through the hole in the wall, filling the room right to the ceiling. Suddenly sounds were all she had. The deep roar of the storm mixing with William's hoarse shouts and, above it all, the canary trilling away like a crazed soloist.

She hated the dark. She'd hated it ever since being a little girl. From its depths, her mind had always been able to conjure such terrible things. Taloned fingers curling round the wardrobe door. Vampires, staring in through the thin panes of her bedroom window. Calm, keep calm, she told herself. The torch would be where it should be, downstairs, on the shelf by the junction box in the cellar. Just think about this logically and you'll find it. She got up and looked over her shoulder.

A dark grey square, vague and indistinct, floated behind her. The window, she realised. She did a quarter-turn and stretched her hands out. Her fingers made contact with the end of the open door. She felt her way along it, extending a foot until her toe bumped against the carpeted step. Something close by made a noise. A light scrape. It sounded as if it had come from within the wall behind her. Bad person poke fingers. Stop it! Just stop it, Laura, she told herself. For God's sake. The corridor will be next and, at the end on the right, will be the stairs. Go down them, turn left and you'll end up in the kitchen. After that, aim left again. On the far side of the room will be the cellar door. Easy.

With a hand on each side of the doorframe, she stepped up into the corridor. Behind her she heard the slow scrape of a brick being moved. No, she desperately insisted, you didn't. She swallowed hard. Imagination, that was all.

She wanted so badly to run. Pressing her right hand against the corridor wall, she battled with the urge. To run, she thought, will be to give my fear control. Instead she took small controlled steps, like walking en pointe across the stage. Yes, she said to herself. En pointe. You're on stage and this is all just a performance. Make believe. Her left hand was waving rapidly to and fro before her. She thought her eyes must be adjusting to the dark: now she could discern the slightest variation in the blackness in front. A faint suggestion of light. Washing up from the front hall.

She passed the door to the bathroom and, a few steps further, the wall on her right ended. She wafted a palm downwards until it touched the banisters. Her eyes were as wide as she could make them and she was just able to see the outline of the hallway window below. Normally from this angle, she thought, there was a sprinkle of lights visible beyond a dip in the hills. Nothing. The power to all of Oldknow was out. Down the hallway, back in her studio, she heard a low moan. Wind, it was wind, probably catching in the chimney.

Carefully she descended the steps, counting each one. She was on number thirteen when her foot touched the hallway floor. Good, she thought, this is good. I'm halfway there. Her inability to see left her craving something tangible. She stamped her feet on the floorboards. The sound reassured her. Solid ground. Progress. Moving forward.

A strong draft was coming from the direction of the kitchen. She turned and walked into the flow of cool air. Her foot came down on something soft and fleshy. Even though she was wearing walking boots, she somehow knew it was moist. Her mind's eye could see a fat tongue, protruding from the mouth of an ogre. He was lying there, chin on the floor, waiting patiently. Her next step would be into the creature's gaping maw. Teeth like tombstones would clamp her shin, slowly splintering it.

She had to know what her foot was on – it was the only way to halt the pictures forming in her head. Suppressing a sob, she bent her knees and reached down with both hands. Her fingers touched something cold and wet and soft. Instinctively, she recoiled from it. Come on, Laura, she thought, making the voice in her head sound stern. Find out what it is. Her fingers reached out once more. Cold, saturated material. William's slipper, she realised, with a sense of triumph. He only had one on. It was a victory for her rational mind, but she was not stopping to savour it. Upstairs, the stupid part of her was saying, something just thudded against the studio floor.

The step down into the kitchen was exactly where she anticipated it would be. Another grey smear in the pitch black; the back door, wide open. It allowed her to get her bearings. By staring at where the door was and waving her hand before her face, she could just make out the movement of her fingers. That made her feel better. She headed for the corner where she knew the cellar door would be.

She heard the knock of wood and her mind was just registering pain in her knee when something to her right tipped and smashed. The vase of lilies, she realised. I've walked into the kitchen table. That's OK. It's no problem. She ran a hand along the edge of it, ignoring the waves of pain travelling up her leg. You wanted something solid, she thought to herself.

Cupping the corner of the table with one hand, she skirted round it. The kitchen door was now off to her right. Wind was making the bits of paper on the noticeboard flap. A set of keys chinked on their hook. She batted at the air with her left hand. Unvarnished wood brushed her fingers. The cellar door. She slid her hand lower and the smooth contour of the door knob glided into her palm.

Seven steps down. Maybe eight. That was all. She imagined the torch in her hand, its heavy criss-cross grip against her palm. The beam of light it could throw out. White and strong and pure.

The doorknob rotated with a metal rasp. She pushed it fully open and looked down. It had felt dark before, but it wasn't. In front of her was real darkness: so complete and utter she imagined reaching down and scooping it out with her hands.

CHAPTER 37

She inched her toes forward until she felt the rim of the top step. She extended her other foot and began to lower it down. But before it connected with the next step she lost her nerve. It was like dipping a toe into an abyss.

She turned round, got on all fours and stretched one leg back. The tip of her boot made contact with a hard edge further down and she brought her knee in until it eased onto the step directly below. That's one.

The stone was freezing but at least, she thought, I can't lose my footing. Climbing down this way also had the advantage of letting her focus on the suggestion of light coming through the kitchen door. She shuffled her way on to the next step and looked over her shoulder into the yawning blackness. That was two.

She realised the birdsong now sounded different. It was no louder, but it was somehow less muffled. Even with the wind raging outside.

She kept count each time she dropped down a step. Three, four, five. It was growing noticeably colder and she sensed she was not seeing into the kitchen any more. If the cellar door swings shut now, she thought, and the lock somehow engages...stop it! She shouted the words in her head as loud as she could. Stop it! Six steps, seven, eight. Oh Jesus, where's the bloody bottom? She stretched her foot back once more and it touched a flat surface straight away. The cellar floor. I've reached it.

She felt up the wall with both hands. The cracked and papery surface caught on her fingers. Paint flaked beneath her nails. Leaves rustled behind her and a scream almost broke from her lips. It's only the toads! Don't be such an idiot! But she was unable to stop the whine twisting in her throat. The smooth plastic of the junction box bumped the back of her hand and her fingers immediately spidered to the left.

Leaves rustled again and she could picture a scarecrow rising jerkily out of the coal pit, lopsided hat, button eyes, twig-fingers raking the air...She felt the edge of the shelf. Please, she prayed. Please be here. You must be here. She touched curved metal and clamped down on it with both hands. The torch! Oh thank God. The scarecrow was closer, now. Almost within touching distance. Her breast banged hollowly, as if her heart had knocked all her other organs aside. She located the button near the top and swung the torch round as she pressed with her thumb. The cellar jumped into view. There was no scarecrow tottering towards her. Just an empty cellar. The leaves rustled again. When this is over, she said to herself, I'll get the window-hatch properly sealed.

Sweeping every corner of the cellar with the bright beam, she couldn't help smiling. It was like she was cleansing the place. Purifying it. I have light, she declared. And my fears have lost their power. They are nothing. Nothing!

A thought struck her: William was still out there. Howling in the darkness like a soul in torment. She decided to find him first. Then they'd find the bloody cage together. Whatever else was in the wall could wait until the police got here. Or Owen. Whoever arrived first.

As she brought the torch round to shine it up the steps, the shelving at her side was momentarily revealed. She froze, not wanting to believe what she'd just glimpsed. Perhaps, she tried to persuade herself, I was wrong. Perhaps the small, square-shaped object sitting on the shelf wasn't the canary's cage. The spot of light was shaking as she directed it back. Oh no, Owen. Why? Why did you bring it down here? You said it wasn't staying in the house. You said.

She now knew why the clarity of the canary song had increased when she'd opened the cellar door. Staring at the dry lump behind the bars, she realised William – blundering about in the blizzard – had stood no chance of ever locating it.

The song changed. Now it was just a single piercing note, held for a second then repeated. She fixed on the faded mass of feathers, the stiff half-open beak. The noise was coming from it and it wasn't. It surrounded her, enveloped her. It was elemental. A component of the air. Why now this single note? Why?

From nowhere, an awful, nameless dread swamped her. She felt her scalp tighten, pulling her eyes wider. The torch was suddenly greasy in her hand and a voice in her head screamed to get out. Get out! She had to get away from this...this dead thing, lying in its cage, calling over and over and over. Realisation was starting to dawn; I was wrong. So terribly wrong.

She pictured the open fields by the cottage. Grass, air, sky. That's where she needed to be. Not down in a cellar. She was about to run back up the steps when she heard a new noise. A dull thud, like the one she'd heard coming from upstairs. She wanted to move, but she couldn't. She wished the birdsong would stop so she could listen properly. It came again. A single footstep. It was above her, in the house. Was it William? Had he come back inside? She was about to shout out that she'd found the cage when another part of her urged silence. William's words reverberated in her head. The bad person will come. Put birdy back or the bad person will come. Poke fingers. She now understood what he meant: poke fingers through the hole in the bedroom wall. Except the hole was no longer a small one. She'd made it bigger. Big enough to climb through. Oh God.

She knew what the canary's steadily repeated note was: a beacon. A homing signal. And now the slow, leaden footsteps were in the kitchen, directly over her head. It was coming for the canary and she was down here with it. No way out.

Terror sent trembles through her hands, but her mind was remarkably calm as she laid the torch on the bottom step. It rolled to the left, lens kissing the wall. Muted light bounced back. She didn't know what was coming, but she understood it was evil. She could feel waves of it flowing onto her, like dry ice from a stage. She backed away from the stone steps. The low wall of the coal pit connected with the rear of her calf muscles as the ponderous footsteps halted at the cellar door.

She kept her eyes on the pool of light being thrown out by the torch as she climbed into the coal pit and silently lowered herself into the pile of dead leaves. The canary continued to call but, in the brief pause between each note, she could also hear a groaning noise. It was low and guttural. A harrowing growl of despair: just like the sound the woman on the psychiatric ward used to make. That woman's children had been suffocated by their father.

She wriggled lower into the leaves. Something cold with slack, leathery skin shifted away from her hand. Chill flesh against hers. She didn't care. The leaves smelled of dust, of the grave. She submerged her head gladly beneath them. There was a slight gap between the bricks which she could see through.

First one shoe, then another came into view. She knew that, up in the studio, her fingers had brushed against their laces. Her breathing had reduced to a tiny pant. She felt on the brink of passing out. A glimpse of a stockinged ankle before the heavy hem of a velvet dress dropped over it. Each step was laborious and stiff. She saw the edge of a petticoat at one point. It was dirty and a strip along the bottom of it was missing. The dress obscured it again. The heavy material wasn't velvet; mould had enveloped it in a furry layer. Laura wanted to shut her eyes, but she couldn't. She didn't dare.

It was now halfway down. The voluminous folds were a bustle. She didn't want to look above the pinched waist. Long strands of hair were hanging down. Laura's eyes crept higher. Its bosom was massive. Hair covered the face like a veil. Laura knew she was looking at the woman in the black-and-white photo from the estate agent's file. The canary breeder's wife. The angle of the head was wrong. Too sharp, almost resting on a shoulder. The head lolled slightly as it looked about. Laura was crushing the backs of her fingers against her mouth. I must not scream, she ordered herself. I must not make a sound. I must not. Was it looking in her direction? Laura couldn't tell: hair hid its eyes.

Slowly it turned to the shelves.

The canary's long, single notes were suddenly replaced by song, a triumphant soaring. Glorious noise, so wrong. A pair of hands with black nails and skin like parchment lifted the cage. Then the figure turned about and started lumbering back up the stairs, cage held before it.

The canary song slowly lost strength. Laura couldn't move. Had it gone? No, the singing was becoming louder once more. She turned her head, brushing leaves from her face to look fearfully up at the hatch near the ceiling. A pair of legs shuffled past. It had left the house. The canary song grew fainter until, finally, the sound was swallowed by the storm.

CHAPTER 38

'Hello? Mrs Wilkinson! It's the police! Can you hear me?'

Laura didn't know how long she'd lain there before the voices came. Long enough for the torch's batteries to have almost died. She'd watched through the crack in the bricks as the beam gradually lost strength. Dreading the blackness coming back. The storm blew over at some point. She wasn't sure what she'd do when the torch went out completely. That thing was up there, somewhere. She hoped with all her heart that William had run away.

With their voices came light, flickering, at first, beyond the coal hatch above her. Soon, they were in the kitchen.

'Mrs Wilkinson! Hello! Is anyone here?'

'This door's been kicked in.'

'I know, the kitchen table's wrong. Broken vase on the floor. Mrs Wilkinson! Can you hear us?'

'I don't like this, I really don't. Let's wait for the fire engine to get up here.'

'Sod that. Her call was logged almost two hours ago. She could be dying in there.'

Were they, Laura thought, real? They sounded real. The light showing down the cellar steps seemed real. She wondered whether to answer.

'They'll have moved that Audi blocking the lane soon. I reckon we should wait.'

'Turn your torch off a second.'

'You what?'

'Turn it off. There – look.'

'What is it?'

'That's the door to the cellar. Something's down there, giving off light.'

Footsteps, slow and cautious. Bright beams cut the air above her. One angled down.

'It's a torch. I can see it on the bottom step.'

'Mrs Wilkinson? Are you down there?'

She sat up, deciding they were real. 'Here. I'm down here.' Light blinded her and she shut her eyes.

'Jesus Christ. Are you OK?'

She nodded. Tears were leaking from her closed eyes. Their shoes scraped on the stone steps.

'Are you hurt? Can you stand?'

She tried to get up. Hands helped her. Strong hands. She clutched at one, pressing it to her cheek. It was warm. It was the hand of a living person.

'Let's get you out of there.'

She opened her eyes and stepped unsteadily from the pit. Leaves dropped from her.

'Were you hiding?'

She nodded.

'Who was here, Mrs Wilkinson? Was it William Hall?'

She nodded again.

'Is he still in the house?'

She shook her head. She heard the colleague start talking into his handset. 'Alpha One, this is Tango Three. Receiving?'

'Go ahead Tango Three.'

'We're at Lantern Cottage on Coal Lane. We have confirmation William Hall was here, but is no longer at the scene.'

'Who from?'

'Laura Wilkinson. No obvious injuries but she appears to be in shock.'

'Ambulance?'

'Yes.'

She looked at the officer whose hand she was clutching. He was the same one who came out when William last broke in. 'I don't know where he went.'

'OK, don't worry. Are you all right?'

'Cold.'

'Andy? Get upstairs, find a coat or something.'

The other officer took the stairs two at a time.

'Can you climb these?' His arm was around her. She gripped his waist.

'Yes.'

He kept the torch on their feet as, step by step, they went up. As they emerged into the kitchen, a blue light started strobing the windows. Andy had found her jacket. 'Careful of the broken glass by the table,' he said, wrapping it round her shoulders as she sat.

The fire engine's diesel chug had a reassuring quality to it. It was all hard metal and moving parts – no one could dispute its existence. A firefighter clumped in through the door, lumps of snow sticking to his boots. He was holding some kind of hurricane lamp that lit the room from one end to the other.

After seeing her, he turned to the policeman. 'Did you ask?'

The policeman shook his head and she saw the nervousness of the glance he sent in her direction.

She looked questioningly at their faces.

The policeman coughed. 'There was a vehicle blocking the bottom of the lane. It's registered to this property. A black Audi?'

'Yes – that's Owen's car...' She stopped speaking. His phone message from earlier. He said he was on his way home. How long had passed since then? 'What time is it?'

'Almost half-past six.'

She got up and their hands shot out, as if she was about to fall over. 'I'm OK.'

'You're not,' one of them answered.

'My mobile; it's there by the laptop. There was a

message from him on it...'

Andy passed it over and she brought the call up. It had been made at 3.15. Owen's voice started speaking into her ear.

Laura, I've just come off the phone to Doctor Ford. Obviously you're not there. No one knows where you are. Christ, Laura. I...I haven't been telling you everything and Dr Ford's afraid you've jumped to some conclusions.

Laura, the reason I was seeing him today was not about you. It was because of my hearing. He tested me and it seems...well...it's failing. I'm losing my hearing, Laura. It's started to go.

The wobble in his voice made her vision swim.

The problems in rehearsals. The sopranos? It was all down to me. I came back here to apologise to the orchestra and choir, to see if we can salvage this performance. We can. We can! But where are you? I'm coming back. I should never have left you on your own. Please wait for me in the cottage. I'll wrap things up here. I'm coming.

'He should have been here ages ago,' Laura announced woodenly.

The policeman was concentrating closely on her face. 'What did he say?'

'He...' Oh, Owen, your hearing. That explained so much. 'He set off from Manchester hours ago.'

The fireman stepped forward. 'My colleagues are looking already. What's he wearing?'

'I don't know...just a thin jacket. And normal shoes. He's not dressed for weather like this!'

'It's OK, don't worry. We'll find him.' The firefighter turned away and stared speaking into his radio.

She shrugged her ski jacket on properly as she spoke to the policeman. 'And William, he's out there somewhere. He was in the garden, over near the bins.'

'Who the hell's William?' The firefighter was now looking at the policeman.

'He's a...a vulnerable young adult. Late teens, but not all there. Up here.' He tapped his temple. 'He lives out at the Skylark Trust.'

The firefighter didn't look happy as he turned to Laura. 'You say he was in the back garden. How long ago was this?'

'An hour ago. Maybe more.'

'I'm bloody tempted to get the High Peak Mountain Rescue Team over with their search dog,' he said to the policeman. 'You sit tight here, madam. We'll sort it out.'

'No, I need to help. I want to help.' She stepped towards the door but the policeman blocked her path.

'Mrs Wilkinson, you could well be suffering from shock. Let us take care of this. An ambulance is on its way for you.'

You're not, she thought, leaving me in here alone. That thing I saw might come back. 'I'm fine.'

He didn't step aside. 'Sorry to say this, but you are not fine. Please, stay here.'

'This is all my fault. Listen, I know where he was. Let me at least show you.'

He glanced at the window overlooking the back garden.

'It was here,' she said, stepping round him and toward the kitchen door.

He let her pass, a hand hovering indecisively at his side. 'Just that, then. You shouldn't be...'

'It's here. Follow me.' She looked out the door. The snow was so deep! Five inches, easily. There were three more firefighters by the engine. The cover of its side panel had been rolled down. Two of them were removing equipment. The other was sitting in the doorway of vehicle's rear compartment. He was tearing lengths off a paper roll and stuffing them in a cardboard box. Molly Maystock's dad. He looked over. 'This isn't your kitten?'

'Mouse?' The snow on the path was churned up where they'd been walking. She sprang from one footprint to the next. 'Mouse? You've found Mouse?'

'Down the lane. This it?'

He bent the flap back and she looked inside. Mouse stared up at her, shivering, eyes as wide as ever. 'Oh my God, Mouse. I thought I'd lost you. Oh Mouse!'

'Are the bins round here?' The policeman and fire fighter were moving to the far corner of the cottage, torches shining into the back garden. One beam picked out the bird table, now leaning drunkenly to the side.

'Yes.' She followed, calling back to Steve Maystock. 'Keep an eye on her, can you? I'll come back...'

They were standing on the patio directing their torches towards the fence.

'The bins are over here, but I think...' Her words petered out. There was no need to check the rear of the house. No need for any search dog. The layer of snow showed a clear trail of footprints. They led up to the top of the garden but then they come back towards the house. Halfway they stopped. Footprints overlapped each other to form an uneven patch in the grass. It was like he'd been shuffling on the spot, unsure which direction to take.

But then the trial cut to the left. A single line of steps went straight to the fence then out into the field.

'That way,' the firefighter announced glumly, crossing the lawn.

Laura followed.

CHAPTER 39

She didn't like the way William's footprints were so close together. If he was fleeing, as he should have been doing, there would have been more of a space between each step. But there wasn't. When she took similar size steps her walk reduced to little more than a shuffle.

The two men started to draw ahead of her as she looked about. The thick layer of cloud had started to dissipate, and though the moon was still hidden from view, the pale landscape didn't need much light to reveal itself. A dark line was away to her left: the dry-stone wall running along the top edge of the field. Beyond it, the copse of trees where the badgers lived was nothing more than a faint smudge.

She was now a good twenty metres behind the two men. Speeding to catch up, she said, 'He's heading towards the canal. This field leads down to it – you can just make out the line of trees at the water's edge.'

Neither replied for a bit. She could hear the sound of their breathing, see it churning in the still air above their heads. The clean white snow creaked with each step. The land was so quiet. Too quiet. She wanted to scream William's name. Owen's. Where were they? Were they all right?

When she drew level with them the policeman glanced at her. 'Was he only wearing one shoe? The right print; I can see an outline of toes.'

'He was wearing slippers. The other one came off in the front hall.'

'He got here from the Skylark Trust in just his slippers?' He looked incredulous.

The line of steps started drifting to the right. The slope grew more pronounced. To their side was the shallow mound topped by a circular stone where she'd stood earlier. Now it was just a soft lump. As they passed it, she could picture William stumbling down to the canal. Why, she thought, did I let him out of the house? That dank water, so horribly cold...

But the beam of the firefighter's torch swung off to the left. The trail of steps now cut across the slope of the hill, heading in the direction of the copse of trees where the badgers had dug their holes. They followed the footsteps for a few seconds, gradually drawing closer to the dry-stone wall.

'Oh bloody hell, no,' the firefighter murmured as he came to a sudden stop.

Laura stepped out from behind him and saw another mound, similar to the one they'd just passed. But the snow from the top of this one had been scraped away. Something large and round was halfway down it. A giant disc of stone. From the way its lower edge had driven up a motionless wave of snow, it had slid there. Or had been pushed.

William's footprints led straight up to it.

'He hasn't managed to shift that, has he?'

'What is it?' Laura asked.

'I bloody hope not,' the policeman replied, starting forward again.

She tried again. 'What is it?' But they were both approaching the little mound, oblivious to her question.

She looked about, studying the perimeters of the field for any sign of whatever had come down into the cellar. Wherever it was, she thought, it caused this to happen. She searched for the lopsided head watching from behind the dry-stone wall. She scanned for its silhouette on the crest of the hill. It was still close by, she was certain.

'Oh shit, oh shit.'

It was the fireman's voice. She turned: they were both standing by the circular slab, torches shining straight down. She felt herself walking forward once more, almost stumbling as the ground started to rise.

'How on earth did he move the cap?' The policeman sounded dismayed.

The firefighter heaved a great sigh. 'Poor lad. What made him do something like that?'

There was an opening in the ground, not circular – more the shape of an egg. The rim was of bricks but, as she drew closer to the edge, she saw the sides of the vertical shaft turned to bare rock after about twelve feet. Her eye continued to travel down the bumpy surface. The gap narrowed. Just before William's body came into view, she realised she'd gazed at this scene many times before. Her dream. William was jammed head down, one arm bent behind his neck, knees splayed out to the sides. His other slipper had come off and the soles of his feet were pointing up. A light layer of snow covered them.

Her entire body started to quiver and the ground tilted beneath her feet. This couldn't be. How could this be? She staggered into the policeman.

'Get her back!' The firefighter yelled, stretching an arm out.

The policeman gripped her by the shoulders.

'What is he in?' She was trying to resist, wanting another view as he lifted her clear of the ground and carried her down the incline. 'It was her!'

'You should never have let her come!' The firefighter growled angrily, yanking a walkie-talkie from his front pocket.

'Mrs Wilkinson, it's not safe.' The policeman's voice was right in her ear. He was trying to sound soothing, but his grip didn't loosen. 'Let's come away, that's it. Good.'

'She did it,' Laura gasped. 'It was her!'

'Who's that, then?' His tone was indulgent as he lowered her down, well away from the cleft in the ground.

'The woman from Lantern Cottage! She climbed out of the wall. William said the bad person would come.'

He positioned himself between her and the hole. 'You're saying someone else was in the cottage earlier on?'

'Yes!'

'Who?'

'A woman.'

A hard edge had crept into the policeman's voice. 'There was a woman in Lantern Cottage? Who?'

Now you're listening, Laura thought. 'I don't know! But she had the canary; it was singing. Then she left the house with it. While William was outside in the garden!'

'OK, hang on. We'll get back to the cottage and you can tell me properly. You say this woman was alone?'

'Yes. William was terrified; she wanted to hurt him, I'm certain. She did this! She led him here and killed him!'

He reached for his handset. 'Can you give me a description of this woman? How old she was, what she was wearing.'

'Yes, she was– '

The firefighter's voice cut in. 'Constable?'

He dragged his eyes from Laura.

'How many sets of footprints did we just follow to get here?'

The officer opened his mouth to answer, then closed it. He lowered his handset and looked back at Laura. 'Mrs Wilkinson, only William's footprints lead here. We need to get you somewhere warm. You really shouldn't be outside.'

'You don't believe me? I can show you precisely where she was.'

'OK, you come and show me.' His patronising tone was back. 'Back at the cottage, yes?'

She nodded. 'Behind a wall upstairs.'

CHAPTER 40

An ambulance was now parked behind the fire engine. The vehicle's flashing lights combined with the fire engine's, making her feel unbalanced. Shielding her eyes, she could see the hills opposite were still totally black. 'Have you found my husband?' she asked the shadowy forms by the vehicles. A paramedic started toward her but she waved him away. 'We need light! Another of those big lamps the fireman had.'

No one seemed willing to move.

'Mrs Wilkinson,' the policeman said gently. 'Why don't we sit down a minute? The ambulance is warm. You can get some warm fluids on board...lie down, if you want.'

'I need to show you where she was. It's upstairs.'

The paramedic was shaking out a silver blanket. 'Come on, love. This way.'

'Don't you touch me!' Her hands were up, ready to slap at him. She was shaking. The policeman and paramedic looked at each other.

A radio went off. Something about the bottom field. The policeman lifted his handset and also started to speak. He mentioned an uncapped ventilation shaft. The need for winching gear.

Laura turned to Molly Maystock's dad. 'You know the lamp I mean. Please.'

He gestured to the policeman. 'I think there's one in the back. It'll be fully charged.'

The policeman lowered his radio and sent a pained look at the paramedic, who gave a slight shrug.

'I'll put the blanket round me,' Laura said. 'If you let me show you upstairs. After that I'll get in the ambulance.'

That seemed to appease the officer. 'OK.'

She whipped the blanket from the paramedic and wrapped it about her shoulders like a cape. Molly's dad turned round and removed a lamp from the side compartment. She could see the box Mouse was in. At least the kitten was safe. That was something. 'We need another of those things – as back-up.'

He pointed apologetically down the lane. 'They're all being used.'

I'm not going in with only one light, Laura thought. If it fails the darkness will take over once more. That thing came out when everything went dark.

'I've got flashlights,' Molly's dad said, removing a couple.

'Thanks.' She took one and clicked it on. The brilliant spot glided smoothly over the trampled snow as she led the policeman into the house. Steve Maystock followed, hurricane lamp held at shoulder height.

She blasted the darkness from the corridor beyond the kitchen with her torch beam. William's slipper was lying there, black and glistening like an enormous slug. At the bottom step, she shone the light up. Steve moved into the hallway behind her, hurricane lamp causing the last of the shadows to evaporate.

'Let me go first,' the policeman said, unhooking something from his belt. A baton extended out from his hand. 'Which way at the top?'

'Left.'

Safely bathed in light, they climbed the stairs in single file. None spoke. A mini-procession of pilgrims. Laura's silver cloak rustled like a giant packet of crisps. The policeman's torch beam went to the carpet. 'That's blood.'

'Mine. I cut my foot earlier.'

'And the walls?'

He'd spotted her handprints, too. 'All mine. It's that end room – straight ahead.'

The policeman's torch beam joined hers. They approached the wide-open door.

'Something's covering the floor.' Now he was speaking in barely a whisper.

'A mirror broke. It's glass. What I cut my foot on – I tried to sweep it back.' She wanted to check the spare room behind them. It could be in there, crouching among the boxes. She wondered whether to ask Steve to take a look, but the policeman started moving forward.

'Hello? Police...' he called out uncertainly. 'Is anyone here?'

Silence.

He pointed his torch into the studio and Laura was momentarily dazzled when the beam caught in the window.

'Bloody hell, what happened in here?' he asked.

Alongside the broken glass, fragments of brick and plaster now littered the floor. Smears of blood showed through the mess. She looked at the hole in the wall. 'I...I tried to move a mirror. It fell. Behind it, there was an opening in the plaster. I made it bigger.'

He stepped down into the room, torch now pointing at the jagged opening. Laura took a deep breath and followed. Steve squeezed in behind them. The space she'd cleared earlier wasn't quite big enough for the three of them and he pushed granules of glass back with the toe of his boot. The sound grated inside Laura's skull.

'Someone was hiding in there?' the policeman asked.

She looked at the hole. Did I really make that? She couldn't remember dislodging so many bricks. 'Not hiding. She...I heard her come down the stairs. I was in the cellar looking for the torch. The one that was at the bottom of the steps. She came into the kitchen above me.'

'You only heard her? You didn't actually see where she

came from?'

'Where else could she have come from? Besides, once the hole was big enough, I reached in with my hand – just before the power went off. I could feel the ends of her shoes.'

'Her shoes?'

'Yes.'

'She was already in there, behind the wall?'

'Yes.'

'You made a hole in the wall and discovered her already in there?'

'Yes.'

His eyes shifted to Steve Maystock. She glanced back: the firefighter looked sad. He didn't meet her eyes. She turned to the opening. 'There!' She pointed down. 'See that bit of lace? That's part of her petticoat. It came away in my hand. She was over in the corner, it's a cavity leading to the chimney shaft.'

The policeman turned his torch off, crouched down and picked up the scrap of material. 'I see.'

Laura could tell he didn't believe a word of what she was saying.

'And this person, hiding inside the wall, she didn't move when you reached in and started pulling at her clothing?' he asked, going on one knee. He leaned forward and brought his head close to the hole.

She saw his forehead wrinkle into a frown. He turned his torch back on and shone it inside, directing it off to the left. His shoulders stiffened. Then he was drawing back, fumbling for his radio as he looked up at Laura. 'Alpha One, this is Tango Three.'

'Go ahead, Tango Three.'

'Um...this is serious, but not urgent. We have the remains of a female in Lantern Cottage.' His voice was high and shaky. 'In a wall cavity.'

'A wall cavity?'

'Yes. Concealed in a wall. It appears to have been there

for quite some time.'

'How long?'

'I...I don't know. Hang on.' Face pale, he directed the torch in again. 'Years, I'd say. The dress looks...Victorian.'

CHAPTER 41

They were back in the kitchen when – without any warning – the lights came on. The fridge-freezer juddered briefly then settled back to its customary quiet hum. Laura thought the zeros of the microwave's clock looked like a row of blinking eyes. *What time is it? How long have I been asleep?*

'Thank God for that,' the police officer muttered, turning his torch off. 'Power's back.'

Laura watched him anxiously. He wouldn't say anything about the woman's body. She tried again. 'Officer, you still haven't answered my question. William was terrified of the bad person coming.'

He looked at her with a mixture of incomprehension and barely hidden annoyance. 'Mrs Wilkinson, my job is to secure the property. Other people will come and work out what went on. Specialists in that sort of thing.'

'Yes, but –'

'Laura?'

The voice robbed her of her own. She closed her mouth and turned her head. It was him. Doctor Ford stood in the doorway, long black overcoat hanging to below his knees.

'Laura, are you OK? We've been trying to find you.'

The policeman stepped eagerly towards him. 'Doctor Ford, are you Mrs Wilkinson's GP?'

He nodded. 'And Owen Wilkinson's. Is he here also?'

239

The officer ignored the question. 'I think Mrs Wilkinson needs some – you know – attention. She's been through a terrible experience.'

Dr Ford's head swivelled back to her. 'Laura?'

'I'm fine,' she replied, clutching the foil blanket tighter. 'They're waiting for me outside. I want the paramedics to look at me.'

'Well,' he lifted his carry case. 'I'd be more than happy to do that.'

She started across the room. 'No thank you. My husband is still out there somewhere, I'd prefer you take care of him.'

***

The three men watched as Laura left the room.

Once she was outside, Steve Maystock turned to the police officer. 'I'd better report back. See if they need me in the bottom field.'

'Hang on,' the officer replied, stepping over to the door. He made an attempt to close it before turning round. 'They've found him already.'

'Who?' Steve asked. 'The husband?'

The officer nodded. 'By a dry-stone wall. In a field near the bottom of the lane – where the ground levels out.'

Doctor Ford's leather case creaked as he adjusted his grip. 'I'd better head down there, then.'

The police officer shook his head. 'Doctor, you can't help – he's dead.'

'I beg your pardon?'

'He's dead.'

'Oh, good God.' Dr Ford looked at the crooked door. 'Oh, good God.'

'I heard earlier, when we got back from searching the fields. But I couldn't say anything to the wife, she's semi-delusional as it is.'

'Are you certain he's dead?' Doctor Ford whispered, face ashen.

'The boys have checked, Doctor. Could you...' he gestured at the corridor behind. 'We've got three bodies. No idea when the pathologist can get here. Can you nip upstairs and pronounce the one there? Then I can at least seal the place for forensics.'

'Three bodies?' Doctor Ford sounded lost.

'William Hall: his body's down a ventilation shaft across the fields.'

The doctor stared at the policeman. 'I don't understand.'

'Nor do we, Doctor, nor do we. Let's start here, then we'll take you to where the other two are.'

'Who is upstairs?' Doctor Ford quietly asked.

'I've no idea, but the corpse has been there for quite some time.'

'Minging, it is,' Steve said, fiddling with the hurricane lamp.

Doctor Ford looked from one man to the other. 'Where?'

The police officer sighed. 'It's been concealed in the wall cavity. Someone hid it in there.'

The doctor looked dumbfounded. 'Is...is it male or female?'

'Female,' the officer replied. 'Doctor, it's just a formality. She was bricked up in there decades ago.'

CHRIS SIMMS

CHAPTER 42

'Cor, your toes are like ice! Trevor, you should feel these.'

'Chilly, are they?' The ambulance driver's cheerful response carried back into the rear of the vehicle. 'Are they blue? If they're blue, I'll turn the heating back there to full. Can't have blue toes in my ambulance.'

They had secured Laura to a gurney. The straps were, they'd cheerfully said, only to ensure she didn't fall off during the journey. Maybe, she thought, that's what they told me the other time I was in an ambulance. But her mind had shut those memories out.

'Not blue. Well maybe a pale...I don't know what the word is for pale blue.' He grinned at her from his perch at the foot of the gurney.

Cyan, possibly, she thought. Or maybe a washed-out aquamarine, like the shade you see on the undersides of icebergs. I like icebergs. So slow and placid. Dangerous, though. The *Titanic* was proof of that. 'How long before a human succumbs to the cold?' she asked, thinking about Owen.

He continued to rub at her feet, increasing the circular motions to encompass her ankles. 'Don't you worry about that. There you go, this'll get the blood flowing back round.'

She thought about how long she'd spent lying in the coal pit beneath the brittle layer of leaves. The memory of her descent started to reassemble itself in her mind. The stiff way the thing's feet had connected with the stone steps. A juddering great sigh set her teeth against each other.

'Hey, now,' the paramedic said more softly, the forced jolliness now gone from his voice. 'We've got you, OK? Everything will be fine.' He reached up and tucked in the folds of the red blanket more tightly. The gurney's grey nylon straps cut across the blanket at regular intervals. She wasn't sure if everything would be fine. She was clear of the cellar, that was true. But she was trapped all the same. Trapped in the medical system, now.

'Lights in the valley look like jewels,' commented the ambulance driver. 'Sprinkled there in the dark.'

His colleague was back working Laura's feet. It felt so nice, so soothing. She wondered if it would be acceptable to perhaps have a nap. But as soon as she let her eyes close, she saw William's upturned feet, the thin layer of snow across the soles...

Her eyes snapped opened and she caught the paramedic staring at her with a look of concern. He attempted an unconvincing smile. 'Would you like some more of that drink, Laura?'

She considered the bottle of lemon-flavoured liquid on the shelf. It had left a powdery residue on her tongue. Glucose, paracetamol, electrolytes and a little salt; that's all it was, he'd assured her. She'd watched him mix it with water, making sure he hadn't slipped anything else in. She shook her head.

'OK. Not long now. Trevor, how long until the A6?'

'Five minutes.'

'There you go, Laura. Not long.'

Five minutes, she thought. Five minutes until we arrive at A&E, where I'll be wheeled past a crowded waiting area straight into a side room. And while you occupy me with light-hearted banter, your colleague will be at the front desk asking for the psychiatric nurse.

Doctor Ford climbed the stairs with the police officer two steps behind. 'Is it left?'

'Yup. Left and along to the end. She's wrecked the room, Doctor. Broke a massive mirror, sliced open her foot. That blood on the carpet? It's all hers. And the palm prints on the walls. She was very agitated. Pretty much hysterical, I'd say.'

'Oh.' Doctor Ford peered into the end room.

'She'd convinced herself the woman – the one in the wall – had climbed out and lured William to the ventilation shaft.'

Doctor Ford stepped down onto the floorboards. 'The body's in there, is it?'

'Correct. To the left. Here, you can use my torch.' As he handed it over, his radio came to life. Tango Three, this is Alpha One. Receiving?

Unhooking it from his tunic, he stepped back out into the corridor. 'Go ahead Alpha one, this is Tango Three.'

After making sure there were no fragments of glass on the floor before him, Doctor Ford knelt at the gaping hole in the wall. He opened his medical case then turned the torch on. The inner surface of the cavity had been coated in a thin, hard, greyish substance. He tapped a fingernail against it. Limestone, he was fairly certain. When turned to powder, mixed with water and left in the open air, a chemical reaction transformed it into a rudimentary form of cement. Someone had carefully prepared the space before placing the body inside. Although a musty aroma permeated the space, no foul-smelling fluids would have seeped into the floorboards.

Looking further in, he saw the officer was correct. The body had been placed against a column of bricks that rose up to the roof: the chimney shaft. He lowered the beam of light back down. The corpse was that of a bulky-looking adult female. The head lay at an unnatural angle on the right shoulder, a dirty veil of hair concealing the face. Wanting to see how dried-out the body had become, the doctor reached out to push the hair aside. But the thought of looking into her face made him shudder. Instead, he decided to examine her hands, which lay in her lap, concealed by bunched folds of dress. As he smoothed the material down, his eyes widened.

The woman was clutching a small cage. He held the torch closer. Something was inside the cage. Pale, creamy feathers stood out in the bright beam. A dead bird. A canary.

Thoughts rose up in Doctor Ford's head, each one jostling for attention. William had talked for years about Tweetie-Pie. Laura had insisted she'd heard a canary, too. Why could William and Laura hear a canary when they were in the cottage? Owen had never heard it...but the reason for that was obvious. He'd lost the upper-range of his hearing. Don't be ridiculous, the doctor chided himself, William and Laura hadn't heard an actual sound. That was impossible. Utterly impossible. Yet they'd both somehow – independently –claimed they could hear a canary singing.

He eased the cage from the female's stiff fingers. It was definitely a canary in there. Long dead and dried out, just like the woman. A canary. It...it...defied all explanation. No, he corrected himself. It defied all obvious explanation. That was all. But there would be an explanation, he insisted to himself. He just couldn't see it yet.

Leaning back, he checked the police officer was still in the corridor. Then he placed the cage in his medical case, closed it and relocked the clasps. 'The person is deceased,' he called out, regaining his feet and moving to the door.

The policeman was looking into the bathroom further down the corridor. 'Thanks, Doctor. I'll get on to base and let them know.'

CHAPTER 43

Twelve days later

All birdsong made Laura cower now. As soon as she heard it, she started looking around. She had to locate the actual bird. Had to. Once she'd done that – once she'd seen it – her shoulders sank back. Her pulse slowed.

It had given her a strained, edgy appearance. She didn't move easily any more. Sometimes she caught sight of herself – in a mirror or a shop window. Usually a mirror as she didn't really go out so much. She looked like she was in constant fear of someone suddenly screaming at her: shoulders permanently on the verge of hunching, head ready to duck.

It was a terrible posture, but she couldn't help it. Her periods still hadn't come back.

She had yet to decide if moving back to Richmond was a good idea. It was only a small flat and she'd only signed a six-month lease. She chose it because it overlooked the park. Just like the house where Owen and she used to live.

Poor Owen. She often thought of him. When his car couldn't get up the snow-covered lane, he'd abandoned it. Her guess why he went into the field was because his shoes were no good in snow. A trudge up a grassy slope would have been easier than slippery asphalt.

He'd tried to climb over a dry stone wall and the top had given way. The drop wasn't big, but his head had connected with one of the rocks. Cause of death was given as exposure. At least, she'd concluded, he'd been unconscious when he died.

It seemed strange to her that she had to wait until his death before getting a true picture of his health. The print-outs she'd found in the study had been part of his dawning realisation that his hearing was no longer perfect.

Presbycusis; that's the word Dr Ford had written in Owen's notes. Hearing loss that comes with old age. The simple audiogram Dr Ford had performed on the day she'd seen her husband driving off from the practice had proved it. The cells of his cochlea – a part deep in the ear that looks like a snail shell – had degraded. He'd been unable to pick out high-frequency sounds. Ones between 4000 and 8000 hertz. Like sopranos singing. Especially if his ears were still ringing from the crescendo immediately prior to the chorus coming in. Other high-pitched sounds he wouldn't have been able to make out included the ring of a mobile phone and the soft jangle of keys. Or the faint singing of a bird.

Though Doctor Ford was obliged to hand over her husband's medical notes, the same didn't apply to William's. In their final meeting, she'd asked again if he knew about William's preoccupation with the birdy. Tweetie Pie. Something that warbled away from its hiding place behind the bedroom wall.

The man had looked anywhere than at her as he declined to answer. 'Tell me,' she'd demanded. 'Did you know that William heard a bird singing, too?'

'You know I cannot discuss another patient with you.'

'Even if he's dead?'

He'd lifted a fist at that point – as if to smash it down on his desk. But a forefinger extended and he'd pointed at her instead. 'I tried to get you out of that bloody house! But you wouldn't go. I tried to make you stay here when you came charging in!' His wrist drooped and his arm fell to his lap. 'I tried.'

A parakeet cried out. Their squawks always made her flinch; but their bright green plumage was easy to spot. The bird arrowed past, aiming for a large oak tree where, she suspected, it had a home in the trunk. She tried not to think of holes, or hollow places. Cavities, shafts or chimneys. All of those things.

Mouse stirred in her lap. At least, Laura thought, she loves it here. How much had she grown since getting here? Lots. She looked at the letter from Martin Flowers again.

Dear Laura,

Thank you for your phone call last week. It was a pleasure, and I'd like to say, a comfort to hear you sounding so well. I feel I got to know you in the time you spent in Oldknow and you have constantly been in my thoughts since you left.

Obviously, the recent terrible events have given rise to many issues up here. Activity is very much ongoing. I had the dubious honour, a few days ago, of holding a burial service for poor William Hall. (The coroner agreed to release his body immediately the pathologist's findings came in. Suicide, as we all expected.)

His grave is on the western edge of the cemetery where the views are across to Manchester and towards Wales. Owen's grave is a mass of flowers, by the way. People continue to pay their respects on a daily basis.

This brings me to the questions you posed in your phone call. I will, if I may, address each one in turn (insofar as I have been able to obtain answers for you). The female remains from Lantern Cottage were taken to a secure facility adjoining the mortuary at Cale Green hospital. I also enquired about the whereabouts of a cage containing a canary; the officer concerned assured me all items from within the wall cavity would have been taken to the same secure facility.

You were also concerned to know what will happen to those remains once all necessary procedures have been completed. The same officer informed me that, where no surviving relatives can be identified (which seems likely in this case), the remains are disposed of in the hospital incinerator.

When she'd read that part of the letter, she'd been consumed with such intense feelings, tears had started from her eyes. That thing she'd seen – and its grotesque accomplice in its cage – were to be reduced to particles of ash. Some would float from the incinerator's chimney to be dispersed on the wind. What remained would be scraped from the furnace, bagged up and buried. She would never walk again.

Once more, she let her thoughts linger on that. It was over. She turned back to the last part of the letter.

By the way, the storage facility for the remains now also houses everything recovered from the archaeological dig by the church. In all, they found five skeletons – three children and two adults – and bones that belonged to a sheep (which certainly didn't date back to the Iron Age, apparently). Speaking to Adrian the other day (he sends his regards, by the way) he told me they now believe the three children were peacetime burials whereas the two adults, unfortunately, met a more violent end. Exactly what happened, we'll never know. But to use Adrian's words, life, in those days, was nasty, brutal and short.

The reason why all the remains are at the same facility is because they are currently being examined by one of the country's leading forensic archaeologists. She is just back from examining recently discovered bones on the coast of Japan. (Tsunami victims, the authorities over there suspect.)

This is all terribly macabre so I will dwell on it no further.

Some more positive news: Molly flew to America at the weekend! We are all so excited to know that she will finally receive the treatment she needs. I greatly look forward to giving you all the details when I see you on Monday. Of course, it would never have been possible without your generosity and I am proud to make the journey down to London bearing a token of gratitude created by Molly herself!

I look forward to seeing you then.

May God go with you, Laura,

My kindest regards,
Martin Flowers

She hadn't been able to refuse his request to visit – especially since he was bringing her news of Molly. But, she knew, he didn't need to travel all the way to south of London to tell her that. She couldn't help wondering if there was some other purpose to his visit.

Paying for Molly's treatment had been no problem. She didn't need the money: Owen had left her more in his will than she'd ever spend. Better to give Molly a life that she could enjoy.

The doorbell rang and the sudden sound made her shoulders jerk. Mouse's eyes opened and she stretches out her front paws. 'That'll be him.' Laura scooped the kitten up and went to the door.

CHAPTER 44

Miriam Nash keyed in the combination that unlocked the outer door of Cale Green hospital's mortuary. Before her, a short corridor led to a set of imposing double doors. Notices on them gave warning that, beyond, full hygiene procedures must be adhered to. A row of lockers for coats and bags were to the left of the doors. Dispensers for plastic overshoes and hairnets were mounted on the wall to the right. Below them was a bin with a one-way trapdoor for their disposal. From the ceiling above her, a CCTV camera silently watched.

But Miriam didn't go into the main room where autopsies on recently deceased bodies were performed. Instead, she swiped her card on the reader of a door to her right. This gave access to another corridor that led to a small office. She could hear two voices inside; Malcolm, the rather slow assistant she'd been assigned for the labelling and cataloguing of the remains from Oldknow. Probably wasting time chatting to a porter. It seemed his favourite part of the job.

'No mate, Japan. She was in Japan. The tidal wave, remember it?'

'Oh, from that earthquake out at sea?'

'Give that man a biscuit! They keep finding bits and pieces on beaches, in coves, all over. So Miriam, she's one of the best there is, the Japanese government paid for her to go out there– '

She stepped into the doorway with a cheerful hello.

The porter hastily put the statue she'd purchased in Tokyo back on her desk.

'Morning, chief,' Malcolm quipped.

She wished he'd drop that way of greeting her. Not that she expected a madam or ma'am. Miriam would do just fine. As she took off her coat, she glanced through the large plate-glass window into the examination room beyond.

The five skeletons from the hill fort by Oldknow church were neatly laid out on trestle tables draped in white cotton sheeting. Every single bone had been meticulously labelled. The best three – two juveniles and an adult which bore striation marks across its collarbone and upper vertebrae – were being shipped to the Manchester Museum. The fate of the other two was still undecided.

Her eyes travelled to the room's far corner. 'Why are the sheep bones still here?'

The porter looked at Malcolm, who was now turning to the window. 'The sheep? That went to the incinerator last night.'

Miriam stepped up to the glass. 'Isn't that it on the corner table with the yellow label on the bag? Yellow for incineration?'

'Those are the female remains. The ones from inside the wall of that cottage.'

'No, her remains should be on table six, which is now bare. I didn't ask for her remains to be incinerated. I asked you to bag the clothing and shoes she was found in for incineration, but not her.'

'But you'd signed off on cause of death being hanging.'

'Correct, but I hadn't signed off on the incineration of her remains. Where are her clothes?'

The porter piped up. 'According to my sheet, one bag – with a yellow label – was collected for incineration last night.'

Miriam shot a glance at Malcolm. 'We'd better check what's on that corner table.'

He nodded meekly as Miriam opened the inner door of the office. Snapping on a pair of latex gloves, she walked briskly over to the heavy-duty plastic bag on the corner table and undid the zip.

From inside, she removed a bone about eight inches in length that widened at one end. 'The lower tibia and upper hoof of an ungulate. Malcolm, this is the sheep.'

He gestured weakly at table six. 'I really don't remember attaching a yellow label to that bag. I...I put the dress and stuff...' He ran a hand through his receding hair. 'No, wait...I gathered up the skeleton of that sheep —'

'Malcolm?' Miriam's voice cut him dead. 'If her remains haven't gone into the furnace, would you like to tell me where the hell they are?'

CHAPTER 45

Laura could see him through the spy-hole. Funny, she thought. I once found him mildly attractive. Now he seemed so young. He had an apprehensive expression and was holding a large bouquet of flowers.

She opened the door and tried to smile. It was immediately there in his eyes: shock. He doesn't look younger, she realised. I am older. My eyes are more sunken, my mouth more pinched.

'Laura, it's so good to see you.'

She retreated, waving a hand. 'How was your trip down?'

'Fine. So fast – the train hurtles along.' His eyes were darting about the flat as he stepped inside. 'It's a nice place you have here. These are from Molly's dad. He's made me promise not to leave without getting a date for you to visit.'

'They're lovely,' she said, putting Mouse in the armchair, taking the flowers and going through to the kitchen.

'Seriously, Laura. They're due home in another fortnight.' He was speaking from the doorway behind her as she filled a jug. It reminded her of the church-hall kitchen at Oldknow. The two of them chatting. 'He wants you to stay with them.'

Steve had mentioned as much over the phone to her before they'd left. He'd even said about visiting them in

America. Tamsin – in one of her many emails – had also invited her to stay in San Francisco. Molly was receiving her treatment at a hospital in Los Angeles. Not that far between the two cities, Laura understood, if you flew. She'd considered a trip over but, in the end, had decided against it. The thought of flying was nice. She always loved to gaze down onto a fairytale land of clouds. But the thought of the noise; engines whining, signs pinging, seat belts clicking. She didn't think she'd cope.

'So, do you think you'll come up to Oldknow and see them when they get back?'

'I don't know.'

He removed an envelope from his bag. 'Molly made you a card before they left.'

'How did she seem to you about going all the way there?'

'Fine. Excited. Apparently making arrangements for the flight over was tricky.'

Laura knew that; the airline had insisted on her being accompanied by a nurse. Laura had quietly signed the cheque for that, too. 'But she was in good spirits?'

'When is she ever not?'

She took the card. Molly had drawn some flowers. Her message was sweet.

Thank you, Laura, for helping me. You are very kind and I will be grateful to you forever. All my love, Molly. XXX. PS Please come and see me when you feel like it!

'Aaah,' Laura murmured. 'She's so gorgeous.'

'Isn't she?'

His smile was brittle. The worried look hadn't entirely left his eyes. She speculated again on why he'd really come to visit. If it was to press for more details about that night, he wouldn't get them. Laura liked the psychiatric nurse's theory at the hospital near Stockport best. According to him, she'd had some kind of psychotic episode. She'd looked into the cavity and seen the woman's body propped against the shaft of the chimney just as the electricity failed. Down in the cellar, the episode had got worse. Bad enough to make her climb into a coal pit crawling with toads. Her mind had then created the vision of the dead woman to explain her overwhelming sense of panic and dread.

It was rubbish, of course. But Laura had enthusiastically agreed: it meant getting out of hospital far more quickly. What the theory didn't explain was how she knew it was a fully-grown female in the wall, when all she'd felt were the ends of some shoes. Shoes alone wouldn't have let her tell the woman was the same heavily-built one from the photo. How I knew, Laura thought, was because I saw her coming slowly down those cellar stairs, moaning and – 'Would you like some tea?'

'No, I'm fine, thank you.' Martin's voice was stilted as he glanced nervously into the front room. 'It's a nice place you have here.'

He's said that already, Laura thought. 'Yes. Shall we sit down?'

'Please.' He settled on the edge of the little sofa. His thumbs rubbed at one another.

She plonked Mouse back on her lap and looked at him.

'Erm, Laura, I...' He cleared his throat. 'This isn't easy. But I need to tell you something. Can...can I please tell you something?'

She wasn't sure if he was about to proposition her. Or was he seeking some kind of absolution? It felt like she was the representative of God here, not him. She hesitated. There was such a look of torment on his face, she wasn't sure she wanted to hear what he had to say.

'Please. I...' His head dropped. 'I don't know who to turn to. But you deserve to know this...' He looked up. She was astonished to see he was almost crying.

'What is it?' She kept her hands on Mouse, enjoying the smooth fur and – more than that – the warmth the animal gave off.

The sides of Martin's nose flexed as he dragged in air. 'When I took over Oldknow church, the vicar who was retiring sat me down. It was on the day he was actually leaving. He'd already gone through all the standard things during the handover period. This...this was something different.'

The air in the flat seemed to have become very heavy. Only Mouse's contented purr broke the silence. 'Go on.'

'Well,' he looked up at the ceiling. Or maybe to heaven, she thought, seeking strength. 'His name was Tim Dobby. When he took over the church, the previous vicar sat him down and told him the exact same story. He described it as a kind of tradition – I wasn't sure what to make of it, to be honest.' His thumbs wrestled one another once more. 'It was in the strictest confidence...I was only ever meant to pass it to whoever took over the church from me. That was how it worked. Dobby made me swear – but I cannot keep silent.' His eyes met hers. 'Not now.'

She lifted her eyebrows in encouragement. This secret was clearly tearing him apart.

'When Dobby told me what I'm about to tell you, he didn't name the actual cottage. But...but now I think he was referring to Lantern Cottage,' he blurted.

'You're talking about the canary breeder who was hanged at Strangeways?'

His mouth fell open. 'You knew about that?'

She gave Mouse another stroke as the conversation with Adrian Moore came back. She realised Martin hadn't been in the church hall when it had taken place. She remembered Moore telling her how the canary breeder had confessed to killing his wife and burning her body. Only now Laura knew he didn't wheel her to the limekilns in the dead of night and put her body inside. She could feel the tips of those shoes once more.

Martin's hands were now pressed between his knees. 'On the morning of his execution the canary breeder summoned the vicar of Oldknow at that time. Once they were alone, the canary breeder admitted that he hadn't killed his wife. You see, for years, she'd been desperate for children. They'd tried but, as time went by, it became obvious that they would never be blessed.'

She looked away; he could be talking about me.

'Gradually, her feelings soured to a deep loathing. She'd sit brooding in the cottage and listen to children from the village as they came to see the canaries. She'd pace the moors above the cottage, sometimes pulling at her own hair. Then, one evening, she came back from one of her walks carrying the male canary in its cage. The males are the ones who sing. She told her husband she'd used the bird to coax a young lad from the outskirts of the village.'

Mouse squirmed and Laura realised she'd stopped stroking the animal. Her fingernails were beginning to dig at the cat's fur. She lifted her hand but didn't look back up.

'She led him into the fields above Lantern Cottage, where the mineworkings used to be. The boy followed, entranced by the canary's singing. As you know, a lot of the mines had ventilation shafts sunk into them. Back then, with many of the mines active, most shafts hadn't been capped. She led him right to the edge of one and she...she...' His shoulders spasmed as he got the words out. 'Pushed him in.'

Laura shut her eyes. Part of her wanted him to be quiet. It wanted him to get out of the flat. She stayed silent.

'After telling her husband what she'd done, she went upstairs to the room she'd so painstakingly prepared as a nursery. She'd refused to allow him to use it for anything else. He rushed out to check the shafts nearest to the cottage, but could find no sign of any boy. When he got back, he went upstairs to ask if she'd been telling the truth. He found her hanging from the rafter.'

The rafter. Only one upstairs room had an exposed beam, she thought. Owen and I had used it as our bedroom. We'd been sleeping in the room where she'd hanged herself. She thought of how crooked the neck of the thing in the cellar was. The way it rested on a shoulder. She whispered down at Mouse, 'So why did they hang the canary breeder?'

'He told the vicar he'd never admit the truth. He felt so ashamed – and that he was to blame for not being able to give her the child she so craved. He didn't want her to be remembered as a monster. He preferred to have that epithet for himself. So he went to the police and said he'd killed her and burned the body.'

She ran her hand down Mouse's back, returned it to the top of the cat's head and repeated the action. She kept doing it. 'I thought the canary breeder was some kind of paedophile. I thought he killed the child.'

'No, I understood he was harmless. It was her who has full of poison and bile. She made life a misery for him, always going on at him for not being a man.'

Laura could hear that bitter, shrill voice again. The one that ridiculed Owen at every opportunity. 'But why didn't the vicar do something?'

Martin took a moment to answer. 'Maybe it was too late for the wheels of justice to be stopped. I think the vicar froze. I don't think he knew what to do. So he kept quiet and the hanging went ahead.'

Laura knew what she was hearing was the truth. 'And the canary breeder wouldn't say where he really put his wife's body?'

'He just told the vicar it was with the canary. The one she'd used to lure the young boy to his death.'

She supposed it made sense, placing his wife as close as possible to the nursery she so treasured. Every night we slept in that house, Laura thought, she'd been just behind us. She and the canary, inches from our heads. She looked up at the vicar.

He held her gaze for a second and broke eye contact. 'I'm sorry, Laura. I think it was her, who you found in the wall.'

Yes, she thought to herself. It was. The thing that came out of the wall hated children. So it used the canary once more. Used its song to lure William away.

Another thought spun off. And the implication of this one was strong enough to make her swallow. She wondered for a second whether to say anything. Of course she had to. She had no choice. 'I need to go back.'

The vicar blinked. He shifted in his seat. 'To do what? I mean...will telling what I've just told you achieve anything?'

The selfishness of the comment left her momentarily speechless. She lifted her chin higher. 'You come here with all this and then expect me to keep quiet?' Anger made her forearms tingle. 'You hoped to make yourself feel better by unloading the secret on me?'

'No...I...' He couldn't look at her properly. 'I just thought...'

The man was weak, she thought. He and all the vicars before him. They'd done nothing. 'You and I are going back because I know where the child is.'

'The child?'

'I know where he is.'

'Which child?'

The ventilation shaft might have been too narrow for William. But someone smaller would have fallen right to the bottom of it. 'The one she murdered first.'

CHAPTER 46

Dr Robert Ford sat in his study. There was an unread newspaper spread across his lap as he stared at the small cage. For more years than he could remember he'd done exactly the same thing; worked up all his patient notes at the surgery, locked the building, returned home, eaten a meal and retired to his study with a tot of whisky. There, he would sit quietly and read.

But now the little object had changed all that. He wished he had never taken the thing. It was a stupid, impulsive thing to have done. He was still not quite sure why he'd snatched it. By doing so, he'd broken the law, risked everything – but that wasn't the reason why he could no longer concentrate on his journals or that day's news.

As the fire crackled in the grate and the clock ticked on the mantelpiece above it, his eyes rested on the dead bird beyond the thin bars. He kept turning his head, first to one side then the other. Straining to catch a faint echo of song. He'd now done the same thing for thirteen nights. He reached for the decanter beside him and poured another measure. It had to stop: he was drinking too much, sleeping badly, waking early. His mind felt fogged and slow every morning.

The memory of Owen in that field came back. His body half-covered with snow. There had been a trickle of blood leading from one nostril and his eyes were slightly open. What a terrible thing to have happened. And all, he thought, because of you. He gazed at the bird's corpse as he sipped again. Somehow, because of you. This was stupid. Maudlin. Worse than maudlin: it bordered on fanciful. He put the half-finished glass down and yawned. He should toss the thing on the fire and have done with it. There was no song associated with it. How the hell could there be? But he didn't pick it up. One more night, he decided. I will listen for one more night. That will make a fortnight. Then I'll burn it.

He struggled forward in the leather armchair with its headrest that curled in on either side. At the door – finger on the light switch – he checked the room a final time. The cage sat on his footstool, lit by flames that were growing fainter behind the fireguard. The clock ticked on. He turned the light off, did the same in the kitchen and made for the stairs.

He was on the third step when a trickle of notes floated past his ears. His foot froze and his head turned. Silence. Had he imagined it? He didn't think so. The movement felt unnatural as he walked backwards down the stairs, one hand on the banister to steady himself.

He stood in the study doorway. The cage and his footstool were bathed by the fire's warm glow. Beyond them, shadows lay thick. Unable to shake the impression of hearing something, he took his seat and resumed his vigil. The clock ticked on. After a few minutes, he finished off the glass of whisky and allowed his head to rest against the armchair's soft leather.

When he woke, several things had changed. The room was cold, so cold he was shivering. He looked blearily at the clock. A single long note was repeating itself. A car alarm, somewhere out on the close? 11.53. He'd only been asleep for twenty minutes. The fire had died down but the embers still burned brightly; tiny pulses scurrying back and forth across the amber surface. It shouldn't be this cold, he thought, confusedly beginning to sit forward. As he realised the shrill noise was not coming from the street outside, he became aware of a figure standing next to his armchair.

His bladder opened. Hot urine spread beneath his buttocks and thighs. She was naked and huge; the dry flesh of her massive breasts mottled with black. The sheet of dirty hair that hung before her face reminded him of the fibrous layer that filled the mouths of baleen whales; there to filter sustenance from the ocean's sunless depths. It was her. The woman he'd seen inside the wall at Lantern Cottage. Curls of steam began to rise from his lap and a childlike whimper escaped him.

The noise caused her head to loll in his direction. Slowly, she shuffled forward and bent towards the armchair. As she did so, a section of hair slipped to the side and he looked in at an empty eye socket, nothing there but the optic nerve's withered root. He shut his own eyes and felt the tips of her hair brushing the backs of his hands as she sniffed him.

And even as he sensed her draw back, and even as he heard the scrape of her leathery soles against the floorboards, and even as the canary's exuberant song moved further and further away, he kept his eyes shut and he would never open them again.

267

CHAPTER 47

The men stared at the hole in grim silence.

Laura turned away from the hushed group to gaze across the dull field at a finger of bright snow. It clung stubbornly to life in the shadow of a dry-stone wall. She realised, wrapping her shawl more tightly about herself, it was the last visible evidence of the brutal storm from a fortnight before.

From below their feet a disembodied voice called out. 'OK, carry on!'

The firefighter holding the winch started turning it once more, winding in a length of rope that dropped like a plumb line into the dark cleft.

The heads of his colleagues stayed bowed, as did those of three policemen, a man in an overcoat and Martin Flowers. A funeral, she thought. It looks just like a funeral. But no body was being buried. The reverse, in fact.

A yellowish glow broke the blackness at their feet. She looked on impassively as the dirt-smeared head and shoulders of a man rose slowly out of the ground. In the harsh light of day, the lamp on his miner's helmet was suddenly useless. His arms came into view. They were cradling something loosely wrapped in blue plastic sheeting.

She knew exactly what it was.

The man had now been winched high enough to get a knee on the brick-lined rim. He held the bundle out.

Reluctantly, a policeman took it. Without looking at it properly, he laid it on the wiry turf and backed away.

All eyes went to the man in the overcoat. After sending an uncomfortable glance in Laura's direction, he crouched down and tentatively lifted the corner. A collective jolt passed through the group and Martin Flower's legs suddenly folded. He sat down in the long cold grass and started to claw at his dog collar, only stopping when his shirt was torn open. Moaning weakly, he turned in the Laura's direction.

But she was already striding away, shawl now pulled over her head. A veil.

As she picked her way across the unkempt field she couldn't stop checking the periphery of her vision, even though she knew the woman's body – and the canary's – were safely locked within a mortuary. For all she knew, they'd been incinerated already. She hoped they had.

But, like how the last finger of snow nearby hinted at the recent storm, a sense of her still persisted. Laura trudged swiftly forward and Lantern Cottage came into view. The vile chimney parodying the human form proudly stood above the slightly sagging roof. Even though chipboard now filled all the windows, she found herself checking them, half-expecting to see the woman's silhouette in the room Owen and her had shared.

The room the woman had once dreamed of being a nursery for a child that never was.

I will have the thing demolished, Laura decided. Torn down, razed, obliterated. Let the turf reclaim it and sheep pepper the ground where it once stood with their shit.

Her hire car was parked alongside the emergency services' vehicles. As she climbed in, she glanced at the clock. Almost two hours before her train left for London. Plenty of time to nip back to the village. She wanted to see Doctor Ford's reaction when she told him of the discovery. Why should he enjoy the comfort of having it broken to him gently by someone else? He should have been here – in person – to see the remains brought up. When Martin Flowers had rung him yesterday to explain what was happening, the doctor had promised he'd come.

As the car approached the cottage, she refused to look at it. She liked to think its hold on her was broken. But, as she neared the front porch, she wished she'd locked the car doors before setting off. What if the thing was there, staring out? Worse: what if it came lumbering onto the road?

The solitary building slid slowly past and the lane in front seemed to narrow where the thick hedge reared up on each side. As she entered its eternal twilight, her mind wandered to Molly. All being well, the young girl was due back in another couple of weeks. How, Laura wondered, do I explain that she must come to visit me down south? That I never intend to return to this place?

The nose of the car dipped as it began to descend the short, sharp slope. The red of berries in the twisting undergrowth stood out. Behind them, the evergreen foliage merged into a dark and fecund wall.

Just beyond, in the field on her left, was where Owen died. The thought – the realisation she was so near to the spot, the tragedy of him having got so close to home, the cold and lonely way he'd left this world – caused her vision to dissolve. She had to apply the brakes, and as she did, something bulky moved in the hedge beside her car.

Laura's heart wrenched in her chest.

No. Not her, please, not her. As she blinked rapidly to clear her sight, a large form separated itself from the screen of leaves. A badger, old and grizzled and stiff of limb. It stepped down the bank and paused to regard her with contemptuous, piggy eyes. You're right, Laura thought. I don't belong here. No one belongs up here. This is your place.

Before she got to it, the door to the GP's surgery opened with a ding. A woman, mid-twenties, struggling with a buggy. Laura grasped the door handle to stop it swinging back and the mum passed with a nod of thanks.

Laura was wondering whether to continue straight to Doctor Ford's room when the low, urgent words being spoken from behind the reception hatch to her right began to register.

'Doctor Hedley went over to his house to check about half an hour ago. She called the ambulance from there.'

'And he hadn't rung asking us to cancel his patients?'

'No, there were three waiting before I thought something wasn't right. His eight o'clock had been sitting there for twenty minutes.'

Laura realised that, by remaining just inside the door, the receptionists couldn't see her. They had no idea she was there.

'He's never off sick. Well, maybe twice in all the years I've been here.'

'Precisely. I tried to ring him: no answer. When I let Doctor Hedley know, she drove over. It's awful. Some kind of breakdown, she said. He won't even speak– '

The bell above the door made Laura jump as someone opened it. The receptionists' conversation stopped and one leaned forward to look through the hatch. She saw Laura and the welcoming expression left her face.

'Excuse me?' The voice came from behind Laura.

She turned to see an elderly gentleman. 'Sorry.'

The receptionist continued to stare, her lips thin and tight, as Laura slipped back out.

Doctor Ford's house was located on a cul-de-sac off the road leading towards the A6. Laura spotted the ambulance immediately. There was an estate parked with two wheels on the pavement beyond it. A sign on its roof said Doctor.

Pulling up in front of the neighbour's house, she wondered what to do. From what she'd overheard, he was unwell. Too unwell to let him know what had been at the bottom of that ventilation shaft? The answer quickly became apparent as the front door opened.

He was in a wheelchair with a blanket tucked in around his torso and legs. Straps had been fastened across his chest and thighs. She could see his toes poking out; he was wearing socks. She realised his eyes were closed. But there was nothing serene about his face. The skin of his eyelids was bunched, the lips twisted back in a grimace. Was he in pain?

As the paramedics negotiated the front step, the wheelchair had to be tipped forward. No part of the doctor moved. He was totally rigid. The knuckles of his hands were white where they clutched the armrests.

The sight of him made Laura uneasy. What had happened? Something traumatic enough for him to try and shut out the world. Deny its existence. She found her eyes sweeping the surrounding gardens. The feeling of disquiet suddenly grew stronger. It wasn't that thing, Laura told herself as she put the car into reverse. Don't be stupid.

Yet, as she turned back on to the main road and started accelerating up the hill and away from the little village, it was with a profound sense of relief.

EPILOGUE

Six weeks later

'Race you!' Molly Maystock jumped from the swing and ran towards the seesaw. She liked to run. Since her operation it had got easier and easier. Since arriving home from America, she could already run from one end of the playground to the other and back again.

The brook that cut through the middle of the park chattered noisily to itself. Dusk had closed in and orange light shone down from the lamp posts dotting the pathways. The bell of Oldknow church began to toll, noise funnelling down the valley and through the village. Six rings. It would be time to go in soon.

Jemma caught up with her and they reached the see-saw together. Giggling, Molly took the end of it nearest to the line of trees. Her friend sat down on the other end and, for a moment, they resembled a pair of frogs, knees bent in readiness to spring.

Molly glanced back over her shoulder. 'What was that?'

'What?' Jemma asked.

The succession of notes came again. High and floaty.

'That,' Molly stated.

'Oh, yes.' Jemma looked intrigued as she climbed off the see-saw. Molly's end sank back down to the ground. 'Was it in the trees?'

Molly stood up and turned round. 'I think so.'

The gaps between the dark pine trunks were very gloomy. It looked a bit scary in there. The sound came again. A cheerful sound. The girls looked uncertainly at one another.

'Shall we go and see?' Jemma asked.

One of Molly's knees turned inward as the toe of her foot rotated against the tarmac. 'I don't know...'

The bursts of song were now coming faster. An enchanting trickle.

'Fairy music,' Jemma murmured, edging closer to the low fence at the playground's edge. 'It might be fairies.' She looked back at Molly. 'Come on.'

Molly watched her friend start to climb over. She began to follow.

'Molly! Time to go in!'

She stepped back. Her dad was standing at the main gate, beckoning with one hand.

'Jemma, you too. I told your mum we'll walk you home.'

The other girl looked disappointed as they crossed the playground together. When they reached Steve, he gave them a questioning smile. 'What were you up to, anyway? Playing hide-and-seek or something?'

'Didn't you hear the fairy?' Jemma asked. 'It was singing.'

Steve shook his head. 'I can hear the stream. That's pretty noisy.'

'It was over in the trees,' Molly said.

'Really?' Steve was turning his back on the playground. 'That's nice. And is it still there now?'

The two girls listened for a moment.

'No,' Molly said. 'It's stopped now.'

'Good.' He'd already set off for the nearby houses. 'Because it's almost time you two were asleep.'

THE END

ACKNOWLEDGEMENTS

Only one person's advice was needed in writing this novel: Dr Ian Collyer – for everything orchestra-related. All inaccuracies are my own.

OUTSIDE THE WHITE LINES
A NOVEL

'One of the genre's all time great debuts.'
Lee Child

Don't drive at night. Don't drive alone. If you break down, do not open the door to anyone - even if you believe they're there to help you.

There's a Killer on the roads masquerading as a breakdown rescuer. Roaming the motorways at night looking for victims, even he doesn't know where and when his next murder will be. But when he does strike, it is with terrifying brutality.

Andy, a young recruit to the traffic police, is determined to hunt the Killer down, jeopardising his own police career in the process. After the third victim is found, he believes he's seen something crucial - but his partner won't believe him. Increasingly alienated from his colleagues, Andy becomes obsessed with finding the murderer.

The Searcher is an outcast from society; lonely and misunderstood he unwittingly links Andy and the Killer through his midnight solitary searches of the motorway system.

As the police fail in their search for the Killer and the murders continue - increasingly savage and unprovoked - Andy is determined to bring them to a halt. The actions he takes bring all three together in the most chilling of finales.

PRAISE FOR

OUTSIDE THE WHITE LINES

'A gritty, suspense-filled first novel. . . here is a new crime writer who really knows his stuff – a compulsive and compelling read.'

Publishing News

'Simms' fresh approach, and the way the story weaves between three viewpoints, makes this one of the most promising debuts in crime for some time. From the prologue's brutal first pages to the satisfying crunch of the final chapter, the prose is spare, lean and mean.'

City Life

'Anyone reading this will do so in one sitting…Simms is really a name to watch out for.'

Deadly Pleasures Magazine

PROLOGUE

As the tiny voice began to speak another huge lorry thundered past. Spray-laden swirls swept around his lower legs, flattening damp trousers against his shins. 'I'm sorry, I didn't catch that,' the man said.

Patiently, the voice resumed. 'I said, try and get your head right into the telephone casing. It will cut out a lot of background noise.'

He did as he was asked and instantly appreciated the advice as the voice clearly said, 'Can you hear me better now?'

'Yes, much,' he replied and stopped pressing the telephone receiver quite so hard against the gristle of his ear.

'Ok, sir, could you tell me what number is on the inside of the door?'

He angled his head to the side and read out the luminous white number.

There was a pause then the voice said 'Right – so you're just beyond junction 14?

He didn't know, but trusting whatever information the voice had to hand replied, 'Yes, that sounds about right.'

The voice then went on to ask him various questions about his vehicle, before finishing with, 'Ok, sir, have you got breakdown cover with any motoring organisation?'

'I have,' he answered, and pre-empting the next question continued 'Shall I read out my membership details?'

'Please.'

He held the card down at arm's length, and using the orange flash of his hazards, read out four numbers with each blink of light.

Drips from the telephone casing fell steadily on to the back of his head as his details were processed. While waiting he reflected on his situation, stranded in the middle of the night on a deserted and unlit stretch of motorway. There was no way he was getting any more than a couple of hours' sleep before work the next day. Today, in fact, since morning was now only a few hours off. He felt frustrated at the way his car's failure had also rendered him completely powerless; up until now he'd always been one of the warm and cosy drivers speeding past the dark, cold cars parked on the hard shoulder. Suddenly he appreciated just why these telephones were called SOS points: no one stops to help on a motorway.

He'd counted 127 flashes of his hazards before the voice spoke to him again. 'OK, sir – you're down as a priority case, so a van should be with you in just under an hour. I know the conditions are bad tonight but I must advise you and your passenger to remain outside your vehicle, preferably well clear of it and up the grass verge.'

'Right, thanks for your help, is that everything?' he asked.

'Yes,' the voice replied. 'Of course, if there's no sign of any van after an hour feel free to call us again.' The line clicked dead.

'Thanks,' he said, feeling strangely vulnerable now the voice had gone. He replaced the receiver on the blank grey telephone, shut the little orange door and stepped back towards his car. With one hand on the roof, he looked through the rear passenger window at his sleeping daughter. Way off to his right, lights began to pierce the darkness. Squinting into the rain, he watched them grow in strength until a lorry rumbled past, rocking the car beneath his hand. To his relief she stayed fast asleep in the booster seat. Moving her outside the car was ridiculous, he thought, glancing uneasily at the - for now - empty lanes. Guiltily, he climbed into the front passenger seat and quietly pulled the door shut. The dashboard clock read 3.18 a.m.

Coarse blades of wet grass poked into his face, the tiny serrations on their edges making a virtually imperceptible rasp on the skin of his cheek. On rainy nights like this the moisture seemed to free the acrid deposits from exhausts trapped in the greenery around him. Even though the smell made his nostrils itch and smart, he resisted the temptation to wipe his sleeve across his nose because he knew it would remove the carefully-applied camouflage cream coating his face. Barely twelve feet from his head a car raced past, wet tyres hissing on the tarmac, headlights flickering between the crash barrier's struts like an ancient cinema projector. He wondered if the grass could have drawn blood.

Pushing his left forearm out, he bent the clump backwards. Keeping himself perfectly flat, he wriggled over the top. Beyond, a dip in the ground offered improved cover and he inched his body forward into the depression. As he did so his elbow knocked against a can. He stopped moving at the hollow metallic noise. Fingers probed the vegetation until the object was located. Holding it in front of his face, he used his other hand to twist the pencil torch gripped in his teeth. Insulation tape over its end reduced the beam to laser-like proportions. Using his tongue he played the pinpoint of light over the metal surface: a standard coke can, not even from outside the EU. He discarded it, turned the torch off and then lay motionless for a while with his eyes shut, waiting for his night vision to return.

He relished these visits more than anything else in his life. This was his territory, free from any other humans through their very proximity within hurtling metal cages. He imagined the unkempt stretches of grass on the central reservations to be islands and the motorway lanes surrounding them an impenetrable grey moat. This was his little kingdom, shared only with the vermin, scavengers and foraging creatures of the night. He knew they also came here because he'd find their pathetically smeared remains where they'd tried to cross back over the hard expanse of tarmac into the normal countryside beyond.

Field-mice, dormice, voles, shrews, hedgehogs, weasels, rats and stoats – he'd collected all manner of corpses, or what was left of them after the cars had crushed them and the crows had taken their pick.

Another vehicle shot past, this time on his right-hand side, going in the opposite direction. By now the rain had begun to soak through his army surplus all-in-one suit. He wondered how much searching he had left before it started getting light. Opening his eyes he craned his head back, looking for any sign of the full moon. He wasn't able to see the unbroken cloud covering the sky, just sense its weight in the blackness above. Reluctantly he undid the Velcro clasp on his cuff and glanced at the luminous-tipped hands of his watch: they read 3.21 a.m.

The driver's window suddenly hummed into life, destroying the peace that had slowly settled over the two occupants. As glass slid into the door, cold air and spatters of rain immediately began blowing in. He looked questioningly at the man slouched before the steering wheel, hands resting on his paunch.

'I'd lower yours too – I've just dropped one.'

'Jesus,' he replied, scrabbling in the dark before the first whiffs hit him.

'This,' the driver announced, 'is going to be a right shag

of a night. Pissing rain and stinking wind – I wouldn't be in your shoes on this shift.' He popped the last two tablets from a blister pack and tossed the empty sheet of plastic through the open window. 'Bloody indigestion,' he said, swallowing the two pills. 'Do you know, I have to sleep sitting up in bed? It's the only way of stopping the acid from burning the back of my throat.'

The passenger grimaced in sympathy and poked his nose into the cold stream of air coming through the gap in his window. The driver stared out of the motionless police car's windscreen and drummed his fat fingers on the steering wheel.

Suddenly the radio spat static and a buzzing voice, said 'Base to 1820F4, RTA involving two vehicles reported off the slip road at junction 8, northbound. Please attend.'

The response came almost immediately. '1820 to base, will be at the scene in about six minutes.'

'Roger 1820. Be advised a member of the public has already called for an ambulance.'

The younger man listened intently. Four days into his attachment and he still couldn't make out half of what was being said over the car radio.

'Well, that's bog-all to do with us – and it's too far to go just to give you a bit of roadside experience, son,' said the driver, closing his window. 'I reckon we'll go and get a coffee at the services. I could do with a dump and all.'

'Aren't we meant to be checking on all breakdowns at the moment, Sarge?' asked the passenger.

The driver glanced disdainfully across at the car marooned on the opposite hard shoulder. 'Yeah – but we'll check on him later. I can't be shagged driving to the next exit and coming all the way back now.'

Not waiting for his passenger to respond, he started the engine and turned on the lights. The patrol car rolled slowly down the concealed ramp onto the hard shoulder and pulled away. As they moved off, the younger man watched the flashing hazard lights from the car on the other side of the motorway slowly disappear. When the 'Services 8 miles' sign drifted lazily past he glanced at the dashboard clock: 3.26 a.m.

'Too many bastard cars,' he cursed to himself. Forced to take the M25 at rush hour he'd crawled round it at little more than walking pace. With every click of his dashboard clock more money had escaped him. He thought of the brown envelopes with their machine-gun type and angry red demands gathering back home and then strained his eyes looking ahead – but there were only cars in front; no gaps, no way through.

Trapped there, he'd scrutinised other drivers in the lanes alongside as they sat, motionless and resigned, watching with glazed eyes as their lives slipped slowly by. Almost all were selfish wankers who, if they weren't so lazy, could easily have found an alternative way into work. Did none of them live near a fucking train station? The only sympathy he had was for fellow drivers like himself. Vans, trucks, lorries – people using the roads for proper work purposes. Not like these twats, alone in their cars, sat on their fat arses and getting in his way.

When he'd finally got off the M25 and onto the M26, he'd been able to put his foot down a bit. Feel more in control. He'd smilingly taken out a couple of crows pecking at something dead on the hard shoulder. The vulture-like bastards never expected a vehicle to jink across the white lines; too late they struggled into the air, ragged wingtips clawing desperately at the flat sky. Puff. He'd turned them into broken balls of black feathers. No doubt their mates were on the carcasses in minutes.

But finding the garage where he was dropping the components off had then taken ages too. After that came the paperwork. And so here he was, making the return trip halfway through the frigging night, having made piss all from the job. The fury had built in him all day and now it constricted his chest like a giant tubi-grip. He bit on the last piece of banana then unwound his window and hurled the skin out. As soon as it crossed the window frame the roar snatched it, sending it flapping through the air on to the central reservation.

Bollocks, he decided. Even if it was pouring with rain he needed some sport, and the bad weather only increased his chances of success. He pulled his van into the approach road for the services then, avoiding the feeder lanes luring him to the welcoming glow of the restaurant car park, carried round on a smaller, unlit service road to the rear of the buildings. Pulling up in the shadows, he jumped from the van and slid back the side door. From a holdall he removed a grey boiler suit and neon waist jacket and put them on. Then he took out a torch, magnetic siren light, and toolbox containing a heavy-duty monkey wrench. Placing it all on the front passenger seat, he restarted the engine and, in seconds, was back on the motorway system searching for prey.

The steady blink of hazard lights let him know of the stranded vehicle long before he could actually see it. Instantly he slowed and checked in his rear-view mirror that the road behind was still deserted. Then he unwound the window and placed the magnetic siren light on the cab roof. Waves of adrenaline surged through his thick arms as the lamp began flashing yellow above him. He eased smoothly onto the hard shoulder, and, as he crossed the white line, the ridges made a sharp drilling noise through his tyres. He dropped his speed still further and stopped fifteen feet behind the solitary car.

Its passenger door opened and a man got out. With one hand he shielded his eyes from the glare of the van's lights, with the other he made a kind of awkward salute. Darts of rain flashed through the headlights in a steady flow.

The van driver sat motionless. From behind his dark windscreen he scanned the interior of the car for the silhouettes of any other heads. Seeing none, a delicious rush played up his spine. Flicking his headlights off and hazards on, he jumped eagerly from the van and grabbed the torch and toolbox.

Confidently, he strode up to the man with his first line ready prepared, but the car driver cut in first. 'Great to see you! I wasn't expecting you for at least another half hour or so.'

That was his first question answered: no rescue van due for a while. He cut straight to the next part of his speech. 'You're in luck, mate. All the regular vans are busy with this bad weather. So they've sent me from a garage down the road.'

'Oh, right, I wondered why there were no logos and things painted on your vehicle. I'm still covered or any repairs though?'

'Oh, yeah, pal,' course,' he replied, quickly walking round to the front of the car. 'Let's get it sorted and you on your way.'

'Superb. The bonnet's already popped.'

'Cheers,' the van driver replied, already disliking the man's eager politeness. He secured the bonnet with the metal arm and turned his torch on. The beam cut across the top of the engine, throwing wires and tubes into stark relief and creating exaggerated shadow between the engine parts behind. He needed the driver right by him and not standing off to the side like some spare part. 'Right, what was the problem again, sir?' he called over while starting to pull gently at the spark plugs.

The car driver glanced at him and then stepped to within talking distance. 'Well, as I outlined to the phone operator, I thought I was running out of petrol at first. The needle started dropping but then so did all the power. Nothing too sudden – I was able to pull up right next to the phone, but now the engine's totally dead.'

'Mmmm. Ok, could you just keep the torch pointed right on that spot, sir?' the van driver asked. The man had to bend forward right into the jaws of the open bonnet. Casually, the van driver removed the monkey wrench from the tool box at his feet, and with a quick glance to check no traffic was approaching, said in a voice pinched with excitement, 'Great, hold it right there.'

With a sharp chopping motion, he brought the wrench down on the back of the man's skull. He fell forward onto the edge of the bonnet, torch dropping into the engine, beam pointing wildly off to the side. Before he could slide back, the van driver grabbed him by the belt, and with one arm heaved him easily off the engine so he dropped to the tarmac by the side of the car.

Quickly the man in the boiler suit stepped around the vehicle, placed a foot on either side of his victim's outstretched legs, and crouched down so he was hidden from any passing traffic. He knew dispatching someone wasn't a quick and clean job, like it was in the films. But he'd expected at least some slurred begging, some groggy attempts at fending off the wrench as he smashed it into the face. That was how it had gone with the other two. But this one was just trying to wriggle back towards his car door. Did he really think he could find safety there?

He watched, fascinated, as the man frantically struggled to raise himself up on his elbows. The blow to the back of his head must have split the skin – blood was flowing from his hair, coursing down his neck. Bending forwards, he looked over the prostrate man's shoulder and saw drips falling steadily off his nose and chin. He placed a knee on the man's buttocks to pin him down and then playfully batted the wrench across the side of his head. It jerked to one side and the skull itself shifted shape. The wounded man sagged back on to his stomach, then slowly started trying to edge forward again. And he began mumbling a name, Laura? Lauren? Probably calling for his fucking mum.

He shook his head in disgust, switched the wrench to his left hand and cracked him across the other side of his skull. The plates of his skull parted properly this time and a membranous lump began bulging through. That stopped his snivelling. He lay still now, except for one hand clawing frantically at the tarmac. The rasping of his nails was his last ever sound as, more firmly this time, the van driver brought the cast-iron tool down on the top of his head and watched as flabby bits of grey jelly tumbled out over his collar. When the body began its nervous twitching, he stood back up.

Next he snatched his torch from the car's hard innards, lowered the bonnet back down and retrieved his toolbox. He stepped round the side of the car and played the beam of light over the man's head. It lay ruined in an oil slick of blood.

'Fucking ignorant prick,' he murmured, taking the first step back towards his van.

The small white face stared at him from behind the glistening window, pads of little fingers pressed against the glass. The van driver froze mid-step, and their eyes locked. In that instant before conscious thought, terrible realisations passed between them. A microsecond later and the van driver's elation completely vanished.

His brain slowed and then began to stall, desperately trying to work out what to do. Secretly knowing the answer already. Realising he had to get moving, he snapped the rear door open, unclipped her harness and plucked her from the car. She didn't make a sound, just kicked her little legs in the air.

Bundling her into the passenger foot-well of the van, he sprang across into the driver's seat, unaware of one of her shoes lying on the ground by the van's front tyre. No headlights approaching from behind. He grabbed the siren light off the roof, started the engine and crossed back on to the motorway lanes.

He sat slumped back in his plastic chair, one hand rotating

an empty Styrofoam cup on the cigarette-singed Formica surface, the other turning an unopened sugar sachet end over end over end.

Opposite sat his young colleague, hands folded in his lap, as he tried not to look bored. But under the table his forefinger and thumb plucked like a vindictive chicken at the skin of his other palm. Black windows pressed in on all sides, reflecting back the interior lights, making the café feel smaller. In the kitchen behind them a radio quietly sounded the four o'clock pips.

The older man abruptly blew out his cheeks and glanced at his watch. 'Well, suppose we'd better make a move.' He announced, reaching for his cap on the seat beside him.

'Cheers for all the advice, Sarge,' the younger man replied, straightening his shoulders.

'No problem, you need to know the ins and outs of how the game's played. But like I told you, say anything to certain people and it goes straight…'

The handset on the table between them burst into life as a voice announced, 'All units in the vicinity of junction 14 on the M40, we have a report from a motorway assistance vehicle of a body next to a broken-down vehicle, eastbound hard shoulder. No other vehicles involved. Please respond.'

'Shit. That's us, come on,' said the driver, struggling to slide his gut out from under the bolted down table. 'Not a word about us being in here, all right?' he said, once they were outside and marching across the car park. 'Roger base, driver 1214F4 responding, ten minutes away.'

'Junction 14, where's that from here?' the younger man asked as they pulled out of the car park and onto the roundabout, heading for the eastbound turn-off.

'Just about opposite where we were sat half an hour ago.'

'We saw that car!' he shouted excitedly. 'No other vehicles involved. What do you reckon?'

'Exactly – he's done it again.' The driver paused for a moment, then added, 'And Andy?'

'Yeah?' he replied eagerly.

'Calm the fuck down.'

With eyes shut, he remained absolutely motionless, relying totally on his sense of hearing. On his right the sound of the siren reached a painful peak as it passed his head. And then it was receding, suddenly growing fainter like some stereo effect heard in a giant cinema. His eyelids opened a fraction. At first he could see no difference but, as they widened, the broad leaves of dandelions showed their black outlines against the fractionally lighter sky. He began pressing forward again, nostrils flared for any unusual aromas. Sometimes he'd find the boxed and rotting remains of pizza slung onto his land. He'd pore over the mouldy lumps with his torch and note down the number of the shop. Once, he'd rung one from a callbox and listened to the voice repeatedly asking for an order before eventually it hung up.

The sound of the siren still hadn't completely evaporated into the night air. He estimated he had another hour of foraging before dawn began to break. Time enough to cover a couple of hundred metres more. Just as well, he though, since tonight had only produced two items worth adding to his collection. The siren now seemed to be coming back. He concentrated on the sound and then realised it was another, approaching from the same direction as the first. He closed his eyes once again and settled flat on his stomach, head slightly up, ears clear of the soaking grass. The second siren passed him and from its tone, he knew it was a different type of emergency vehicle. With the first one never having fully faded away, it was time to call off the forage.

He hated the end of his searches, when he was forced to lift himself from his belly and resume his existence on two feet. He hated leaving the debris that littered his territory like so much rubbish washed up on a deserted beach. Regretfully he returned the pencil torch to the zip-up pocket on the upper arm of his overalls, then, favouring his left elbow and knee, he burrowed off to the side until the crash barrier loomed above his head.

From the gap below the lowest strip of metal he peered out to his left. Twin points of approaching light caused him to shrink back into the shadows. A few seconds later the white van hurtled by, easily doing over a hundred. He glimpsed the crop-haired driver bent forward, massive arms gripping the wheel, willing the vehicle to go even faster.

He waited a bit, then, looking again, saw the lanes were empty. Far beyond the motorway's gentle curve, the faint flicker of stationary blue lights pulsed. Checking that the lanes behind him were also deserted, he quickly vaulted over the barrier and scuttled, legs stiff and crab-like, across the tarmac strip. Reaching the hard shoulder he didn't slow down, climbing the grassy slope in quick strides until he reached the edge of the field at the top. Glancing back at the central reservation, he resolved to return and complete his search of this particular stretch another time. And then he was over the fence and away into the night.

Made in the USA
Charleston, SC
07 October 2015